Praise for Linda Winfree's
Truth and Consequences

"The heat is great . . . the characters in this book are worth the time . . . interesting, sympathetic . . . The story just teetered on the edge of frustration, the way a suspense is supposed to."

~ *author Kate Rothwell/ Summer Devon*

"A terrific read... very realistic, gritty situations... definitely not your stereotypical romance hero."

~ *author Sharon Long/ Maya Banks*

"Jason is a very well-developed character. He's an appealing mix of issues and heroism, with his crush on Kathleen being most sweet indeed...Jason comes off like someone who is determined to do the right thing. He's a good guy with some issues which he tries his best to get over."

~ *Mrs. Giggles, mrsgiggles.com*

"...a first rate suspense thriller with an excellent romantic component that hooks the reader from the very beginning... quintessentially a story about doing the right thing and it's so well told that I'm in a hurry to read it again. I give it my highest recommendation."

~ *Aviana, Two Lips Reviews*

"Ms. Winfree has done a spectacular job of setting up a great read. . .the story unfolded before me and kept me enthralled until the very end. Anyone who loves romantic suspense will want this book..."

~ *Shara, My Book Cravings*

"But in the south, we also have men like Jason who are patriotic, law abiding, loyal, caring, family men...Thank you, Ms. Winfree, for a character that is a real southern man. I also enjoyed Kathleen's tough girl, independent, take no prisoners attitude...the embodiment of a southern woman...*Truth and Consequences* is an exciting, pulse-pounding, suspense story."

~ *Stephanie B, Fallen Angel Reviews*

Truth and Consequences

Linda Winfree

A Samhain Publishing, Ltd. publication.

Samhain Publishing, Ltd.
577 Mulberry Street, Suite 1520
Macon, GA 31201
www.samhainpublishing.com

Truth and Consequences

Print ISBN: 1-59998-771-6
Digital ISBN: 1-59998-513-6

Editing by Anne Scott
Cover by Anne Cain

First Samhain Publishing, Ltd. electronic publication: June 2007
First Samhain Publishing, Ltd. print publication: April 2008

Dedication

Again, to Rick for answering fifteen million law enforcement questions.

For Carol, because you know this book wouldn't be without you, my IR. And for Mama, Felicia and April – some of my best supporters.

To Elisabeth, because Jason has always been her favorite.

Finally, for Mary. I'm hoping this one will bring you completely over to the dark side!

Chapter One

"Altee, do you have a bad feeling about this?"

Kathleen Palmer put the car in park and stared at the chaos. In the distance, heat mirages danced on the Georgia highway, an ebb and flow of nonexistent water. Patrol cars from two counties lined the two-lane blacktop road, and a battered, gray S-10 pickup slanted into the ditch at a wild angle. She flexed her fingers on the steering wheel, nerves jumping in her stomach.

Her partner Altee Price smoothed the collar of her navy polo shirt, emblazoned on the left chest with the emblem of the Georgia Bureau of Investigation. Altee smiled, temporarily creasing skin the color of polished pecan wood. "It's me and you and a bunch of white country boys. What do you think?"

"Can you actually smell the testosterone?" Opening the door of the unmarked Crown Victoria, Kathleen grinned. With the number of male law enforcement officers milling around, the hormone would be in ample supply.

"That would be a good thing if we were at the Cue Club." Altee slammed her door. "Here, it makes me nervous. Real nervous."

Kathleen made sure the back of her own polo was tucked into her khakis. "You want to be in charge this time?"

"No, I'll leave it to you. That way if it does blow up in our faces, I can blame you."

"Thanks."

Altee nudged Kathleen's shoulder with her own. "What are partners for, girl?"

Around the patrol units, deputies stood in two groups and exchanged territorial glares. Muttered curses and insults filled the hot, still afternoon air. "Why don't you just go back to your own county, Farr? Go chase a chicken or something. You might actually catch one of those."

Kathleen sighed. A pissing contest. Just what she wanted to deal with today. "Come on. Let's get this over with."

Blue lights whirled atop the cars, while headlights sparked in an alternating pattern. As she drew closer to the wrecked truck, her stomach clenched. Blood and bits of bone spattered the cracked windshield. She straightened, walking taller. This situation was going to be ugly and she couldn't afford to show any weakness.

As she and Altee approached, the hostility quieted. Kathleen stopped a few feet away and nodded. "Gentlemen."

The murmured responses to her greeting held subdued resentment. She refused to respond to the antipathy and eyed the men. The April sun glittered off brass decorating crisp tan uniforms. They appeared to be Georgia's finest, ready to protect and serve.

Two-thirds of them were corrupt sons of bitches.

"Something we said?" Altee murmured, her lips barely moving.

"More like the fact we have breasts to go with our badges."

She glanced down the highway, the sign marking the Haynes County line within sight. Why couldn't this chase have ended in Chandler County where it started? A tingle shivered down her neck and she looked up to find a deputy staring at her. He leaned against a Haynes County patrol car, arms folded over his chest, face expressionless.

A frisson of awareness slid along her nerves. She didn't know him, and that made her nervous. She knew every man here on a first-name basis. The watchful look in his green eyes left her feeling naked, exposed. Cold and hot all over at the same time.

With a deliberate motion, she turned her head away. She didn't have time to waste on a Haynes County deputy. She glanced toward the officers assembled from Chandler County. "Calvert, you want to tell me what happened?"

Before the tall investigator could answer, Jim Ed Reese, Haynes County's chief deputy, stepped forward. "They crashed the truck, got desperate and blew their brains out."

Visible tension tightened Tick Calvert's lean frame. "I think the lady asked me, Reese."

Jim Ed shook his head and spat into the weeds along the roadside. "You're not a Fed anymore, Calvert. You're not in charge."

Kathleen shoved down the urge to wipe the smirk from Jim Ed's face. She didn't have to join in their little alpha male party—she *was* the one in charge. The GBI investigated any death occurring while a suspect was in custody or during a pursuit.

Ignoring Jim Ed, she looked at Calvert again. "Tick?"

He jerked a hand through his dark hair. "They held up the stop-and-rob out on Highway 19. Troy Lee cut them off at the Flint crossroads—"

"Condensed version, please."

"Troy Lee lost them at the Hopewell city limits because his engine ran hot, but one of their city units picked up the chase. Haynes had units waiting for them when they crossed the line and Hopewell dropped out there. Reese radioed that the suspect vehicle had gone 10-50. When I got here, the boys were dead."

Jim Ed's square chin jutted at a pugnacious angle. "You left out the part about them shooting at your boy. They were young, stupid and scared, and it was easier to eat a gun than face up to what they done."

Kathleen glanced over her shoulder at Altee. The theory Jim Ed offered seemed plausible enough, but she'd learned a long time ago to look beyond surface explanations, especially where Jim Ed or any other Haynes County deputy was concerned.

She caught Altee's calm gaze. "Radio Moultrie, please, and have them send the van over."

"I told you what happened." Jim Ed's voice lowered, vibrating with tension. "We don't need the crime scene van here."

Still very much a politician's daughter, Kathleen smiled at him. "Maybe you don't. I do."

And that's what counts.

As she turned toward the truck, her gaze clashed with that of the unknown deputy again. His pale green eyes glowed against his tan. Admiration flashed across his face before the expressionless mask returned.

Pulling her attention back to her responsibilities, she walked away from Jim Ed and Tick, being careful to keep her gaze on the truck. Not looking at him didn't help—her mind conjured pictures of him, light glinting off his sun-streaked hair, his eyes hot and stormy.

Focus. And not on him.

The fascination was ridiculous. She didn't fall prey to instant attraction—ever. Hell, she couldn't remember the last time she'd fallen prey to any type of attraction. She didn't allow it. And he was a Haynes County boy. The dictionary definition of a corrupt cop.

The scene inside the small truck wiped away all thoughts of inappropriate attraction. She suppressed a horrified gasp, knowing she was still in the men's auditory range. For a second, she forgot to breathe through her mouth and the overwhelming smell of drying blood swamped her. A fly buzzed along the edge of the open window and she brushed it away.

Slumped in the cab, the two boys wore jeans and T-shirts. One no longer had a face; the other was missing half his head. Two teeth, bloody roots pointed toward the sky, rested on the dashboard. Bile pushed up in Kathleen's throat. Always the same reaction to a violent crime scene, always the same procedure. Lock the shock and horror away and do the job. Focus on the facts. Give in to the revulsion later, when no one was around to witness the weakness.

"The crime scene van's on the way." Altee spoke behind her, and Kathleen nodded.

"Would you start taking statements?"

"Sure thing. Who's first?"

Kathleen looked across the gulf of the ditch. Tick Calvert leaned against his car, smoking a cigarette and talking to a young deputy. Jim Ed had gathered his deputies and seemed in the middle of a lecture, shooting occasional glances at the truck. "Reese. Just don't expect to get very far. Give me a second here and I'll start on the other Haynes boys."

"Take your time."

With a deep breath, she took a visual inventory of the truck cab. A high-powered rifle lay between the two boys. Among the fast food wrappers littering the floorboard, a small handgun rested next to the passenger's foot. Blood-spattered CD cases lined the dash. Kathleen eyed the massive wounds, the blood spray and the rifle.

Suicide, my ass.

Stress tightened every nerve in Jason Harding's body. The sensation recalled memories of being a green army private, sitting in the sands of Kuwait and Iraq, and waiting. Waiting for something to happen, being afraid of what that something would bring.

If anything, the arrival of the two agents from the Georgia Bureau of Investigation increased the tension. Jim Ed still espoused the belief that women belonged in two places, the kitchen and the bedroom, and Jason suppressed a grin, watching his cousin chafe under Agent Price's questioning. Judging from her expression, she knew Jim Ed was pissed off and she enjoyed his discomfort. Maybe that was why his interview had taken longer than any of the others—the entire thirty minutes until the crime scene unit from Moultrie arrived.

"Deputy? I'd like to ask you a few questions."

Still leaning against his unit, he glanced at Agent Palmer. The sunlight picked out golden streaks in her shaggy copper hair. He figured she had a temper to go with those fiery strands.

He dropped his gaze down her trim form and another grin quirked at his mouth. If the standard issue GBI uniform of khaki slacks and navy polo shirt was supposed to hide her femininity, make her just another one of the boys, it failed. Firm breasts pushed at the cotton fabric and the khakis nipped in at a small waist above slim hips. All the uniform did was make him want to find out what was underneath.

He glanced up, meeting narrowed eyes the color of rich coffee. An angry flush danced along her cheekbones. She knew what he was thinking and she didn't like it. That was plain and Jason glanced away, shrugging off the sensation that he'd joined a long line of jerks who'd given her the same once-over. Apparently she hadn't thought much of him already and now he'd dropped a couple rungs in her estimation. That was fine—just the way it was supposed to be.

But he still didn't appreciate the way she looked at him, like something beneath her, gum smeared on the bottom of the expensive loafers she wore. How many times had he seen that expression before? The admiration he'd felt earlier watching her handle Jim Ed faded into a cold, hard lump of disappointment in his gut.

Resisting the ingrained urge to respond to her authoritative stance, he crossed his arms over his chest and maintained his negligent posture. "Ask away."

Those dark eyes narrowed further. Obviously, she was accustomed to men snapping to at her approach. She inclined her head toward the truck in the ditch. The technicians from Moultrie's crime scene lab swarmed the vehicle. "Tell me what you know about that."

He shot a glance at the truck. "It's two dead boys in a really ugly truck."

Irritation pinched her full mouth. "I suppose if I ask you how they got that way, you're going to say because of a gun."

This time he let the grin curve his mouth. "Well..."

She didn't appear amused. "When did you arrive? Before or after they crashed?"

Arguing with the woman would be a rush, almost as good as making up after. Jason smothered the images taking over his mind. Unlikely he'd ever get the chance to have a real argument with her, let alone make up. "After. I was second on scene for Haynes County. Jim Ed got here first."

She flipped open a small notebook, her long, slender fingers caressing the leather. Her nails were short, a practical length, but lacquered a passionate red. Another image flashed in his brain—those slim, red-tipped fingers sliding over his skin. He cleared his throat.

Palmer glanced up at him. "Before the Chandler County units."

Jason shrugged. "Yeah. They showed up right after I did."

She shot a look at his nameplate and jotted a note. "What did Deputy Reese say on the radio?"

"Nothing much."

"Which means he said something." Palmer shifted her weight, her relaxed manner stating she didn't mind standing here all day if he didn't. He could think of worse things than looking at her, letting her voice wash over him, a cool contrast to the heat. Sweat trickled down his back, his undershirt clinging to his skin beneath the bulk of his bulletproof vest.

"He asked Chandler what he needed to do to stop them."

"Who responded?"

Jason gestured toward the youngest Chandler County deputy. "The kid. He said the suspects shot and wounded a store owner and had been shooting at his unit."

The pen scribbled across the pad again. "What was Reese's response to that?"

"10-4."

"This was just before he radioed them 10-50."

"Right."

"Do you think they committed suicide?"

The question came at him with the same rapid-fire, no-nonsense delivery of the others and almost caught him off-guard. Admiration stirred in him again. She would be lethal in an interrogation.

Jason met her watchful, dark gaze, sure she'd seen more in his face than he'd wanted her to. "Jim Ed says they did."

She snapped the notebook closed. "What's your first name, Deputy Harding?"

"Jason."

She nodded and glanced over her shoulder at Jim Ed, still being questioned by her partner. His face was red, jaw set with anger. "How long have you been with the sheriff's department?"

"Six months." He straightened, bringing him a step closer to her. Some elusive scent, clean and old-fashioned, tickled his nose. Ivory soap. She smelled of Ivory soap. "How long have you been with the GBI?"

That brought her attention back to him. Her expression tightened—mouth pulling into a thin line, neat brows angled into a slight frown. Obviously, she wasn't used to being on the receiving end of a questioning. "Long enough. Are you from around here?"

The double-edged question hung between them. She was interested in more than his address. She wanted to know if he was as corrupt as the men he worked with. "I grew up here. Graduated from Haynes-Chandler High School."

Squinting, she studied his face. "So did I. I don't remember you."

Why would she? He'd been invisible back then. Still was, in too many ways to count. Invisibility was his strong suit. Jason forced his body to relax.

Hooking his thumbs in his gun belt, he stared down at her. "I doubt we moved in the same social circle, Agent Palmer."

"Or maybe I was just classes ahead of you." She broke eye contact first, glancing toward Jim Ed and Price again. Price had motioned Calvert over, and Jim Ed was talking, waving his hands in the air. "How did you come to work for the sheriff's office?"

"Jim Ed's my cousin." With that statement, he had her immediate attention. She pursed her lips, sizing him up, Jason knew, tarring him with the same brush. The thought made him ill, his gut clenching. "He helped me get on with the department."

Jim Ed's voice, suffused with anger, carried to them, the words indistinguishable with the commotion.

Palmer slipped her pen inside the leather notebook. Her teeth worried her lower lip for a second before the tip of her tongue soothed the spot. Heat flashed through Jason's belly and he hoped it didn't show on his face when she looked at him again.

She lifted an eyebrow. "Were you in law enforcement somewhere else?"

"No." Lord, he wished this interest was in him as a man, not as a potential witness to a possible murder. Or a suspect. "Army."

"You need to shut your damn mouth, Reese!" Calvert's deep voice carried over the din of squawking police radios and male conversations.

Palmer spun and took a step toward the others. Calvert turned away, heading for his car, and the tight line of Palmer's shoulders relaxed. Watching the smug smirk creep across Jim Ed's face, Jason tensed. He knew that smile. It was the same one he'd seen Jim Ed wear as a kid, when he was hatching some minor act of cruelty, like stuffing kittens into Pringles cans to roll them down a hill or flicking firecrackers at the neighbor's chained-up dog.

Jim Ed hooked his thumbs in his pockets and spat into the weeds at the side of the road. "Hey, Calvert. Forgot to ask. How's your sister? I should pay her a little visit one of these days."

Calvert stiffened and stalked back to Jim Ed, talking so quietly that his words didn't carry this time. Price placed an arm between them. "All right, boys, that's enough."

An ugly laugh rent the air and Jim Ed shoved Price's arm away. "Boy? How big do they grow the men where you come from, Price? Calvert might be a boy, but I'm all man, baby."

"Yeah," Calvert drawled. "It takes a big man to shoot a couple of kids."

Jim Ed's face darkened, and he stepped forward, hands clenching, unclenching, clenching again at his sides. "Shut up."

"Oh, hell." Palmer strode toward the two men and Jason started after her. Although he had no doubt the agent could hold her own, he knew Jim Ed, and he didn't want Palmer caught in this. Two distinct groups of deputies gathered to watch the confrontation.

"Tick, back off." Palmer's voice indicated she didn't intend to be disobeyed. "Get in your car."

Calvert took a step back, his gaze locked on Jim Ed. "You're a disgrace to your badge, Reese."

Jim Ed laughed. "I'm not the one taking orders from a woman. Still a mama's boy at heart, aren't you?"

Her face stiff with anger, Palmer wrapped a hand around Calvert's upper arm. "Move, Tick. In the car. Now."

Calvert didn't budge. "Speaking of mama's boys, Jim Ed, the next time you visit Billy up at the state prison, tell him I said hey."

With a snarled curse, Jim Ed slammed a punch into Calvert's jaw, missing Palmer by inches. A startled expression on her face, she stepped back. Calvert staggered, but didn't fall. Jim Ed got one more punch in and the hard right caught Calvert in the face. Jason winced at the sound of bone against bone. With an inarticulate growl, Calvert lunged and both men hit the ground with a thud, rolling in the dusty gravel.

Disgust twisting her face, Palmer strode toward the two, and Jason didn't miss the incredulous glance Price shot her way. "I know you're not going to try to break that up."

Palmer threw her hands up. "I suppose we should just let them kill each other?"

Sighing, Jason signaled for a couple of deputies to help him. He'd pulled Jim Ed out of fights before. What was one more?

His movement collided with Palmer's step back. Her feet tangled with his and she pitched forward. Jason reached out, snagged an arm around Palmer's waist and pulled her upright. She was lighter than he expected, and the force of his tug brought the line of her back into direct contact with his chest. Her clean scent filled his nostrils and warmth flashed along his nerves.

Deputies moved in to separate the two men. Palmer attempted to wriggle free of his hold, her hip brushing his groin. Jason swallowed a groan and tightened his arm around her waist. "Stop. You almost—"

"Let go of me." The words emerged on an enraged growl and she shoved his arm, stepping away from his body. She glared, disdain curling her mouth. "I don't need to be protected, Harding."

Jason stepped back, hands aloft. "Sorry I tried, Palmer. Next time I'll let you fall on your ass."

She turned her icy stare on Jim Ed and Calvert. Two Haynes County deputies held Jim Ed, blood, sweat and dust covering his face. Sporting what would be one killer black eye, Calvert stood on his own, the young officer from Chandler County keeping a restraining hand on his arm.

"Real professional behavior, gentlemen. I expected better from you, Tick." Palmer cast one last disgusted look at them. "Get off this scene before I arrest both of you."

Spinning, she walked toward the crime scene technicians, who stared, open-mouthed. Jason watched her go, still tingling from the brief feel of her body against his.

ଓଃ

Jason set a can of soda in front of Jim Ed before popping the tab on his own can. A small icy spray hit his fingers and he took a long sip. Jim Ed rolled his can across his swollen lip. "Son of a bitch has one coming for this."

Deciding not to comment on Jim Ed's starting the fight, Jason settled into a battered vinyl chair. They were alone in the squad room. Behind them, the television played the twenty-four-hour news channel, providing a kind of white noise.

He lifted an eyebrow at his cousin. "You still hold a grudge against him?"

Jim Ed's face darkened in a vicious scowl. "Billy's sitting in prison, doing a life sentence, for charges that son of a bitch trumped up."

Forget the DNA evidence that had everything to do with the four rape convictions. Forget that Calvert's sister had been only nineteen when Billy attacked her. Jason sipped his soda again and tried to look sympathetic. "Do you think—"

"I hope the other boy looks worse than you, Jim Ed." Sheriff Bill Thatcher's booming words obliterated the background noise from the television.

His voice thick, Jim Ed muttered something else about that "son of a bitch Calvert". Jason dropped his head back, wishing his cousin had a broader vocabulary.

Thatcher's heavy hand slapped Jason on the shoulder. "Guess you just missed all the excitement of that chase, didn't you, boy?"

Opening his eyes, Jason sat up. "Yes, sir."

Thatcher leaned on the scarred table and studied his clean, blunt nails. "Jim Ed says that Palmer girl had a lot of questions for you."

Jason blew out a disgusted sigh. "It was bull."

"She can be awful persistent. Gets it from her daddy." Thatcher lifted his gaze, pinning Jason with a sharp look. "So how much of that chase did you see?"

Jason shrugged. "I didn't see nothing. When I got there, it was all over."

"Is that what you told Palmer?"

"Yes, sir."

Thatcher grinned, his rugged face younger than his sixty-odd years. "Good boy. With that attitude, you should go far around here."

"Thank you, sir." Feeling like a dog patted on the head by an indulgent master, Jason waited until Thatcher retreated to his office. "Who is Palmer's daddy?"

Jim Ed made a disparaging sound in his throat. "She's Talley Palmer's daughter. Playing at law enforcement."

"Talley Palmer, the state representative?"

Jim Ed nodded. "Yeah."

Jason stared at him. "That was Kathleen Palmer?"

"Yeah." Jim Ed shot him a sly look. "Why? She get you hard the way she did back in high school, prancing around in that little cheerleader outfit?"

He ignored the gibe. "I thought she married some law student from Mercer."

That had been his sophomore year of high school, the year after Kathleen graduated. He was still trying to reconcile the cold agent with the bubbly, popular girl from high school. Man, had he been wrong when he'd said they moved in different social circles back then. More like different universes.

"It didn't last." Jim Ed drained his soda, grimacing. "Wish it had. Then she wouldn't be here, being a pain in the ass. She's not gonna let this mess with these boys lie, either. Mark my words, she'll try to stir something up."

A shiver traveled over Jason's skin at Jim Ed's dark look. Jason remembered the sun shining on Kathleen's hair. For her sake, he hoped she left well enough alone this time.

Chapter Two

Kathleen surveyed the contents of her refrigerator. Why did she always buy so much? She couldn't stand to open the fridge and find nothing, but this was ridiculous. Enough food for two small armies in here. Pushing the orange-cranberry juice aside, she found the six-pack of diet soda hiding behind two longnecks she'd bought Lord knew when.

"Altee? You want beer or soda?"

"Soda." Altee's contented voice drifted through the open patio doors. Kathleen grinned. Her partner lived just across the lake, but swore the view was better on Kathleen's deck. Probably because the view included the two muscular college kids who lived next door.

Grabbing two diet sodas, Kathleen padded barefoot onto the deck. She set the cans on the table and took the plate Altee proffered. The spicy aroma of onions and peppers rose from the open pizza box on the table. Her stomach growled and she took one more piece than usual.

Settled into her chair, she rested her feet on the deck railing and watched several ducks weave between the cypress trees on the lake below. A breeze wafted in, cooling the evening air and tickling her toes. She tried to let the normalcy soothe her—the lake, her home, Altee's presence—but calm didn't come. Nerves continued to jump in her stomach; images continued to replay in her mind. "Was that a mess today or what?"

"Which part? The dead bodies or Reese and Calvert acting like middle school boys?"

"Both." Irritation curled through her again. Let her show the least amount of bitchiness and accusations of PMS rained down. But male officers could act like Neanderthals and no one said a thing. The contrast would be funny if it weren't so pitiful. "You know that wasn't a suicide."

Altee snorted. "Gee, what gave it away? The fact the gun in the floorboard was a throwaway with no prints? You know, the gun they shot themselves with. Or the mere fact that Jim Ed Reese is involved?"

After a sip of soda, Kathleen settled deeper into the chair and leaned her head back. "This is going to be the case from hell. No witnesses, so everything hinges on the forensics. That'll be fun to explain to a Haynes County jury. We'll be lucky if Tom even agrees to take it to trial."

"He's a DA. If the evidence is there, it's his duty to take it to trial." Altee's husky voice held equal amounts of idealism and frustration.

Kathleen shot her a wry look. "He's a politician and it's an election year. Haynes County makes up at least a third of his district. Sure, he's going to take an iffy case against their chief deputy to trial."

Grinning, Altee waved a slice of pizza at her. "Careful. You're starting to sound like a bitter ex-wife."

"It's been over too long for me to be bitter." Kathleen savored a bite of pizza. The girl who'd married Tom McMillian had been another person, had lived another life. She didn't remember that girl any longer.

That same girl had gone to high school with Jason Harding. The recollection of his face came too easily, and she tried to place his sun-streaked hair and light green eyes on a younger face. The effort failed, because in her mind she saw his stubborn jaw and the fine lines fanned out from his eyes, remembered the way his mouth moved when he talked, revealing white teeth. She rubbed a finger down the side of her soda can, droplets of condensation scattering in her wake. He'd claimed they'd moved in different social circles; maybe that was why she couldn't remember him. The next time she was at Mama's, she'd have to look for him in one of her old yearbooks...

Hold up there, Kathleen. What the hell are you thinking? You're not looking for anything where this guy is concerned, except maybe the truth.

And she wouldn't find that in any old yearbook.

"We're not sure there weren't any witnesses." Altee's matter-of-fact voice dragged Kathleen from her reverie.

"What do you mean?"

"Harding said he arrived basically the same time as Calvert."

"Right."

"Haynes and honesty don't exactly go together, remember? What if he got there a few minutes or even seconds earlier? What if he saw something and just doesn't want to rat out good ol' Jim Ed?"

A faint unease stirred in Kathleen and she frowned. "Did we ask Calvert about Harding's statement?"

Altee's playful grin did little to settle Kathleen's anxiety. "No. He was too busy leaving to escape your wrath."

Kathleen snorted and dropped her feet to the deck. "Right. What do you say we go ask him?"

ઉ৪

The décor of Tick Calvert's office at the Chandler County Sheriff's Department consisted of a rusty metal desk and a stack of storage boxes. A stuffed bass already graced the wall and his FBI award leaned on a wooden bookshelf next to a photo of another prize-winning catch. Although it was after six and his shift had ended at three with rotation of duty, Kathleen wasn't surprised to find him working. The man had two obsessions—fishing and work.

He waved Kathleen and Altee to two mismatched chairs in front of his desk. "Y'all have to excuse the mess. Stanton and I are still getting our stuff moved down from the FBI offices in Albany."

Kathleen eyed the bruising around his left eye. He'd be lucky if it wasn't swollen shut tomorrow. "So how does Stanton like being sheriff?"

Grinning, Tick dropped into his ancient desk chair. "I don't think the reality has sunk in yet. The jail is outdated, the records are in a mess, and since he released the entire staff when he was appointed, he's been trying to fill positions. Today was the first day off he's had since he's been in office—he went to Tallahassee to see his kids."

Altee smiled, a teasing expression. "And as soon as his back is turned, you boys get into a high-speed chase."

Tick chuckled and leaned back in his chair. "Pretty much."

Hands folded in her lap, Kathleen crossed her legs. "We've got a couple more questions about what happened today."

"Shoot."

"Do you know Deputy Harding from Haynes County?"

Tick's jaw tensed. "I know who he is, but I don't *know* him. There's not a lot of love lost between us and them."

"He says he arrived on scene the same time you did. Did he?"

"I don't know." Tick shrugged. "He was there. I wasn't paying attention to when he actually arrived. To be honest, I was too busy chewing Troy Lee out for blowing the engine in his squad car."

Kathleen narrowed her eyes at him. Super-observant Tick Calvert not paying attention to what went on at a crime scene? Sure. And her daddy wasn't the best fundraiser in his political circle. "So he could have been there before you arrived?"

Another negligent shrug. "He could have been, I guess, but I can't say for sure whether he was or wasn't."

"I understand." Kathleen glanced at her partner. Altee stared at Calvert as if he'd sprouted a pair of green antennae. She turned her head and looked at Kathleen, unspoken communication passing between them: *Do you believe this crock of bull?* "I appreciate your seeing us on such short notice."

"No problem. Anytime." He rose and lifted a stack of file folders from the desk. "Anything else? I hate to rush you, but I've got to get over to the women's center to teach that new self-defense class they're offering."

"If we need anything else, we'll call." Kathleen waited half a beat, knowing Altee would pick up her cue.

Altee jingled the keys. "I'll pull the car around."

"How's your mama?" Kathleen asked, accompanying Tick down the hall.

He grinned. "Good. Crocheting a blanket for that new grandbaby."

She stopped at the door. "You know there's more to this than Jim Ed said, right?"

Blowing out a rough sigh, he shifted the folders from one hand to the other. "Look, Kath, I want Thatcher and his boys out of power as much as you do. Hell, more. But sometimes we go looking for stuff that's not there. Maybe all there is here is just what Jim Ed said."

She stared. "I don't believe what I'm hearing. What have you done with the real Lamar Eugene Calvert, Jr.?"

"Come on, just listen. Reese is dangerous. You can't go making accusations without anything to back them up. Hell, Kathleen, I'd hate to see something bad happen to you. Just stay away from Harding and Reese. See what the forensics turns up, but don't be surprised if it's nothing. I've never seen people cover their tracks the way these sons of bitches do."

"Weren't you the one accusing Jim Ed of shooting those boys?"

He tugged his free hand through his hair, the dark strands falling forward onto his forehead. "Damn it, I was pissed off."

"If you know something, even if it seems inconsequential, like Harding already being on scene when you got there, I need to know." Irritation with his obstinate nature stirred in her. Good Lord, he *was* as stubborn as a tick on a hound dog. His daddy had known what he was doing when he'd bestowed that particular nickname.

The Crown Victoria cruised to a stop in front of the steps and the horn beeped twice. Kathleen straightened her shirt. "Thanks anyway, Tick. Tell your mama I said hey."

He shoved the door open for her. "Yeah. Take care."

Sliding into the passenger seat, Kathleen turned the vents to let the chilly breeze of the air conditioner cool her flushed cheeks. In the mirror, she watched Tick saunter to his truck.

Altee shifted into drive. "Did he say anything else?"

"Yeah. He warned me off Reese and Harding."

"Deputy Goodbody?" A grin quirking at her lips, Altee merged into the sparse traffic. The early evening sun glinted off the spire of the First Baptist Church. A pair of women speedwalked along the sidewalk. "He thought you were some kind of fine."

Annoyance crawled over Kathleen's nerves. Altee was too good at reading the opposite sex, but Kathleen only wanted to think of Jason Harding in a professional sense. She didn't want to think about how he looked at her. The desire to ask Altee exactly how he'd looked at her made her feel like a high school girl with a crush and that bothered her even more.

She pushed the aggravation into her voice. "What are you talking about?"

"Couldn't keep his eyes off you. Hands, either, obviously." With one finger, Altee smoothed her precise, sideswept bangs, not a hair out of place on her sleek bob.

"Altee. He's a Haynes County deputy. Why would I want anything of his on me?" His hands had been strong, warm even through her clothes. A shiver trickled down her body. With his arm around her waist and her back pressed to his chest, she'd experienced his strength. She refused to acknowledge that for a second she'd felt sheltered and intensely feminine.

"I'm just saying...he was hot for you." At a traffic light, Altee slowed to a stop behind a chicken truck. Fat birds sat in cages, oblivious to their destiny—a trip to the chicken plant and a transformation into chicken nuggets.

"Don't say it. I don't want to think about that."

"Okay." A knowing grin played about Altee's rose-glossed lips.

"He's just a possible witness. A possible suspect. If I have any dealings with him, it's on a purely professional basis. That's all."

"Okay." The grin widened. Anger pricked at Kathleen's nerves.

"It would suit me just fine if I never had to see him again."

"I hear you." A full-fledged smile bloomed.

"Would you stop smiling like that?" Kathleen sighed. "You know he saw something."

"Oh, yeah." Altee remained silent for a long moment. "That means you're going to have to see him again."

"Me? I think you mean *we.*" Kathleen glared at the passing scenery. That was not a flare of anticipation in her stomach. She was *not* looking forward to seeing Jason Harding once more. And if she did have to see him, her interest would be merely that of an agent investigating a case.

Certainly not that of a woman.

ଔଓ

"Hey, you coming to the house for supper?"

Surprised by Jim Ed's voice, Jason jerked upright, his head colliding with the open truck hood. Pain shot through his skull and he cursed. Holding a hand to his scalp, he glared at his cousin. For a big guy, he sure moved quietly. "What?"

Chuckling, Jim Ed reached over and tightened the battery cable Jason had been fiddling with. "I asked if you planned to eat supper with us."

"Sounds good. You don't think Stacy will mind?" Jason's fingers crept over the small lump growing under his hair. The old ghost of feeling like a charity case drifted through his mind, but he shrugged it off. Jim Ed hadn't ever made an issue out of the meals Jason had taken at the Reese home or the hand-me-down clothes and toys he'd received. No, that had been Billy, taunting him about being poor.

And fatherless. Billy had always held that over his head, how his father had taken off, leaving him and his mother alone.

Jim Ed shrugged. "Why would she mind? She cooks a huge supper, and if you come, I won't have to eat leftovers tomorrow. Is that pile of junk gonna start or do you need a ride?"

"It'll start." Jason slammed the hood and tried to view the old Chevy through his cousin's eyes. Rust showed through the faded blue paint and a cracked spider web radiated out from a small hole in the windshield. The tires were as bald as Sheriff Thatcher's head. Yeah, it needed to be put out of its misery and, if it was all he could afford, he was in pretty bad shape. Poor and desperate.

"Well, come on then. You look like you could use a good meal and we don't want it to get cold." Jim Ed clapped him on the shoulder, and Jason struggled to keep the anger and resentment from showing.

Following Jim Ed along the back roads, he let the mental guard down and allowed his thoughts to roam. He didn't want to remember, but the image of Kathleen Palmer's classic face, pinched with disdain, filled his mind. Full, pretty mouth, big brown eyes, straight nose, creamy skin—every cliché in the book. But a gorgeous cliché. He flexed his fingers on the steering wheel. No wonder he'd found himself fixated on her from the second she appeared at that crime scene.

Back in high school, Billy, Jim Ed and the rest of his buddies had gone for the blonde babe cheerleaders. The ones most likely to put out. Not him. He'd watched Kathleen and seen purity, polish, perfection. And he'd ached to have that in his life.

Kathleen Palmer was his Holy Grail. Ultimately desired. Ultimately unattainable.

Unattainable because he sure as hell wasn't Galahad, the perfect knight. More like Lancelot, who brought down the kingdom because he wanted what he shouldn't have.

But a guy could dream. Could lose himself in the memory of the scent of Ivory soap lingering on pale skin. Get caught up in wondering if those spiky wisps of copper framing her face felt as soft as they looked. Imagine what it would be like to make her lose that awesome control. Heat flushed his body and settled in his groin.

The celibacy is catching up to you, Harding. Get a grip, would you? It's a freaking fantasy. That's all Kathleen Palmer will ever be to you. Something not real.

His truck bounced up Jim Ed's long, rutted drive. Young pecan trees rose on either side, casting cool shade on the red clay. Atop the hill, cradled by tall pines, sat Jim Ed's brick, two-story Tudor-style house. Killing the engine, Jason stared. Stacy had to have chosen the plans. Jim Ed's pretensions ran to his toys—the flashy new 4x4 pickup he drove, the sleek bass boat parked under the shed, the extensive gun collection.

Jason climbed out of the truck, his feet sinking into new sod. A liver-spotted bird dog raced across the yard, yapping with wild affection. After a brisk rub behind the ears from Jim Ed, it collapsed on the grass in a contented heap.

Jim Ed passed a thumb over his split lip and winced. "Did I show you my new project?"

Jason shook his head. "Nope."

A cross between a grin and a grimace twisted Jim Ed's face. "C'mon. You'll love it."

As they walked toward the detached garage, the side door to the house slammed open and a pigtailed dynamo tumbled out. Jason grinned, watching his cousin's youngest tear across the lawn, yelling, "Daddy! Daddy!"

"Hey, hot rod." Jim Ed laughed and caught the little girl, swinging her up to settle on his hip. He rubbed his stubbled jaw against her cheek, and she erupted into wild giggles.

She patted his face. "You've got a booboo."

Jim Ed's expression hardened for a moment, then he smiled. A chill slid over Jason's spine.

"Yeah, Daddy's got a booboo. Give me a kiss and make it better." She laid a smacking kiss on his cheek. Jim Ed laughed again and turned her in Jason's direction. "Laurel, can you tell Uncle Jason hello?"

The little girl ducked her head against her father's shoulder. "Hey, Uncle Jason."

Uncle.

Family. A brief spurt of shame flared in his chest and he shoved his hands in his back pockets, forcing a smile for the four-year-old. "Hey, Laurel."

An answering beam shaped Cupid's-bow lips. "Daddy brought me a new kitty. His name's Mims."

Jim Ed let the little girl slide to the ground. He tugged the end of one pigtail. "Go tell Mama we'll be right in."

She flashed another smile in Jason's direction, showing tiny, pearly teeth. "Okay."

Jason watched her tear across the lawn toward the house. "She sure loves her daddy."

Clapping him on the shoulder again, Jim Ed rumbled with laughter. "That she does. And I'm wrapped around that pretty little finger, too. Come on."

The garage door lifted to reveal an immaculate floor and organized storage areas. Tools not only hung on pegboards, but red outlines showed where each should reside. A long table ran along the back wall, holding an array of woodworking tools. A half-finished dollhouse stood at one end.

"This is my baby." Jim Ed reached for the canvas cover on the car parked in the third bay. He pulled it away to reveal a 1970 Chevelle SS. With the hood removed, the chromed engine glimmered in the dim light.

Jason whistled and ran his hand down the right front quarter panel, the metallic blue paint slick and cool. The mingled scents of grease and oil tickled his nostrils, bringing back memories of his youth, hours spent piecing together junk cars with his cousins and their father. Envy shimmered under his skin. "Bet she set you back a penny or two, didn't she?"

Jim Ed patted a headlight. "She's worth it, though. Here, fire her up."

Anticipation licking at him, Jason caught the keys in midair and opened the driver's door. New vinyl and air freshener enveloped him, and the roar of the engine rolled along his senses. Fingers wrapped around the steering wheel, he soaked in the sensation of pure power. The urge to go tearing around the back roads of Haynes County swamped him.

Through the windshield, he studied the massive brick home, the new truck, the professional landscaping. How did Jim Ed pay for it all?

The possibilities made him ill. Killing the engine, he swung out of the car and tossed the keys to his cousin. He forced a grin, everything he'd eaten that day sitting in a lump in his gut. "She's great."

"You hang with the department long enough and you'll be able to afford one."

"Yeah." Bitterness rang in his short laugh. Jim Ed had no clue what was in his bank account, but the condescension stung. "Sure."

"Bill Thatcher believes in rewarding loyalty."

Jason glanced at the house. "You must be awful damn loyal."

His cousin didn't laugh. "Listen, Jason, I'm serious. This could be a good thing for you—"

"Jim Ed!" Stacy stood on the deck, hands on her hips, an exasperated look on her pretty face. "Are you coming in or not? Supper's getting cold."

"Wouldn't want that to happen," Jim Ed muttered and slapped Jason on the back. "Let's go before she has a hissy fit."

Jason helped him replace the car cover. As they left the garage, Jim Ed whistled sharply and the bird dog, tongue lolling, raced across the yard to them. With the canine dancing about his legs, Jim Ed fondled its ears once more and clucked his tongue.

At the sound, the dog shot toward a chainlink kennel behind the house. The gate stood open, moving slightly in the soft breeze.

"Come on." Jim Ed ambled to the pen, where the dog waited inside, panting. Jason followed, eyeing the huge deck and professional landscaping behind the house. When Jim Ed reached the gate, he stopped. "Goddamn son of a bitch."

His cousin's low growl sent unease skittering up Jason's spine. "What?"

"I told that boy to clean this pen." Jim Ed stalked away, fists clenched.

Jason surveyed the kennel: neat dog house, white concrete floor, automatic watering system, stainless steel bowl full of kibble. Looked clean enough.

"Jamie." Jim Ed bellowed into the house. "Get your ass out here."

A skinny teenager ducked out the back door. "Yes, sir?"

Jim Ed wrapped a hand around the boy's neck and shoved him in the direction of the kennel. "Look at my goddamn dog pen. I told you to clean it before I got home."

"Daddy, I—"

"Don't fucking argue with me, boy." Jim Ed spoke from between obviously clenched teeth. Jason tensed, ready to step forward and get between his cousin and the kid. Hell if he wasn't different with Jamie. The indulgent father Jason had seen with Laurel was nowhere in existence. "You know what I mean by clean and this ain't it."

Jamie ducked his head, shaggy sandy hair falling forward to hide his eyes. He didn't speak but scuffed one tennis shoe on the grass.

Jim Ed dug his fingers into the boy's thin shoulder and a grimace crossed Jamie's face. "Do you hear me, boy?"

Clearing his throat, Jason shifted his stance. Everything in him wanted to shove his cousin away, make him leave the kid alone.

Everything except the voice telling him to do so would be a fatal mistake. Seeing this side of Jim Ed made him wonder just what had happened that afternoon before he'd arrived.

Had Jim Ed really pulled the trigger on those boys?

"Do you hear me?" Jim Ed's voice deepened to a menacing rumble. His grip tightened until his knuckles glowed white against his tan, and Jamie winced.

"Yes, sir." The words emerged as a whispery mumble.

"I can't hear you."

"Yes, sir." Louder this time, but holding a trace of unshed tears.

Jim Ed released him and stepped into the pen. The dog wagged its tail but he didn't spare it a glance. Instead, he picked up the dog bowl and flung it against the floor. Jamie and the dog flinched from the metallic clanging as kibble rained all over the concrete. Jim Ed didn't look at his son as he strode by him. "Clean it up right this time. Don't come in until it's done."

He slapped Jason on the back as he passed. "Come on. Let's eat."

The joviality had returned to his voice and Jason followed him with one last glance at the teenager kneeling in the kennel, gathering dog food piece by piece.

Jason shook his head. Maybe taking Jim Ed up on this job offer hadn't been such a good idea after all.

What the hell had he gotten himself into?

ꕥ

Kathleen prowled her living room, picking up the remote, flipping through the channels, putting it down again. A magazine received a cursory glance. Finally, she pulled her notebook from her soft-sided briefcase and flipped it open to Jason Harding's statement.

He knew something.

She just didn't know how to get it out of him.

In the morning, she and Altee could drive over, interview him again.

Yeah. Sure.

The key would be catching him off-guard. On his own territory, where he was comfortable, but when he wasn't expecting her. And one-on-one. Somehow, she knew he'd shut down if the conversation involved more than the two of them.

Not giving herself time to regret the decision, she grabbed her keys and notebook and jogged downstairs to her car. Using the interior light, she read his address, trying to remember where the hell Cotton Boll Road was in Haynes County. Wasn't that out behind Dale Jenkins's dairy farm? A quick check of her regional map proved her memory correct.

Trees overshadowed the back roads. Her headlights pierced the dark, bouncing eerily off mist rising from the ill-maintained pavement. Her practicality screamed she was making a mistake. *Wait and take Altee with you.*

Her instinct told her something else entirely, whispering that Jason Harding could be the key to this case.

Her conscience told her she was making excuses, simply to get what she really wanted—and not as a cop, either.

Cotton Boll Road was a generous name for the narrow trail that led into the woods behind the dairy farm. Her SUV handled the rutted dirt road well. When the clay track opened up into a clearing, Kathleen hit the brakes and eyed Jason Harding's home. The place was a tactical dream—for the occupant. The trail circled around the single-wide trailer, one way in and one way out. The isolation pressed in on all sides.

Okay, this had been a bad idea. A really bad idea. Right up there with letting her mother talk her into accepting an engagement ring from Tom. The divorce had taught her it was never too late to get out of a bad situation.

She threw the Wagoneer into reverse. Behind her, headlights swept the tree line. Damn. Too late this time. Resigned to brazening things out, she shifted to drive and pulled up to park in front of the trailer.

The white and green siding glowed under the security light. A crooked stoop had been tacked on to the front. Heavy painter's plastic covered two windows, rippling in the breeze.

This was all he could afford? Obviously, police corruption didn't pay as well at the entry level.

ᏜᏜ

Jason stared at the early model Grand Wagoneer in his driveway. He pulled to one side, steering with one hand while the other unsnapped his holster. No one had any business being on this isolated piece of dirt and this presence had alarm burning in his chest.

They knew who he was. It was all over.

Heck, if they knew who he was, *he* was all over.

Images burned in his brain—the two dead boys, the cold, lifeless expression in Jim Ed's eyes, blood splattered on a cracked windshield.

Stiffening his spine, Jason pushed the truck door open. He'd never been a coward and he wouldn't start now. Hand on his gun, he kept the cab of the truck between him and the Wagoneer, watching. The driver's door opened, he tensed, and the interior light flashed over fiery hair. Fiery, just-tumbled-out-of-bed hair.

For a moment, he relaxed, the awful fear of discovery and retaliation subsiding under a wave of relief. A different fear flooded into the wake. He shot a glance at the trailer where he'd grown up, the only piece of dirt he could say he owned, and compared it to what Kathleen Palmer was accustomed to—her father's acres of hunting land, the big white house she'd grown up in, with its Grecian columns, huge crystal pendant light on the porch and widow's walk. The old inadequacies rushed in on him, waves on a shore.

He grabbed on to his old life preservers, the anger and resentment, and walked around the front of the truck to confront her. Her hair framed her face in a halo of wispy fire. The dim light made it difficult to tell if her eyes were brown or black, but he knew they were a warm brown dappled with gold. God, even her eyes were rich.

His gaze followed hers to the trailer and back to his truck. In those incredible eyes, he was nothing. The ache made him grit his teeth. Thumbs tucked in his gun belt, he slumped in a negligent posture he knew his high school teachers would remember. The poor kid who didn't give a damn.

"Missed me, did you, Palmer?"

She fixed him with a disdainful look. "I have a few more questions. I'd like some straight answers this time."

And he'd like her gone. "I'm busy."

Her mouth tightened. "We can do this here, or I can drag you into Moultrie and make it last all night."

Oh, my God. The words punched into his gut, mental pictures exploding in his head. Here. Elsewhere. All night long. He watched her, remembering her high school reputation as somewhat of a prude, an innocent who blushed at off-color jokes and never allowed a hand to venture to the hallowed ground beneath her cheerleading skirt. He was willing to use any weapon he had, just to get her out of here. For her safety as well as his.

He eyed her, letting his gaze take a lazy exploration of her body. "Baby, I bet you could, too."

Awareness dawned in her eyes and her mouth thinned to a nonexistent line. "Harding—"

"Call me Jason." He poured all the bedroom innuendo he could into the words. Need speared through him. What would his name sound like on her lips?

Furious color played over her cheeks, visible even in the bluish vapor light. Her long indrawn breath was audible and she flipped open that damn notebook again. "You said that you arrived on scene the same time as Investigator Calvert from Chandler County."

He ignored the question and stepped closer. He was going to make her hate him, and regret stabbed at him. What if he'd met her in another life? One where he wasn't a dirt-poor, desperate cop, so desperate he'd cover for a murderer? A life where they were equals, where she could look at him with respect, maybe admiration.

Close enough that her scent of Ivory soap filled his nostrils, he reached out to finger one of those wild wisps. "If you make it last all night, do I get to call you Kathleen? Or is it always Agent Palmer?"

She closed the notebook and took a step back, colliding with the Wagoneer. "You don't get to call me anything."

"Don't you know this county's dangerous?" He leaned closer, his breath mingling with hers. Her eyes dilated and he felt her pull her stomach muscles inward. Avoiding contact with him. Afraid of contamination. Bitterness gnawed at him.

"I'm not afraid of you." Her voice was soft, steady.

Jason rested both hands on the hood, trapping her between his body and her SUV. Her body heat seared him, but the sensation brought no pleasure—just a nauseating knowledge that she'd never let him touch her, not willingly. He forced a smile, using Jim Ed's for a pattern. For a moment, he was afraid he really would throw up.

"Well, sugar, maybe you should be." He held her prisoner a moment longer. Stepping away, he indicated her truck with a flourish worthy of an Arthurian knight. "Go home, Kathleen. Forget about those boys. Just let it go."

She didn't say anything else, but climbed into the Wagoneer and fired the engine. Jason didn't wait to watch her leave. With the sound of her departure following him, he walked into the trailer that had once been his home.

Chapter Three

Jason woke with a headache grinding at his temples and a groan rumbling in his throat. He rolled to sit on the edge of the bed, head buried in his hands. Lack of sleep left him feeling hungover, a result of the wild dreams he'd endured all night—a swirling array of running in the dark, gunshots and Kathleen Palmer's derisive laughter.

Dragging himself into the shower, he tried to force his brain into logical patterns of thought. Fear, lingering from the night before, slithered through him. The paralyzing dread created by her SUV in his drive hammered home the most important point once more: he couldn't afford to be sloppy.

And he couldn't afford to let Kathleen get further involved. He didn't for a second believe he'd scared her off for good. Her tenacity sparked his admiration, but it also scared the living hell out of him. What had she been thinking, showing up at his house, in the wilds and badlands of Haynes County, after dark? Alone. Hell, she'd come alone.

The idea that Jim Ed might have been with him intensified the pounding at his temples.

Didn't she know there were worse things in life than unanswered questions? Was she that naïve, to think simply catching him unawares would push him to answer her? He wouldn't tell her anything he didn't plan for her to know.

The stream of water, which had hit his skin with stinging force, slowed to a trickle, thanks to the well's uneven performance. Cursing, he rinsed the soap from his body the best he could and stepped out. With a thin, rough towel wrapped around his waist, he padded back to his bedroom. At the end of the hall, a closed door marked the room his mother had called her own, where she'd succumbed to the cancer that had ravaged her body with devastating speed.

Not being able to afford basic health care was a freaking bitch. Anger coiled in his gut again. His mother's cancer was eighty-five percent curable if found early enough. She'd avoided regular checkups, using the money for food, electricity, clothing for him. Maybe if his father had bothered to stick around, she would still be alive. Maybe if he'd never been born.

He hurled the towel into a corner and jerked on a pair of underwear. The clock radio clicked on and the deejays at the local country station kept up a steady stream of repartee. "...it's five-forty-five, fifteen until the top of the hour. Bonnie, what does our weather look like today?"

Sunny and too hot to wear the bulletproof vest all day. Jason pulled on an undershirt and the vest anyway. He could hear Jim Ed's mocking voice now. *You scared someone's gonna shoot you?*

Well, yeah. Maybe one of the guys I work with. Maybe you.

He shrugged on the pressed uniform shirt and stepped into his pants. Bonnie's too-cheerful voice chattered from the radio. "Kurt, we have a request this morning that has us digging in the archives. Here's Johnny Cash's 'I Walk the Line'."

With the song's title, tension grabbed his nape and the headache, once subsided to a dull throbbing, returned full force. He shot a glance at the clock. Almost six and he had to sign on at seven. He needed to get moving.

ଔ୪ଓ

Fog shrouded the pecan grove, hanging between the ancient trees like shimmering phantasms. The grass whispered under Jason's steps and the damp mist lingered against his skin. Overhead, trees arched and created an artificial darkness that blotted out the early morning sun. Silence surrounded him, suffocating him in isolation.

A lighter flared, illuminating a face with sharp angles and intelligent dark eyes. An angry purple bruise surrounded one of those eyes. The end of a cigarette glowed red and smoke curled upward before the light went out.

Jason spoke first, keeping his voice quiet. No one should be around, but he couldn't shake the feeling the grove held unseen listeners. "We've got a problem. Kathleen Palmer showed up at my place last night."

"Damn it." Tick Calvert shook his head. "I warned her. That woman wouldn't listen if the Lord Almighty Himself tried to tell her something. Tell me she brought Price with her."

"No. She was alone." A shiver slid over Jason's skin again. Too many things could have happened.

Tick sighed. "Figures. I swear, if I could, I'd—"

"Sounds like you know her pretty well." The words emerged with more sharpness than Jason intended. He pushed down the irrational jealousy. Who knew Kathleen well didn't have anything to do with him.

"Our fathers were close friends. We grew up in each other's houses." Tick darted a look at him and grinned. "Why? You have a crush on her?"

Yeah. One almost twenty years old.

Jason schooled his face into an expressionless mask. "I just don't want to see her dragged into this mess. I wouldn't want her to get hurt."

Tick shrugged. "Kathleen's pretty able to hold her own, but I'll talk to her again. The only problem is that once she gets an idea in her head, she's like an old hound dog with a bone. And she thinks you saw something yesterday."

An unspoken question lingered in Tick's words. Jason stiffened. "Just like I told her. I didn't see anything."

Except the look in Jim Ed's eyes and he didn't care to ever see that soulless expression again. He glanced around the grove. With the fog lifting, the light filtered through the trees and the dark shifted to gray. Time was running out.

"So did you call me out here to ask me that?" Jason rubbed a hand over his neck, the muscles tight and painful under his fingers.

"Thought you might be interested to know that Thatcher checked out your military record Friday. Seemed real interested in your general discharge. Wanted to know why it wasn't honorable." Tick dropped his cigarette butt and ground it beneath his heel.

Jason chuckled, a humorless sound. "Somehow I expect the Bureau made me seem like a corrupt son of a bitch."

"Something about missing equipment and you flashing a lot of cash around."

The idea of anyone, even Bill Thatcher, thinking him a thief left a metallic taste of disgust in his mouth. "I take it my Purple Heart and Meritorious Service Medals no longer exist?"

Tick laughed. "Not in the reality created for you by the FBI. Sorry, bud, but you've got a pretty unimpressive record right now. Actually, if you want the honest truth, Agent Harding, it sucks."

Jason glanced at the other man, a fellow recipient of Quantico's FBI award. Fidelity. Bravery. Integrity. Not words anyone would attach to his current persona. But if Thatcher was checking him out, going deeper than the cursory reference check the department had done six months ago, maybe they were making some headway. Maybe he was about to be invited into the inner circle, become one of Thatcher's tarnished knights. The thought didn't bring the satisfaction it should. He shook off an image of Laurel kissing Jim Ed's cheek, of the family gathered around his cousin's dining room table.

"What's wrong?" Tick's sharp voice cut through the remaining fog.

Great. Now Calvert suspected him of second thoughts, of wavering in his duty. He shook his head and glanced away.

"I know Jim Ed's your cousin. I know he's family, and I know what that means." Low intensity colored Tick's words. "But the man is a crook. Prostitution, drugs, gambling—you name it and Thatcher's boys have their fingers in it somewhere."

Jason glared. "He's a good father."

To Laurel, anyway. To Jamie? That was arguable. And hell, what did Jason know about what made a passable dad? His hadn't hung around long enough to provide much of an example. Besides, Billy and Jim Ed had definitely been hell-raisers as teens. For all Jason knew, maybe there was more to it than cleaning a damn dog kennel. Maybe Jamie had deeper issues Jim Ed was trying to deal with.

The explanations felt weak, even to him.

"He might be a murderer."

"I know." Jason kicked a stray pecan into the side of a tree. "Damn it, I know."

"Harding. You're the only one who can do this. You're the only one we've ever been able to get on the inside. This goes further than just the Haynes sheriff's department. If we can get Thatcher, we can use him to get at a whole segment of the Dixie Mafia. This is the only way. And you're it, man."

"I haven't said I wouldn't do it. I'm here, aren't I?"

"You can't screw this up, Jason. You mess up, you're dead. Don't think that Jim Ed will put loyalty to you over loyalty to Thatcher. You've got to keep your emotions out of this." Calvert's dark eyes glowed with intensity, even in the dimness. "And that includes any feelings you have for Kathleen Palmer."

"I don't have any feelings for her." Not any he could act on anyway. Not any she would care about. "But she's a problem."

"Maybe not." Tick stroked his thumb over his chin. "If she ties Jim Ed to the boys' deaths, we could use that. He'd be facing the death penalty. Maybe he'd turn on Thatcher in exchange for a reduced sentence."

"Maybe." *But I doubt it.*

"You'd be surprised what a man will do when he's desperate."

That's what he was afraid of and if Kathleen pushed this investigation, Jim Ed could get real desperate, real quick.

"Can we get her pulled off the case? Have it reassigned?"

Tick shrugged. "We can try, but all it'll do is piss her off and she'd be investigating on her own. Believe me. She's so stubborn she makes me look wishy-washy. But you're the real FBI guy. I'm just the ex-agent turned lead investigator for a piss-ant sheriff's department. Do you want me to call the OCD?"

Yes. Jason wanted him to call the Bureau's Organized Crime Division, have the FBI contact the GBI and *request* that Agent Palmer be removed from the case. He wanted her safe.

But if Calvert was right, he'd be shoving her directly into danger. The only way to ensure her safety was to keep an eye on her.

"Harding? Do you want me to call them?"

"No. Just help me keep tabs on what she's doing." Jason glanced at his watch. "I've got to get moving. My shift starts in ten minutes."

"Yeah, mine, too."

Jason was feet away when Calvert called his name. He turned to find the other man watching him with a somber expression. "Harding, you're doing the right thing."

"I know." But betraying the only family he had left seemed far from right.

ന്ദ

If Jason Harding thought he could intimidate her into giving up an investigation, he had another think coming. With a loofah saturated with soap suds, Kathleen scrubbed at her skin. Anger burned in her, anger at Harding and herself. Him for being a son of a bitch. Her for giving in to his sleazy, sexual bullying.

She ought to run him in for obstruction, except then she'd have to explain what he'd done in front of Judge Virgil Holton. At the image, a shudder ran down her body. The old boy network would have fun with that one. With imaginary laughter ringing in her head, she rinsed the soap from her body, the rivulets of water too much like caressing fingers. The steam surrounding her echoed the heat from Jason's body and pinpricks of desire flushed through her.

"Stop it. Stop thinking of him that way." She worked shampoo through her hair with punishing force, trying to wash the sensations from her mind. "Think of him as the corrupt jerk he is."

A *lying*, corrupt jerk.

A lying, corrupt jerk with sexy hands and the most compelling green eyes she'd ever seen.

Growling, she stuck her head beneath the spray. Suds burned her eyes and she stood there until the water grew cold. Anything to cool her heated skin.

Wrapped in a towel, she applied light makeup and rubbed the moisture from her hair. With the hair dryer, she dried her shaggy cut, using a styling pomade to piece out sections. She fingered the layers, wondering if she should let it grow again. For fifteen years, she'd kept the copper strands short.

In her teens, her hair had fallen in a shining sheet almost to her waist. Tom had loved her hair, loved wrapping it around his hand when kissing her or when they made love. She'd wanted to cut it, for convenience's sake, but at his protest, she'd given in and left it long.

A memory rose of the tiny bathroom in their Macon apartment, rough sobs shaking her body, silken copper littering the floor as she took the scissors to her hair. Pain swamped her and she gasped, bending forward. Lord, it hurt now the way it had then when she'd peered into—

Screams echoed in her head. Her jerky movements knocked the dryer from its perch and it clattered to the countertop. Leaning against the wall, Kathleen closed her eyes to keep the stinging tears at bay. This was never going away. She didn't deserve to have it go away. She deserved the anguish, deserved it because she'd failed in the worst possible way a woman could.

A few minutes later, she repaired the damage to her makeup and slipped into her standard khakis and GBI polo. Once more buried beneath composed resolve, the ache of grief tried to pulse, and she squashed it. She couldn't change what had happened, but she didn't have to dwell on it. And she didn't have to open herself up to that kind of hurt again.

The worst pain of her life came out of trying to be the woman her husband, her parents, expected her to be. She was infinitely better off being the cop the GBI expected. Failure there meant censure, a mere blow to her pride. Failure as a woman meant so much more.

Jason Harding was dangerous. Dangerous simply because he was associated with the den of rattlesnakes in Haynes County.

Dangerous because he made her feel like a woman again.

ଔଓ

Freshly brewed coffee tickled Kathleen's nose and a couple of voices drifted down the hall, early morning shoptalk, even on a Sunday morning. So she wasn't the only one with an open case, obviously.

She flipped to the next page of the computer printout on her desk. Harding's background was about as impressive as his home. She rubbed a finger over his high school graduation date, three years after her own. A twelve-year stint in the army with no commendations. A general discharge. The last year he'd worked as a security guard and been fired from that job before applying with the sheriff's department in Haynes County.

No arrests, but a string of traffic violations. She eyed the list of speeding tickets from various states. Lord, it was a wonder the man even had a license to drive.

His credit report was atrocious. Collections, garnishments, returned checks, even a repossession.

All of it added up to a man ripe to be seduced by money.

She dropped the paper and rubbed at her temples. Why did she care anyway?

"What are you reading?" Altee set a cup of coffee in front of her.

"Jason Harding's background file." Sipping the sugar- and cream-laden liquid, Kathleen groaned at her partner's knowing expression. "God, Altee, don't look at me like that."

Altee leaned back in her chair, designer loafers propped on the edge of her desk. "You went to see him last night, didn't you?"

"I went to ask him some questions."

"That couldn't have waited until this morning?"

Kathleen placed her cup next to the plant her mother sent for her birthday. She fingered the brown edge of a leaf. "I wanted to catch him off-guard."

"You're lucky you didn't get caught off-guard, going in that county without backup. God, Kath, rookies know better." With a disgusted sigh, Altee straightened in her chair.

"I know." She remembered the mingled fear and excitement incited by being trapped between Harding and her Jeep. Okay, it was official—she'd gone way too long without sex for that to give her a jolly. "It won't happen again. Trust me."

Altee fixed her with a hard look. "Promise me."

"Okay."

"I mean it, Palmer. Those boys don't play. Think about the state trooper who disappeared over there. We never even found his car. Or what about Calvert's daddy? These sons of bitches are good at killing people and getting away with it."

Ice shivered down her spine, but she covered the fear with anger. "Fine."

Altee jumped to her feet and prowled the office, one hand waving in the air. "Damn it, do you even realize what you did? Okay, Harding is sexy as hell, but you can't forget what he is."

"I'm not." Defensiveness stung Kathleen's throat, making it hard to get the words out.

"Right." Altee glared, her full, bee-stung lips compressed to a thin line. "You already did. Maybe we should pass this case off—"

"No."

"But—"

"I said no." She might be a failure in the personal areas of her life, but not as a cop. She could handle this like a professional. She *would* handle this like a professional and she wouldn't let some sick attraction to a corrupt deputy get in the way. "We're not handing it off."

Altee threw up her hands. "Fine."

"Fine." They stared at each other for a long moment and Kathleen dropped her gaze first. "Let's walk down to the lab and see if Whitlock has anything on the truck. I know Williams hasn't even started on the autopsies yet."

ଔ

The S-10 sat alone in the garage, a forlorn last testament to the loss of two lives. The doors stood open, the seat on a table nearby.

"Hey, Whitlock. You around?" Kathleen's voice echoed through the metal building.

Allan Whitlock popped up from the other side of the truck. “Palmer. Price. Report’s not ready yet.”

Altee shrugged. “We just wanted to see if you had any preliminary findings.”

A wry grin twisted Whitlock’s mouth. “Yeah. The kids shot themselves by using astral projection.”

Electric excitement sizzled along Kathleen’s nerves. She exchanged a quick glance with her partner. “What do you mean?”

White lab coat flapping, Whitlock gestured at the cab. “Gunpowder residue. The amount inside is too low.”

“So the shots came from outside the truck.”

“Maybe.” Whitlock shrugged.

Frustrated, Kathleen resisted the urge to smack the lab technician who always talked in circles and riddles. “You just said the gun couldn’t have gone off in the cab.”

“That’s not what I said. The amount seems low, but if the shots were close to the bodies, a lot of the residue will be on the clothing, which hasn’t been checked yet.”

“Whitlock, I hate you.” Altee sighed and stuck her hands in her back pockets. “Would you call us when you have some useful information?”

“Definite useful information,” Kathleen added.

“How’s this for useful?” Whitlock asked, his voice mild. “The swabs we took off Jim Ed Reese’s hands yesterday? Tested positive for residue.”

Kathleen’s excitement, which had subsided, sprang to life again. “Thanks, Whitlock. We’ll check in with you later.”

He waved them off and Kathleen pulled her partner outside. “Let’s take a ride over to Haynes County.”

"It's not enough for a warrant. You know how pissy Judge Holton is about probable cause and we both know this ain't it."

Kathleen smiled. "Yeah, but it's enough to make Reese nervous. He should be on the last day of his rotation this week. Let's go harass him a little at work, see if we can trip him up."

"We might as well go see if we can get Reverend Johnson to say the Second Coming isn't imminent."

Kathleen nudged Altee's shoulder. "Oh, ye of little faith. Don't think Jim Ed's ego will get the better of him?"

"It's not his ego I'm worried about," Altee mumbled. "It's your attraction to Goodbody."

"Altee. Stop it." Kathleen pulled her sunglasses from her pocket and slid them on, seeking protection from the sun as well as her partner's all-seeing eyes. "We covered this. I'm not attracted to him."

"Oh, sure. And Calvert's not the hottest eligible bachelor in Chandler County."

Kathleen forced a laugh. "Calvert's not hot."

"Oh, girl. You *do* have a serious case of denial. You haven't even figured out that it's not Reese you're going to see. It's Harding." Altee slipped on her own sunglasses. "Come on. Let's go stir up a mess of trouble."

ଓଃ

Jason stared at the thick hamburger sitting on the square of greasy waxed paper. His stomach revolted. He pushed the sandwich to one side and reached for his iced tea. A nagging headache lingered at his temples and the noise of the squad room did nothing to relieve it.

"Jim Ed, you got a headache powder?"

“Yeah.” Chewing, his cousin rummaged in the desk drawer and tossed him the small packet.

“Thanks.” Jason tilted his head back and dropped the white powder on his tongue. He grimaced at the bitter taste and gulped tea to wash down the painkiller.

“Look like a flock of vultures to you, Altee?” Kathleen Palmer’s voice filled the room and Jason strangled on the swallow of tea. He coughed, eyes watering, the acidic medicine mingling with the syrupy-sweet tea.

Holy shit. What was she doing *here?*

“No. Vultures have better manners.” Derisive laughter colored Altee’s drawl.

“What do you want, Palmer?” Jim Ed demanded.

Jason lifted his head, gulping from the cup again. Kathleen leaned in the doorway, arms crossed over her chest, an anticipatory smile flirting around her lips. She didn’t look at him, her attention focused on Jim Ed.

“Oh, just stopped by to chat.” She straightened and stepped into the room. The two women moved with the well-oiled timing of a long partnership. The deputies’ lunchtime chatter fell silent, the television providing the only background noise. Nerves jerked in Jason’s stomach.

“We ain’t got time to talk to you.” Anger darkened Jim Ed’s face.

“Really? Not even if I told you we have some very interesting lab results?” If they were vultures, Kathleen was a lioness moving in for the kill. A beautiful lioness with a feral smile.

Jim Ed took another bite of his hamburger. A couple of deputies slipped out of the room.

Altee perched on the edge of the closest desk and Kathleen pulled out a chair. The women exchanged a glance and

Kathleen leaned forward, still smiling. "Don't you want to know what we found, Reese?"

The look Jim Ed shot her way vibrated with hatred. "No."

"What if I told you that yesterday your hand was covered with gunpowder residue?"

With a smile, Jim Ed leaned back in his chair. "I'd say I'd been on the range earlier in the day." He flicked a hand in Jason's direction. "With him."

"You want to know what's really weird, Jim Ed?" Altee's smooth voice slid over Jason's ears. "All that residue on you and hardly any in the cab of that truck. Isn't that strange?"

"Whatever, Price." Rising, Jim Ed tossed his hamburger wrapper in the trash. He pointed at Jason. "You ready to get back to work?"

This time, Kathleen glanced at Jason and he cringed at her disdain. Now he was lower than gum on her shoe. More like dog crap.

Holding her gaze, he stood and discarded his own burger. "Yeah. Let's go."

"Don't let us keep you." Kathleen stood and Altee slid from the desk. "We know how busy you boys are, protecting and serving."

Jim Ed watched the two women leave, his fingers caressing the butt of his gun. He glanced at Jason, sending foreboding crashing through his brain. "We've got to do something about those bitches."

Chapter Four

Kathleen dropped her shoes by the couch and crossed to open the curtains at the wide glass doors. Early morning sunlight spilled into the room. Outside on the lake, the ducks flocked to the deck where Altee had left food for them.

The scent of biscuits and eggs drifted from Kathleen's small kitchen, accompanied by the scraping of a spatula against a skillet. Vicious scraping. Kathleen shook her head. Obviously, Altee wished that cast-iron skillet was some part of Montaine Walker's anatomy.

"So tell me what happened last night," Kathleen called, picking up a magazine from the floor and dropping it back in a basket.

"I went over there, planning to fix him a special dinner since I broke our date last weekend. Used my key to let myself in." The distance between the kitchen and living room did little to soften the hurt anger in Altee's voice. "Should have saved myself the trouble. Montaine already had himself a special dinner."

"How old was she?"

"About nineteen and full of attitude, even buck naked. That's it, Kath. I'm through with men."

"You said that the last time." Kathleen folded the fringed, silk throw, arranging it over the back of the couch. "Maybe you just need to look in different places."

"I found him at my mama's church."

"Oh. Yeah. I forgot about that."

"I'm serious. I'm through looking for Mr. Right and happily ever after. I'm going to go out and have fun until I'm too old and gray, then I'm still going to try to kick up my heels with my wrinkly old ass hanging out of a skirt that's way too short."

"Sounds like a plan." Kathleen wandered into the kitchen.

Altee slid fluffy scrambled eggs onto waiting plates and shot her an irritable look. "I'm not going to stop living because of a man."

Kathleen refused to rise to the bait. "You think I have?"

"Not because of a man, but you've buried yourself under all that grief and guilt you carry around."

Lord, she wished Altee would beat around the bush every once in a while. She poured coffee, her hands shaking. "I have a life."

"No. You have a job that consumes you." Altee dropped mile-high flaky biscuits next to the eggs. "Going out on the occasional duty date your mama sets up is not living. Dancing with Calvert at all those fundraisers you attend for your daddy is not living. Just face it. The real you is in that coffin with—"

"Stop." Kathleen slammed the carafe back on the coffee maker. "Enough. I'm going to get the paper."

Walking down the long hall to the front door, she struggled against the anger and pain. Altee *knew* this subject was off-limits. Everyone did. The problem was, once Altee got on a tear about something, getting her to back off was beyond difficult.

Kathleen did *not* want to spend the entire workday hearing about how she needed a life.

She swung the inner door open and the snake fell on her bare foot. Pure, primal dread trickled down her back.

"God Almighty!" She leapt back, the rattlesnake's body rolling over on the floor. A moment passed before the realization the snake was dead sank into her brain.

"What's wrong?" Footsteps thudded on the floor and concern laced Altee's voice.

"That was in my door." Kathleen nudged the lifeless snake with her toe and revulsion pulsed in her veins.

Trying to conceal the tremors running along her skin, Kathleen turned to face Altee. Her partner stared back, her skin yellow, SIG nine millimeter in hand, eyes huge and dark in her face.

Altee's throat moved with her swallow. "I told you, Kath, these boys don't play."

ଔ

"Someone killed it with one clean shot through the head. A damn good shot." Tick straightened to his feet, gazing down at the dead snake. He slanted a grin in Altee's direction. "Think you could do that after all that extra time you've been spending on the range, Price?"

"Hey, that practice has paid off." Altee leaned against the wall and returned his grin. "But I'm good at lots of stuff, Calvert."

"Really? You might have to show me sometime."

Their meaningless flirtation grated on Kathleen's exposed nerve endings. "Could you two save this for later? Altee, I thought you were swearing off men."

"I'll make an exception for him. He's good to his mama—that says a lot."

Tick chuckled, lifting the snake by its tail and dropping it into an oversized evidence bag. "You and Montaine split up?"

"That's one way to put it."

"He wasn't good enough for you—"

"Hello? This isn't a Sunday social," Kathleen snapped, pacing a few steps down the hall. "Somebody put a freakin' snake in my door!"

Unruffled by her anger, Tick closed the evidence bag. "What do you expect, Kath? You're stepping on Jim Ed's toes. He's not going to send you candy and roses, for God's sake."

She glared at him, arms folded over her chest, as much to contain her fear as her anger. "You sound like you think I should back off and let him get away with murder."

"I didn't say that. I'm just telling you that if you go ahead with this investigation, you can expect things to get even nastier. You can't be naïve and think he's just going to lie down and let you build a capital murder case against him."

"I'm not naïve." At least, she hadn't thought she was, but she'd believed her position with the GBI would protect her. What had she been thinking? Being a US Marshall hadn't protected Tick's father from Bill Thatcher's retaliation.

"This is a typical warning. It's a back-off statement. The next one you're likely to find inside your mailbox. And it'll be alive. You've got to be careful." Tick's voice brooked no arguments. "Both of you."

The storm door swung open, admitting the young deputy who'd accompanied Tick on the call. He eyed the plastic bag Tick held. "I got the prints off the door. Are we dusting the snake for prints, too?"

At Tick's long-suffering expression, Kathleen forced down a hysterical giggle. Tick shook his head. "Yeah, Troy Lee, we're gonna get prints off a damn snake."

Flushing, the young man backed out the door. "I'll put the evidence kit back in the car."

"You do that." Tick waited for him to leave and rested his head against the wall, blowing out a long breath. "I swear, I've seen fence posts with more common sense. I think Stanton hired him just to get even with me for being a pain in the ass when I was a rookie agent."

Altee shot him a questioning look. "Why are you taking the snake?"

He grinned and moved toward the door. "I'm going to turn him into a belt. I'm sending the prints over to the Moultrie crime lab, which means y'all will get the results before I do. But I doubt there'll be any other than the two of you. Remember what I said about being careful."

"I don't think we'll forget." Altee closed the door behind him and turned to fix Kathleen with a stern look. "Come on, Kath. We need to talk."

ଓ୫ଌ

Jason dropped the office copy of his traffic citations in the wire basket. Glad the long, slow day was over, he wanted nothing more than to go home, have a beer, take a hot shower and fall into bed. Driving circles around Haynes County, answering three calls and writing a handful of speeding tickets didn't define his idea of a productive existence.

The sheriff's office door opened and Jim Ed stepped into the squad room, chuckling. The quality of that small laugh raised the hair on Jason's arms.

Jim Ed clapped him on the shoulder and crossed to the coffee station. "Rough day?"

"Boring day."

After filling his mug, Jim Ed leaned against the counter and grinned at Jason over the rim. "I bet our lady friends at the GBI don't share your sentiments."

His breath stopped in his throat. Forcing himself to inhale and exhale, he shrugged. "What do you mean?"

"We left Kathleen Palmer a little calling card this morning. If she has any sense at all, she'll back off."

Jason dropped his citation book on the desk and went to pour himself a cup of coffee. Anything to keep his hands too busy to wrap around Jim Ed's throat. "What kind of calling card?"

"A dead five-foot rattler." Jim Ed chuckled again, a twisted little-kid-at-Christmas sound. "In her front door."

Visions of Kathleen opening a door and a rattler tumbling at her feet assailed him. Jason lifted his cup and scorched coffee assaulted his tongue. "Think it'll scare her off?"

"Who cares? If it doesn't, there are ways."

He didn't even want to think about that statement. He sipped his coffee, pretending to mull over his cousin's words. "You know, there might be another way to get her to back off."

"Yeah?"

"Stacy does what you tell her to, right?"

"She better."

"What if I could convince Kathleen Palmer to do what I told her to?"

Lasciviousness spread across Jim Ed's face. "Boy, you've got it bad, don't you?"

"You got to admit, she looks like a sweet piece." He had to force the words out, thanking Mrs. Louella Hatcher for three years of drama instruction. "Wouldn't be a hardship to get close to her and convince her to do the right thing."

Not to mention getting close to her would allow him to keep an eye on her.

Jim Ed's lips twisted, a thoughtful frown between his eyebrows. "You think she'd look twice at you?"

Anger fired to life in his gut, and he shoved down the impulse to choke his cousin. Instead, he shrugged again. "Won't know unless I try."

With a shake of his head, Jim Ed drained his coffee cup. "Go for it, cousin, but I'm telling you—if you can't get her to back off, I can."

ଓଌ

Kathleen Palmer's home perched on stilts on a small lot overlooking Ocean Lake. The neighborhood was old and many of the homes were in various stages of restoration. The wooden shakes on Kathleen's house sparkled under a new coat of white paint. Bright red geraniums sat in pottery crocks on the front porch and marched up the steps to her back deck. Ferns swung in lazy arcs from the open rafters.

Jason glanced out over the lake, appreciating the view. Man, to have that stretch of fish-rich water in the backyard. Perfect for a boat or jet ski.

A glass-topped metal table and chairs with plush cushions dominated one end of the deck. Jason knocked at the French door and wandered over to study the large square tiles spread atop newspaper on one end of the table. Polished sea glass covered the tiles in a mosaic pattern, the scent of fresh glue heavy in the air. He rubbed his thumb over a bit of bright blue glass.

"What are you doing here?" Ice coated Kathleen's voice.

He spun, hands tucked in the pockets of his uniform pants. She stood in the doorway, legs in an open, aggressive stance. A pair of low-slung denim capris clung to fantastic legs and a pale pink blouse tied at her waist revealed an inch or so of a flat stomach. Following the direction of his gaze, she crossed her arms over her midriff.

Jason lifted his gaze to her face. "I owe you an apology."

One eyebrow arched. Her stance didn't change.

"I was completely out of line the other night."

She didn't reply, but continued to watch him with those gold-flecked eyes. Jason swallowed, tempted for a moment to spill his guts, tell her everything, reveal his true self.

Yeah, that would go over real well with his Bureau chief. This whole crazy idea of getting close to Kathleen to keep her safe was guaranteed to get him called on the carpet, but, really, what could they do? As Calvert said, he was it. The only one they could get inside.

Still she watched him. He swallowed again and rocked back on his heels. "My behavior...my attempt to intimidate you...was inexcusable."

She shrugged. "Fine. You apologized."

The dismissal was plain. "I told you the truth. I didn't see anything the day before yesterday. I arrived the same time as Calvert. I saw *nothing.*"

Her hand on the doorknob, she stepped back. "I doubt you'd know the truth if it jumped up and bit you."

He couldn't let her go, not until she understood the seriousness of the situation. Not until she really understood how far Jim Ed was willing to go. "I know about the snake in your door."

Her face flushed, and her entire body stiffened. "I'm sure you do."

"Kathleen, you don't know what he's capable of."

"Your cousin?" She released the door and stalked across the deck to stand in front of him. "Oh, I think I do. Maybe you're the one who doesn't want to see what he is." She paused, her gaze searching his face. "Or maybe you do see and you're willing to look the other way. Maybe you're in this up to *your* neck as well."

"I'm...not." Not the way she thought, anyway.

She stared at him, minutes ticking away, and he wondered what clicked through her head. She stood close enough that he could see the pulse beating in her throat, smell the Ivory clinging to her skin.

His stomach growled, filling the silence.

Her eyebrow quirked again. "Hungry?"

"I skipped lunch." Breakfast had been a cup of coffee in the squad room. He lived on the actual salary paid to him by the department and, after his utility bill, he had three dollars in his pocket until Friday. Gas money for the truck that got eight miles to the gallon.

She shook her head and turned away. "Come on."

"Excuse me?"

At the door, she paused and sent him an inscrutable look over her shoulder. "I just finished cooking and I've never mastered the art of cooking for one. I'm inviting you to supper."

His pride warred with hunger and the desire to be with her. The hunger and desire triumphed, sending his pride to hide in a corner and lick its nonfatal wounds. Sooner or later it would arise and get its own back. Right now, he was being offered food and Kathleen. His pride could take a hike.

She left the door open, not waiting for him to follow.

Jason stepped over the threshold. He'd expected the house to reflect her monied background. The home was rich, but not with expensive trappings. Rich with what had to be Kathleen. Rich with a sense of home and welcome that tried to wrap seductive tentacles around him.

Textures called out to him, begging to be touched—rough cotton-weave curtains, a leather couch, a silk throw, a sisal carpet over slick wooden floors. Clean, spicy scents filled the living room—cinnamon and something more elusive, mingled with the aroma of baked chicken wafting from the kitchen. Books lined built-in shelves, sharing space with a small television and a smaller stereo.

No photos. Anywhere. None of her family, friends, vacation memories.

Hell, even he kept photos of his time in Kuwait.

"Bathroom is down the hall on the left if you want to wash up." Kathleen's voice filtered from the kitchen.

Photographs lined the hallway—black and white shots of Chandler County landmarks. The courthouse. The ancient Baptist church. An ornate iron fence surrounding a family plot. Her parents' home.

A door stood open on the right, revealing a small office area, striking only by its impersonal air.

When he opened the closed bathroom door, the lingering scent of Ivory enveloped him. Droplets of water glistened on the transparent glass shower and he swallowed, heat curling along his nerves.

A second door, slightly ajar, revealed her bedroom. More textures—cotton comforter and sheets, satin throw pillows, another silk throw, a fluffy rug by the bed. All in white. He had a sudden vision of her coppery hair and creamy skin against that pure white. The heat fired into full-fledged flames.

"Come on, Harding, get it together," he whispered, running cold water over his hands. "Like you're ever gonna make it into that bed. Give it up, man. You're just trying to keep her safe."

He dried his hands on a damp towel and tried not to think about that same towel smoothing water from her long legs.

This meal promised to be even longer and more torturous than his day.

ଔଔ

What was she thinking?

Kathleen stabbed a fork into a potato, then repeated the action on its hapless partner. She shoved the pair into the microwave.

Altee was right. She was crazy.

Actually, the word her partner had used was *obsessed.* Obsessed with the past. Obsessed with this case. Obsessed with Jason Harding.

She and Altee had not parted on good terms at the end of the day.

So what did Altee's obsessed Kathleen go and do? Feed the guy.

Lord, it was just dinner. One meal. And she intended to get answers out of him. It wasn't like she planned to sleep with him.

The creak of his leather gun belt told her he was in the living area again. Plates and cutlery in hand, she stepped out of the kitchen. He stood in front of her bookshelves, studying the titles. Kathleen eyed the line of his back and wondered how much of the shoulder bulk was his and how much belonged to the bulletproof vest.

"I usually eat on the deck."

He spun, not smiling. His pale green eyes drew her in, making her forget who he really was. He gestured at the plates she held. "Want me to set the table?"

"Please." She handed the plates over, careful not to let their fingers brush. Imagining his touch was bad enough. She didn't need the real thing to fixate on.

She returned to the kitchen for the salad bowl and platter of baked chicken breasts. He met her at the French door and took them, a quick grin playing around his mouth. The boyish expression sent an ache through her abdomen again.

This idea was the craziest she'd ever had. Getting to know him in an attempt to persuade him to open up about the chase and its aftermath. Back in the kitchen, she tossed ice in two glasses and grabbed the pitcher of iced tea. She closed her eyes for a moment. *Who are you kidding? You just want to know him, period. He intrigues you, and it's been so long since anyone did that you're willing to risk everything.*

She should tell him it was all a mistake, tell him to go. The lab results would come in, the autopsy reports, and they'd have Jim Ed. She didn't need to do this.

The truth was she wanted to. Her lungs closed, panic rising in her throat. Her career was all she had left, and she was throwing it away with this crazy course of action.

"Anything else?" His tenor drawl jerked her from the abyss.

Her eyes snapped open and she looked at him, sure from his watchful expression that he could see her fear and uncertainty. Feeling raw and exposed, she shoved the glasses at him. "Just these."

He stared down at her for a long moment before turning on his heel and striding out of the kitchen. Kathleen sagged against the counter, her heart pounding a sickening rhythm against her ribs. When had everything gotten so out of control?

ଔ

Kathleen laid her fork down by her plate. A breeze played along the deck, lifting fern fronds, ruffling the edges of Jason's brown hair. He ate with excellent table manners, but also with the appreciation of true hunger. They'd talked during the meal, of topics far removed from what she knew was uppermost in both of their minds.

He described some of the far-flung places the army had sent him and asked questions about novels on her shelves. He was sharply intelligent, possessed a quick wit and cut straight to the heart of a topic. Everything she liked in a man.

She just didn't want to find it in this man.

"Why Haynes County?" she asked and watched him freeze.

He took a sip of his tea and shrugged, and she knew he was giving himself time to formulate an answer. "It's home."

"Jason." He glanced at her, his green eyes guarded. "That's not what I asked and you know it. There are other departments. Stanton Reed has been hiring left and right."

His mouth twisted in a grim semblance of a smile. "Reed's looking for knights in shining armor. Let's just say my background isn't sparkling clean enough."

"But you don't have to—"

"Kathleen." He dropped his fork by his plate, the line of his jaw tight. "I'm no Tick Calvert—you know, local football hero, valedictorian, FBI award recipient. I'm just what I am. A Haynes County boy who didn't make it so good in the real world. I needed a job and Jim Ed came through for me. I owe him."

The words shivered through her. "Enough to lie for him?"

"I told you. I didn't see anything."

"I know what you told me. I want the truth."

"The truth is that I don't know what happened. I didn't see it."

She sat back. "Would you tell me if you had?"

"Do you really want me to answer that?" His mouth firmed. He glanced away, then back at her, his eyes the color of a rough sea. "Look, Kathleen, I want to see you again. But you have to take me for what I am."

Anger flushed through her. Arrogant son of a bitch. "You're assuming a lot, aren't you? This wasn't a date, Harding. I invited you to dinner because...because..."

"Let me guess. Because you felt sorry for me and you thought you'd get out of me the information you think I have." The chair scraped against the deck and he tossed his napkin down. "Thanks for the meal, Palmer."

He strode toward the steps. Kathleen shoved up from the table and followed. The idea was get close to him, use him to get inside Thatcher's operation. Not piss him off and push him away. "Wait."

"Why?" He turned on her, color high on his cheekbones. "You going to offer to screw me to get me to talk?"

Swallowing her fury, Kathleen frowned at him. "Did you mean what you said?"

Confusion glittered in his eyes. "About what?"

"About wanting to see me again." Oh, if Altee found out about this, she was dead.

His eyebrows rose. "Yeah."

"Good. Dinner tomorrow night. Same time."

"You're sure?"

No. Anything but. She nodded. "I'm sure."

A quick nod and he was gone, bounding down the steps, handcuffs and keys jingling against his gun belt. Kathleen watched him go, dread and anticipation mingling in her stomach.

What on earth had she just done?

Chapter Five

"We've got positive IDs and preliminary autopsy results on the boys from the truck."

At Altee's cool voice, Kathleen looked up from the witness statements she was rereading for the umpteenth time that morning. She couldn't concentrate, couldn't convince her mind to stop straying to Jason Harding. Her thoughts wandered to the way his cheek dimpled when he smiled or how his voice rumbled over her nerve endings, instead of considering the repercussions her actions could have, like destroying her career.

"Kath?"

After dropping the statements on her desk, Kathleen rubbed a hand over her eyes. "So who are they?"

"Runaways from Pensacola. The driver took his mom's car the night they left. It was found abandoned in the public parking lot by the beach in Panama City, which, by the way, is where the S-10 was stolen from. The rifle? Belonged to the owner of the truck."

"What about the handgun?"

"Neither set of parents or the truck owner reports a handgun missing."

Kathleen shook her head. “Like anyone would admit to having an untraceable gun with the serial numbers etched off.”

“An untraceable gun with no serial number *and* no fingerprints,” Altee pointed out, her voice wry.

“It doesn’t make sense. Jim Ed’s not that sloppy.” The man was known for his meticulous behavior. The whole thing didn’t make sense. If he’d killed the boys, what was his motive?

“Maybe he’s not. Maybe someone else is. Someone not as experienced at being a corrupt son of a bitch.”

Someone like Jason Harding.

“You said we had positive identifications?” Kathleen tried to banish the unsaid words hanging between them. What if it really wasn’t Jim Ed? What if it were Jason?

God, this case was going to make her insane before it was all over.

Altee handed her a fax printout. “Connor White, age seventeen. Heath Brannon, age fourteen. Although you might as well say fifteen. His birthday would’ve been in a couple of days.”

Two days. April 16. Heath Brannon would have been fifteen on April 16. Kathleen brushed her finger over the smudged characters. So would Everett.

He shared Everett’s birthday.

Pain crashed through her body, freezing the breath in her lungs. She refused to close her eyes, knowing if she did, she’d be confronted with an image of bright brown eyes, sparkling with laughter and golden flecks, a chubby face surrounded by russet hair.

What would that face have looked like at fifteen? Her eyes burned, and she swallowed against the tightening of her throat.

“You want to know what’s really weird?” Altee perched on the edge of her own desk.

Kathleen struggled to bring her attention back to the conversation. "What?"

"Cause of death for both boys was a gunshot wound to the head."

"We knew that without the autopsies."

"The wound damage couldn't have come from that .38. Williams is willing to swear to it in court."

"A defense attorney will argue they shot themselves with the rifle."

Altee smiled. "See, that's the thing. Chandler County reports two shots fired at one of their deputies. We found only two shell casings in the truck. And it gets better. The wounds are to the left side of their heads."

"Okay." Kathleen tried again to focus on her partner's words. She pushed the memories and the pain into their little compartment in her mind and shut the door.

"According to their parents, both boys were right-handed."

"So they shot themselves with the wrong hand with a nonexistent weapon." Kathleen rested her chin on her hands. "I wonder if he's realized yet how badly he screwed up."

"Oh, he's probably scrambling for a way to cover it up. You know what we need to do? Listen to those dispatch tapes."

Kathleen leaned down to pick up a box from the floor by her desk. "One step ahead of you."

They settled in, the tape player on the desk between them, and listened to Chandler County's recording first. Kathleen frowned, tapping a pen against her lips as the dispatch record played out. A shiver of foreboding traveled down her spine.

"Wait. Play that back."

"The whole thing?"

"From where they contact Haynes dispatch."

Altee hit the play button again. Troy Lee's voice held excitement blended with a trace of fear. "Chandler, we're westbound on County Line Road, approximately three miles from Haynes County. Notify Haynes of status."

"Chief Deputy Reese has been monitoring chase on radio, is standing by at county line, C-8."

"What have we got?" Jim Ed's distinctive drawl cut across the static.

"Two armed robbery suspects coming into your county."

"What do we need to do to stop them?"

"He's caused a city unit to 10-50, has tried to ram a unit and is shooting at patrol cars," Troy Lee retorted. "Does that answer your question?"

"10-4."

"This is where his car runs hot," Altee said, fast-forwarding the tape. "Calvert picks him up and..."

"Chandler, we've got C-8. Back in the chase." Tick's calm voice. "Suspect vehicle is back in sight, now in Haynes County. Vehicle is approximately a mile ahead of us."

Kathleen studied the map. "There's a really steep hill at that point. He'd have lost sight of him."

Ten. Fifteen seconds of silence.

"Chandler, suspect vehicle 10-50. Two Haynes units on site."

More silence, then Tick's voice again, the tension higher than before.

"Chandler, notify GBI. We'll be needing the coroner."

Two Haynes units on site. Two. Fifteen seconds. What could happen in fifteen seconds?

Fifteen seconds was long enough to empty a clip from a semi-automatic handgun. Long enough to see who fired two fatal shots. Long enough to tell a lie. Long enough for Jason Harding to have made her forget all of her training.

With a groan, she buried her head in her hands. Disappointment and self-disgust rolled through her. She'd let him blind her to the truth, forget her duty. To Altee's credit, she didn't say, "I told you so."

After a moment, Kathleen lifted her head. "Play the Haynes County one."

The second tape began with Reese's interaction with Troy Lee. The tape crackled, obliterating Reese's voice for a moment. "H-13, what's your twenty?"

The croaking of frogs accompanied Jason's voice. "Highway 112, just north of the Bridgeboro crossroads."

Altee frowned and hit the pause button. "Frogs?"

Kathleen nodded, already figuring the mileage. "There's a pull-off there where the Haynes boys like to run radar. It's right next to the dairy's drainage pond. More frogs than Egypt saw during the plagues."

"So he's how far from where the chase ended?" Altee started the tape again. Jason confirmed he was en route to serve as Jim Ed's backup.

"Three to four miles. He's coming from the opposite direction as Tick." A blend of relief and frustration rolled through her. With the distance involved, Jason would have arrived scant seconds before Tick, but he still could have had time to see what happened. Not enough time to commit the murders himself, but enough time to see them take place. She was no closer now to knowing the truth than she'd been before, but she was closer to losing her heart.

The remainder of the tape confirmed her calculations. His "on scene" call to dispatch came just four seconds before Tick reported seeing both units.

"Well, that was really helpful." Altee snapped off the tape player.

"He was telling the truth about when he arrived."

Eyes narrowed and lips thinned, Altee looked at her. "You really want to believe this guy, don't you?"

Kathleen rose and paced to the window. She leaned against the sill, her fingers clutching it until her knuckles ached. "If he's telling the truth about that, he could be telling the truth about what he saw."

Altee's hands fluttered like angry birds. "Do you *hear* yourself? These guys left a dead snake in your storm door. That's a threat, Kath! And you're giving him the benefit of the doubt."

Everything her partner said made sense and Kathleen could imagine herself saying the same things if their positions were reversed. In her mind, though, she kept hearing Jason swearing he wasn't involved in the snake incident, that he hadn't seen anything the day the boys died. She remembered his enthusiasm as he talked about his time in the army, his quick grin, the way his eyes crinkled at the corners.

Altee was right.

She *wanted* to believe in him.

He was a Haynes County boy and she wanted to believe him so badly she was looking for ways to back up his story.

Hell, she was using a case to get close to him.

What did that say about her?

"Kathleen?"

She closed her eyes briefly, then looked at the woman who'd been closer than any sister ever could be. A frown carved a deep furrow between Altee's brows. Kathleen blew out a long, shaky breath.

Tears pushed up in her throat and she blinked. "This conversation stays between us."

"Of course."

"Girl talk, Altee, not cop talk."

"Just spit it out."

"I don't want him to be involved in this. I want to believe him. God, Altee, I don't know what to do."

"You've got to stay away from him. I don't want to see this blow up in your face, and the whole situation is one of those nasty little things that tend to do that. He's a potential suspect and you're a lead agent."

Kathleen turned away, staring out the window. In the parking lot, a handful of tiny birds fluttered along the ground. In her gut, she knew Altee was right. Jason Harding was trouble waiting to happen. The best thing to do was avoid brewing trouble and cancel her dinner invitation. The right thing to do.

Then why did her chest ache at the mere thought of not seeing him again?

ʚɞ

Whistling an off-tune version of "Ring of Fire", Jason jogged up the steps of the sheriff's department. Thanks to a last-minute call, his shift had run an hour over, but he found himself grateful. Only an hour until he was supposed to be at

Kathleen's—time to clock out, run home to shower and hotfoot it over to her place.

He felt like a seventeen-year-old with a hot date and no matter how many times he told himself this was business, part of his job and not a real date, it did nothing to kill his excitement.

For once, quiet lay over the squad room. Even the television was turned off. Jason moved through his end-of-shift routine with rapid efficiency. He remembered the wild tangle of his mother's tiny rose garden at the trailer. A couple of the overgrown plants bloomed, spilling creamy pink and vibrant red buds on the too-high grass. Maybe he'd cut some of those, stick them in one of the cheap milk-glass vases under the sink. Something to keep him from showing up at Kathleen's door empty-handed.

As he walked to the dispatch area to clock out, pink message slips fluttered on the window separating the small office from the squad room.

Berta, the second-shift dispatcher, waved toward the glass. "You got messages, Harding."

"Yeah?"

Her smirk set the nerves off in his gut. These were not good messages.

The first bore Jim Ed's distinctive scrawl. *Meet me at the rec center ball field.*

The second heaved his stomach straight to his feet. *Kathleen Palmer called. Dinner's off. Permanently.*

ଔ

A cacophony of voices and the soft thuds of baseballs hitting broken-in gloves filled the early evening air. Another month and the temperature would be unbearable at this hour, but tonight a breeze flirted across the Haynes-Chandler rec center's baseball fields. Jason paused by the concession stand, scanning the crowd for Jim Ed's sturdy frame.

The aroma of fresh popcorn tickled his nose and made his mouth water. The bowl of Rice Krispies he'd run home to eat at lunch was long gone. He regretted Kathleen's cancellation of their dinner plans for more than one reason.

Set free from their mothers, a pack of young children ran wild and played chase under and around the bleachers. On the nearest field, a T-ball game was underway, the current batter biting his lip in concentration as he lined the bat up with the ball. A father yelled encouragement from the stands.

Jason smiled, eyeing the strawberry blond curls poking out from under the batting helmet. If he and Kathleen...

Whoa. Hold up, Harding. Where are you going with that? You and Kathleen, nothing. And certainly not kids. Your concern is her safety and helping bring down a section of the Dixie Mafia. Not necessarily in that order either, pal.

But, man, he'd love to have a kid one day, except he wanted to be out there on the field, coaching. Not sitting in the stands, in any aspect of a child's life. *His* son would know he had a father, wouldn't always be the one who stood out because his father was long gone, because he'd been abandoned.

And look at the home Kathleen had created in the small lake house. He'd bet money she'd be an awesome mother. He shook off the daydreams, the ones that had plagued him since dinner the night before. Waking dreams of what it would be like to make a life with Kathleen Palmer.

Maybe when this was all over. When he was himself again. If he didn't make her hate him in the process.

"Come on, Jamie! Catch that ball!"

Yeah, that was Jim Ed's big mouth.

Jason wound through the crowd to the bleachers facing the east field. Jim Ed sat halfway up, empty spaces around him affording a bubble of isolation. Jason chuckled. No one wanted to be near his cousin's foghorn of a yell. Stacy sat a few feet away, chatting with a group of mothers.

He climbed the bleachers to take an empty spot by Jim Ed. "Hey. Dispatch said you wanted to see me."

His cousin's gaze didn't waver from the field where the two teams warmed up. "Saw your message from Palmer. Guess your little plan isn't working."

"It's been one day." Jason stretched his legs out, resting his feet on the empty bench below them. "She doesn't trust me."

"That's the way, Jamie! Great catch!" Jim Ed surged to his feet, clapping loudly for a moment before sitting again. "It was a stupid idea to begin with."

"Thanks a lot. And putting a snake between her doors worked? I don't see her backing off."

He actually felt the angry tremor that ran through the other man. Wonder what the price was for challenging Jim Ed's authority? Jim Ed shot him a look, then, amazingly, began to laugh.

"What?" Jason shook his head.

"You always were scrappy." Jim Ed's gaze wandered back to the field. "Hell, you might just pull this crazy shit off. So what went down last night?"

Jason shrugged. "We had dinner."

"That all?"

"We talked."

"What about?"

"My stint in the army. Books. Stuff like that."

His cousin's gaze swung his way, pinning him like an insect to a biology pan. "She didn't ask you again what you saw?"

"No." Jason refused to look away. "She knows she's gonna keep getting the same answer. I didn't see anything."

"Good." Jim Ed nodded, satisfaction in the smile shaping his mouth. "Keep it that way."

For the next hour and a half, he endured Jim Ed's bellowing and watched the game, trying not to dwell on Kathleen's message.

Permanently.

He shouldn't be surprised that she'd changed her mind about seeing him. He should be surprised she'd considered seeing him in the first place.

The third baseman tagged Jamie out and Jim Ed cursed. Only one run separated the teams, with two outs left in the final inning. Jason glanced toward the other team's dugout, where Tick Calvert leaned against the fence, calling encouragement to the players and conferring with the other volunteer coach.

Calvert was the kind of guy everyone expected Kathleen to want. Educated. Honest. Responsible. Everything he appeared not to be.

A double play between first and second ended the game, and Jason sat, letting the stands empty around him. Jim Ed, his face dark with resentment and bad sportsmanship, glared down at him. "We're going for pizza. You coming?"

Oh, yeah, he wanted in on that little family outing. Even the thought of fresh, steaming pizza with all the trimmings couldn't lure him into sitting through a meal listening to Jim Ed berate Jamie for how he'd played. He shot a glance at Stacy, who waited at the bottom of the bleachers, gathering the children around her like chicks under a protective wing. Her gaze was on Jim Ed and wariness lurked in her blue eyes.

Jason shook his head. "Nah. I'm beat, man. Just gonna go home, shower and hit the bed."

Jim Ed shrugged, a tight, irritable movement. "Suit yourself."

Jason watched him descend the steps. At the bottom, Laurel launched herself at him, blond ponytail bouncing, her face bright with adoration. Jim Ed swung her up to perch on his hip, but his comments were directed at Jamie. The teenager's solemn face tightened, his gaze downcast. Jason shook his head, glad he couldn't hear his cousin's critique of the kid's game.

He waited until Jim Ed's family disappeared into the crowd. On the field, the victorious team gathered, chattering and hooting with exultation. Parents and siblings stood in straggling groups. Every hamburger joint in town would be packed with hungry families and their camaraderie.

Envy tightened his chest. He hadn't experienced that kind of solidarity since he'd left the army. He and the guys in his unit had played softball and football, even in the desert sands, and he'd formed a kind of loose family structure with a few close friends. The rigors of Quantico usually fostered tight friendships, but he'd found it difficult to connect with his classmates, although he was never sure why. Maybe because he knew they'd be going on to standard FBI duty and he'd be disappearing into the dark abyss of his past.

Families reunited and voices blended in cheerful conversation.

"Dad! I'm riding with Riley, okay? We'll meet you at the Dairy Queen."

"Come on, John Ray. Get your glove and let's go."

Jason stood and took the steps two at a time. He pulled his keys from his pocket and threaded through the crowd, invisible in his isolation. The flow of people slowed near the gate, with players and spectators arriving for the next set of games. Beyond the entrance the crowd thinned.

Two preteen boys sprinted by him, playfully jostling each other and trading insults. He saw the impending collision in the seconds before it happened, but couldn't stop it. The boys, focused on each other, careened into a tall brunette, sending her and the contents of her purse sprawling. Jason winced for her as bare knees and palms hit the gravel parking lot.

One of the boys glanced over his shoulder. "Hey, sorry, lady!"

Not sorry enough to stop. The kids kept running.

"Are you okay?" Jason hunched and reached for the woman's arm, meaning to steady her. At his touch, she flinched away with a violent motion.

"I'm fine." She rocked back, still crouched, brushing gravel and dust from her legs. Blood trickled down her shin. A long breath shook her slender frame and she pressed her fingers to her forehead. "Oh, Lord."

"You're sure you're all right?" Jason leaned over, snagged her purse from the ground and began gathering the spilled items. Worried, he eyed her pale face and trembling jaw. Extreme reaction for a minor spill.

She nodded, then shook her head, blowing at the scratches on her palm. Jason dropped a small makeup bag, change purse and a calendar in the purse. Bottle of painkillers. A lipstick. He handed her the tissues. Did all women carry this much stuff with them?

What did Kathleen carry in her purse? Did she carry one at all?

The brunette swiped at a tear, leaving a dusty trail on her cheek. She was crying. Oh, man. He didn't do crying women. He didn't remember his mother ever crying, although she must have had plenty of reason to do so, especially after his father ran off.

Cell phone, pack of gum, mints. A tiny leather-bound New Testament. Good God. He hadn't carried this much equipment on active duty. A photo album. Tampon. He shoved that find in the bag. A set of keys with four cutesy key chains attached.

She took a deep, audible breath. Jason rose, holding the purse in one hand. She brushed back her dark brown hair and stood.

A smile trembled across her lips and she rolled a tissue between her bleeding palms. "Thanks. Sorry for acting like a crazy lady."

"No problem." Jason studied her still-pale face and surveyed the near-deserted parking lot. He couldn't just leave her standing here. "Are you with someone?"

Her dark eyes, oddly familiar, shuttered and she took her own quick appraisal around the lot. Tension tightened her features further. "Yes."

Jason jerked a thumb over his shoulder. "Do you want to walk back and—"

"Tori?"

Jason glanced back to see Tick bearing down on them. He stepped out of the other man's way.

"What happened? What's wrong?" Calvert stopped by the young woman, taking her hand in his, his sharp gaze roving her face, the cuts on her palms, the bloody scrape on her bare leg. He glared at Jason. "Harding? What the hell?"

"A couple of kids knocked me down." Frowning, Tori moved away from Calvert's looming protection. "No big deal."

Jason's eyebrows rose. She'd been in tears and now it was no big deal? He studied her and Calvert, noting the identical eyes, the shape of the jaw, the stubborn set of similar mouths. Siblings. Calvert's sister.

A victim of his other Reese cousin, the rapist.

Oh, hell.

Yeah, his family was a real prize. A rapist and a possible murderer. No wonder Kathleen wanted nothing to do with him.

Jason jerked a hand through his hair and held out her purse. "Glad you're okay."

"Wait." Tori Calvert straightened further. A stronger smile lurked at her mouth. He could actually feel the effort she exerted to pull herself together. "Let me buy you a burger or something. A thank you for rescuing me."

"I didn't—"

"Tori, that's not—"

"I insist." She overrode both their protests and shot a narrow-eyed glance at her brother before beaming at Jason. "I mean it. We were going for something anyway. I'm not as crazy as I appear and you have to eat, right?"

"Tori." Tick's voice held a stern warning.

"Tick. Back off." She turned a dazzling smile on Jason. Man, he did not want to get between these two and the epic power-struggle brewing in the warm evening air. "So what do you say? And ignore my overprotective big brother. He thinks he's in charge of my life."

"Someone needs to be." Tick glanced sharply at Jason.

"I really can't," Jason said, looking around. Just standing here with Calvert, his skin crawled. Being seen with him, no matter how innocent the circumstances, was not a good idea. He searched for an excuse to get him out of the invitation. "I'm expecting a phone call and I need to be at home. Thanks anyway."

He didn't miss Calvert's relieved expression. Tori opened her mouth, probably to protest, but Tick took her arm and steered her toward the lot. "C'mon, Tor. Stop harassing the guy."

In his truck, Jason sat and watched the families trickling in and out of the recreation park. The isolation pushed in on him again and he shrugged off the despondency. During the training he'd received before going undercover, he'd been warned about the sense of remoteness, how dangerous it could be to give in to it. He needed to focus on the outcome.

His cousin in prison. A family destroyed.

Cursing, he fired the truck to life and pulled out of the lot, resisting the compulsion to squeal the tires. He navigated the near-deserted streets, trying not to glance at yards that held playing children and grilling fathers. That wasn't his life, probably never would be. With his luck, this was as good as it got.

The thought chilled him. *Get over yourself, Harding. Enough self-pity.*

He swung into a space in front of the post office. He hadn't checked his mail for three days and didn't know why he bothered now. The only thing awaiting him would be a stack of bills and junk mail.

Fluorescent lights hummed in the lobby. He opened the little metal door and pulled out a handful of envelopes. Power bill. Promotional mailings. A distinctive brown envelope bearing the US Treasury address. *Hot damn.* His tax refund.

He ripped open the envelope. Visions of real food danced in his head. The Winn Dixie cashed refund checks. No more Rice Krispies. Whistling, he tucked the check in his pocket and jogged back to the truck.

His luck was looking up.

Chapter Six

Why was she doing this? Overflowing cupboards at home, and she was in the grocery store, filling a cart. Perusing the bakery selections, Kathleen sighed and tossed a bag of Altee's favorite double-chocolate biscotti in the buggy. She even tried going through the store backward, avoiding the carefully designed flow, but knew it wouldn't work. She'd still end up buying enough food to feed a small third world country.

Losing herself in the soothing mindlessness, she eased along the aisles. In the dairy section, she added ricotta and parmesan to her selections. Maybe she'd make a vegetable lasagna tomorrow night...stop by Mama's and get some of those early-ripening tomatoes Daddy was always bragging about, throw in some spinach and fat portobellos. Add a huge salad and steaming, fluffy rolls.

Guilt nipped her with sharp little pinchers. What had Jason eaten tonight?

That's not your concern. She snagged a bag of frozen shrimp and slung it into her cart. The buy-one-get-one sign caught her eye, and she added a second bag. Potatoes, corn, sausage, crab boil. She'd call Tick, ask him to join her and Altee for a low country boil, maybe tell him to bring his friend, the good-looking chicken farmer along. The farmer had green eyes, and maybe that would make her forget Jason's intense gaze.

Not likely, since she couldn't even remember the farmer's name.

Another lone woman walked by, her cart holding several containers of yogurt, a loaf of wheat bread and a two-liter diet cola. Kathleen shot a glance at the mound of groceries in her buggy. Enough. She was going to the checkout, now.

After nine o'clock on a weeknight, three customers constituted a mob in the Winn Dixie. One checkout counter stood open, with enough customers standing in line to back up into the frozen food section. Kathleen sighed and meandered along the aisle. Heading for the end of the queue, she perused the selection of frozen goods.

"Hush, I told you not until we get home." The young mother in front of Kathleen tried to remove a bag of cookies from the frenzied clutch of a fussy toddler. The child cried louder, and a flush crept up the girl's neck and face. "He missed his nap today."

"He's a handsome boy." Kathleen forced a smile, her face aching. She could imagine her mother offering platitudes and advice, but what could she say? She'd never fussed with her child over a couple of cookies destined to ruin his supper. Swallowing hard, she looked down at her purchases, everything but cookies because they were on the same aisle with the baby items.

"Oh, shoot." Muffled frustration hovered in the girl's voice. "I forgot the eggs. Do you mind if I leave my stuff here? It won't take but a second to run get them and I don't want to lose my place."

"Want me to grab them for you?" Jason's deep drawl slid over Kathleen's raw nerves and her whole body jerked.

The girl's hands stilled on the belt holding her son in place and she gazed over Kathleen's shoulder, an appreciative grin lighting her face. "You don't mind? I just need a dozen."

"Be right back."

Kathleen refused to turn and watch him walk away. The other woman had no such reservations, her bright blue eyes focused on the aisle. She shook her head, bright pink lips curving. "Gosh, he's cute. A nice guy, too. You don't find many of those these days."

Honey, everything isn't always what it seems, either. Nice guy? You have no idea.

Had she ever been that naïve?

Sure she had. She'd married Tom, had a baby, thought they'd live happily ever after.

"Here you go." Jason flashed a grin at the young woman and handed her the pastel pink carton.

"Thanks." Appearing utterly dazzled, she turned away and placed the eggs in her cart. The little boy twisted in the seat and made a grab for the bright container.

His smile dying, Jason walked past Kathleen. He nodded as he passed her. She gripped the cart handle until her knuckles glowed white. She would not turn around. She didn't care what he was doing here or how he felt about her canceling their plans.

Paper rustled behind her and he began a soft whistled tune, a familiar melody that tickled the edges of her memory. She surveyed the stagnant line. The young mother played peek-a-boo with the toddler. In front of her, a couple of men held a twelve-pack under each arm. At the register stood Mrs. Sara Louise McGillicutty with a six-month supply of kitty litter and cat food. She rummaged in her purse, probably looking for coupons and her change purse. Lord help her, they'd be here all night.

The whistling continued, sawing against her nerves. Kathleen sighed and faced him. "Harding, do you have to do that?"

Jason looked up from his newspaper. He lifted one eyebrow. "Do what? Read?"

"That infernal whistling."

"That bad? Was I off-key again?" He folded the paper and leaned against the cart. He didn't smile and Kathleen looked away, her gaze flicking over his buggy's contents.

His basket held more than hers. Unease skittered down her spine. The cart held basics—milk, cheese, eggs, bread. It also held what had to be splurges—a pack of thick rib-eye steaks, a side of cooked ribs, a half-gallon of premium vanilla ice cream, a six-pack of longneck bottles.

She glanced up to find him watching her, a cynical twist to his lips. She swallowed and forced a cool smile. "Looks like you're stocking the cupboard."

His icy green gaze dropped to her buggy. "You, too."

She lifted one shoulder in a tense shrug. "I always buy too much. My grocery expenses are higher than my light bill."

"Must be nice."

The sarcasm stung. "About dinner—"

"Don't worry about it. Your message was pretty darn clear."

"You don't understand. This whole thing—"

"Oh, I understand plenty. Being a little poor doesn't make a guy a lot dumb."

"That's not—"

"Are you moving up?" With a bored expression, he gestured.

She followed the direction of his negligent wave. The line had moved—Mrs. McGillicutty pushed her buggy toward the door, the young men gathered their purchases and the mother unloaded her items while trying to soothe the fussy toddler.

He didn't speak again, but she was intensely aware of him during the few minutes it took to get her own buggy unloaded, her groceries paid for and her purchases bagged.

"You want me to take that out for you?" The teenager bagging groceries popped his gum a couple of times, punctuating his words.

Kathleen shook her head and tucked her checkbook back in her small purse. "I've got it, thanks."

She pushed the cart toward the door and, unable to resist the impulse, peeked back at Jason. He smiled at the clerk, pulled a wad of bills from his pocket and peeled off two hundreds. Her stomach clenched, a chill snaking over her skin.

Waiting for his change, he glanced around, his gaze clashing with hers. Kathleen spun and walked out the door.

☙❧

Anger set up camp in Jason's gut, reaching out tentacles that smothered the thrill he'd gotten from blowing two hundred bucks of his oh-so-convenient tax refund on food.

What did he care what she thought of him? It wasn't like he stood a chance, anyway. Her mind was made up, and any opportunity he'd ever had of her seeing him as something other than just another corrupt cop was long gone. He resisted the urge to shove the cart toward the truck and create another dent in the pockmarked side panel.

Insects flirted and danced against the halogen security lights, casting weird shadows on the parking lot. The spot next to his truck sat empty now, devoid of the massive blue Cadillac parked there earlier. A familiar white and wood-paneled Wagoneer was two spaces away, and Kathleen moved bags from cart to the cargo area with economic speed.

He began unloading his own purchases, aware of her glances in his direction. She slammed the cargo area door closed. After a moment's pause, she approached him, her shoes clicking on the pavement like angry castanets. Jason settled the bag holding his milk and ice cream in the corner of the truck bed and watched her approach.

The bright security light glinted off the elegant silver studs in her ears. Anger glittered in her eyes and he stiffened. She marched up to him, her hands resting at her hips. "It's probably not my place to say this, but I'm going to anyway. This job in Haynes County and your loyalty to your cousin are going to ruin your life. You need to get out, Jason, before you get sucked in."

"Didn't we have this same conversation last night?" He nestled a bag of canned goods in front of his milk. "I need this job. I need the money."

Her gaze flickered toward the bags of groceries and he could sense the thoughts tumbling through her mind. She thought he was already selling out, taking payoffs.

Sadness settled over her features, tugging the corners of her mouth down, wrinkling her brow. "There are other jobs out there. You don't have to do this."

If she only knew. He rubbed the tightness at his nape. "Yeah, I do."

"Why?" She threw her hands skyward. "Just tell me why. Make me understand. And don't give me that crap about family loyalty. The only person Jim Ed has any true loyalty for is himself."

He shrugged. "He's faithful about visiting Billy up at Reidsville."

"Do you really think he's going to look out for you?" She shook her head, dragging her fingers through her hair, the short wisps standing out, begging him to smooth them. "How do you know he's not setting you up to take the fall for some of his shenanigans?"

A bark of laughter escaped him. "Shenanigans? Did anyone ever tell you, Miss Palmer, that you have an old-fashioned vocabulary?"

She muttered a word sure to have offended the old-fashioned English teacher they'd shared in high school.

He lifted his eyebrows and muffled his laugh this time. With a quick shove, he sent the cart into the buggy corral and turned to face her again. "Why do you care? Does it matter whether you're slapping cuffs on me or Jim Ed?"

The question brought her up short. He could tell by her rapid blinking. Finally, she nodded. "Yes, it does. I don't want to see him bring you down, too. You deserve more than that."

The quiet words ricocheted through his brain. She thought he deserved better. No one—*no one*—had ever said that. While he tried to digest the idea that the girl who'd always been out of his reach thought him worthy of more than he had, she stepped forward, a hand gentle on his arm. "You have to get out now. Before it goes any further."

I can't. The words refused to leave his lips, his brain short-circuiting since all he could focus on was the warmth of her hand against his bare skin. He stared at her, her eyes dark and luminous. The muggy air pressed in on them, enveloping them in the silence of the deserted parking lot. Heat radiated from her skin on his, desire invading his blood stream, traveling through his body.

Don't do this, man. Step away. Get in the truck and leave her alone before one of you gets hurt. Or dead.

I can't.

"Jason?" Her lips parted on his name and the desire hit him hard, even weakening his knees for a split second. God, he wanted to taste his name lingering on her full bottom lip.

With a hand on the truck to steady himself, he bent his head and covered those parted lips with his own. Her soft mouth moved against his and her hold tightened on his arm. Making a small noise in the back of her throat, she swayed closer and he drank in her unique taste—mint mingled with something sweet and wild.

His tongue danced across her lips, seeking permission to invade. Her palm moved up his arm, then her arms were around his neck, mouth open under his, her body aligned with his. The tip of her tongue tangled with his, tasting, teasing.

With a groan, he backed her against the truck door, not sure his legs would support him. Wanting pulsed in his abdomen, below his belt, through his entire body. He wanted her naked, stretched out beneath him on the purity of her white sheets, making those same breathy little sounds as he made love to her. The image exploded in his brain and a moment passed before he realized her hands had slid to his chest and she was attempting to lever him away.

He pulled his mouth from hers, his breathing coming in unsteady gasps. She curled her fingers into the oft-washed cotton of his T-shirt. He nuzzled his nose against the curve of her ear. "Go home. Forget this happened."

She slipped closer, heavy breaths pushing her breasts against his chest. Her cheek brushed his and her knuckles moved, an inadvertent caress. Her clean scent filled his head. "Say you'll quit. Get out before it's too late."

"I can't." Forcing his hands from her body, he wrenched the door open, rusty hinges squawking. Feeling her gaze like a continued touch, he climbed into the cab and started the engine. He pulled onto the street, aware of her watching him leave.

ꕥ

At her parents' home, the lights shown brightly in the kitchen. Kathleen parked behind her mother's ancient BMW and grabbed the bag containing her refrigerated items. The scent of roses and gardenias flowed over her on the walk to the back door. She entered without knocking. The glass sunroom off the kitchen was empty.

"Mama?"

"Kathleen?" Her mother's surprised voice drifted from the large kitchen and Kathleen followed it. Her mother sat in the window seat at the other end of the room, a cup of coffee and a novel at hand.

Kathleen put her bag of cheeses in the refrigerator. "Where's Daddy?"

Her mother smiled and stood to envelope her in a hug. "He's at Virgil's, talking politics. What are you doing here, sweetheart?"

"I just left the grocery store and thought I'd see if you were still up." She swiped at a strand of hair falling in her eyes and tried to avoid Mama's all-too-seeing gaze, sure from the heat in her cheeks she was still flushed from Jason's kiss.

"What's wrong?"

"Nothing." Kathleen shook her head and forced a laugh, moving to the coffee maker and pouring a cup. "I can't just stop by because I want to see you?"

"If that was truly your reason for coming, of course." Her mama patted her arm. "And even if it wasn't your real reason."

Silence wrapped around them. Kathleen sipped her coffee, the rich taste lost in the bitterness of her thoughts. She'd come seeking forgetfulness, wanting to put Jason and his kiss out of her mind. Wanting even more to forget he wouldn't turn his back on Haynes County.

Wouldn't turn his back on Jim Ed.

The phone rang, its shrill cry shattering the stillness. Mama moved toward the study. "That's probably your daddy, calling to let me know he's on his way."

Coffee in hand, Kathleen followed her mother into the dark wood and leather retreat. Settled into one of the armchairs, Mama picked up the phone. "Hello? Oh, Lenora. How are you?"

Kathleen scanned the bookshelves, letting Mama's cultured voice soothe her jangling nerves. The classic novels her mother loved shared space with her daddy's law books. Paperbacks lined another shelf—thrillers, mysteries, romances. Below those were her own high school yearbooks and the ones her mother had received as a long-time faculty member.

Leaning down, she pulled out the book released three years after she graduated. She eased into the other armchair and flipped the book open to the senior class. Her fingers slid down the glossy paper, coming to rest by the picture of a solemn boy. *Jason Alex Harding.*

She smiled, albeit unwillingly. He looked so young. His hair was longer, lighter and fell onto his forehead, and he stared out at the world with shuttered, defiant eyes. In the photo, he was unsmiling, and she traced his mouth with a fingertip. Her lips burned with the remembered feel of that mouth moving on hers and tendrils of desire tickled her stomach again.

"He was a good boy."

Startled, Kathleen glanced up, a hot flush stinging her neck. When had Mama hung up the phone? How long had she watched her staring at his picture? Kathleen struggled for an uninterested look. "Who?"

"Jason." Her mother's slender finger tapped the photo. "He used to spend his lunch hours in the library. He claimed he liked to read, but I always thought it had more to do with not having lunch money and having too much pride to apply for free lunch. He was in Louella's drama group, too, at least until his senior year."

Seizing the opportunity to soak up information about him, Kathleen kept her gaze on the yearbook, afraid her eyes would reveal too much. "Why not that year?"

"His mother was ill. She died a few weeks before he graduated. He joined the military right out of school. Louella was bitterly disappointed. She always said the boy had real talent, like he could just climb in a role and wear it as long as he needed."

"Maybe he thought he'd get farther in the military than on Broadway." If he was such an excellent actor, which Jason was real? The down-on-his-luck deputy? Or the man who charmed her with stories of his travels? The one who kissed her and made her feel more than any man had in what felt like forever? Or the one who chose money and corruption over her?

Her mother glanced at her, lips pinched. "It's difficult to watch a child you care about waste talents and opportunities."

Tension crawled up her spine. She closed the yearbook and rose to return it to the shelf, her motions jerky and tight. "You know what, Mama? I'm more tired than I thought, so I won't wait for Daddy. I'm going to head home, but I'll come by Sunday after church."

She crossed the room to embrace her mother, who held on for a moment, a fierce, tight hug. "Kathleen, don't forget there's more to life than the GBI."

Not likely, since Mama reminded her every chance that came along. Her throat closed and she disentangled herself. "I know. Tell Daddy I came by."

ଔ

Hands behind his head, Jason lay on the bed and stared at the ceiling. The rich voice of Johnny Cash filled the room with a song about a man trapped in prison, longing for the freedom offered by a passing train.

Trapped and longing. He could relate to that.

He'd stashed his groceries earlier and eaten a turkey sandwich, satisfying his body's physical hunger. A deeper hunger continued to gnaw at his gut. Damn it, he could still taste her, still feel the warmth of her body aligned with his.

She'd let him kiss her. More than that, she'd kissed him back, moaned into his mouth and swayed into him.

She thought he deserved better. No one, except maybe Mrs. Louella Hatcher, had ever thought that of him.

He closed his eyes, remembering the aching quality of her voice asking him to quit.

Her voice. Just one more taste of his name on her lips. Was that asking too much?

The phone lay on the bedside table. All he had to do was reach for it, punch in a number already memorized, and he could be awash in her voice again.

A sorry substitute for her kisses, but a fix for his craving, the addiction he couldn't let himself satisfy.

Johnny's crooning faded to nothingness and silence descended on the room, crushing in its intensity.

Muttering curses, he rolled over and reached for the phone.

ↂ

With her mother's words beating in her head, Kathleen undressed for bed and removed her makeup. How dare Mama insinuate she was wasting her life? Anger trembled under her skin. She was satisfied. Work was good, her hours were filled—so what if she didn't have the traditional lives her cousins and high school friends had? She'd tried the wife and mother bit, and the failure had almost killed her.

Be honest, Kathleen. It did kill you, way deep down inside. Altee's right. The girl you used to be, the real woman you were going to be, died with Everett.

Shaking off the dismal little voice, she tossed the washcloth in the hamper and snapped off the bathroom light. Thinking about it, dwelling on it, didn't change anything. It just made the nagging sense of hurt and loss worse.

The polished wood cool beneath her feet, she padded across the bedroom and jerked the covers back. Low light spilled from the beaded lamp by the bed and cast colored shadows on the wall. That light would make Jason's tanned skin even darker, highlighted against the snowy sheets.

Stop. That kiss was as far as it was going to go. That kiss alone was too far. *Stop thinking about him.*

The news. Stories about the impending IRS deadline and the local budget deficits would take her mind off everything, including Jason Harding. Settling against the pillows, she reached for the remote.

The phone rang and she frowned at the clock. After eleven. Who on earth? A glance at the caller ID screen revealed a Haynes County number with no name.

She didn't need a name. Her pulse picked up, a distinct thud at her throat.

A second ring, temptation hovering in the room.

Her hand trembling, she picked up the receiver. "Hello?"

Charged silence popped along the line. She swallowed, her mouth suddenly dry, and tried again. "Hello?"

Silence.

"Jason?"

The connection stretched, the sensation one of darkness reaching for her. None of the warmth and passion she'd experienced in his arms. A chill worked its way over her skin. With slow precision, she replaced the receiver. She pulled the comforter over her shoulders and turned her back on the phone.

She couldn't bring herself to turn off the light.

Chapter Seven

"It hasn't changed since the last time you looked at it." Altee mumbled the words around a peppermint. She didn't glance up from her laptop.

Kathleen's gaze remained trained on the diagram and photographs hanging on the wall, but she sighed at her partner's droll tone. She still felt as if she were slogging through mud, mentally and physically. Three cups of coffee hadn't helped either. With one hand, she covered a wide yawn.

"Stop doing that. You're making me do it, too." Altee shook her head. "What kept you up last night?"

"Prank phone call." She'd run the number from her caller ID—a pay phone at a Haynes County gas station. The little trill of nerves tickled down her spine once more. She'd lain awake for hours with the memory of that dark silence hovering over her.

"A prank call?"

"Yes. Just an open line."

"Kath."

"Leave it alone, Altee. It was just a phone call."

"Did you trace it?"

"Straight to a dead end. It's nothing. Just more games. But believe me, I'm being exceedingly careful." She'd altered her morning routine and changed the way she journeyed to work, telling herself paranoid was better than dead. A frown tugged at her brows. “You should be, too.”

“Always.” Altee gestured at the photos pinned to the corkboard wall. “Find anything?”

“Nothing but more dead ends.” Kathleen turned her gaze back to the diagram of the scene, the photos of the little gray truck with its blood-spattered windshield. She fingered the edges of her hair, twisting a couple of thick strands together. “Maybe if it actually made sense.”

Altee’s snort was anything but ladylike. “Remember who we’re talking about.”

“No, listen. The trooper who disappeared? Everyone has always assumed it was because he saw something he shouldn’t. Tick’s daddy? He wasn’t really the target—they wanted the witness he was transporting to Atlanta. Every death we know they caused but can’t tie them to, there’s a reason. There is absolutely no reason here. Why would Jim Ed risk everything to kill these boys?”

“Meanness?”

“I don’t know.”

“Kind of amateurish, don’t you think? Like someone who hasn’t been around that long?”

“Oh, Altee, don’t. Not now. It’s not him.” She gestured at the diagram, marked with vehicle placements and time arrived. “He didn’t have time to shoot them, and I don’t think he saw anything.”

“Meaning you want to believe every word he says.”

“You know, just because he’s working there doesn’t mean he’s like all the others.”

"I would come up with some witty and biting reply, but, Kath, I'm tired of having this conversation with you. It's like listening to Montaine trying to convince me to take him back."

"You're not, are you?"

"No, and I'm not buying that Jason Harding is telling the truth, the whole truth and nothing but the truth. That man is hiding something. You can see it in his eyes."

Her mother's words replayed in her head. *He could put on a role and walk around in it.* What role was he playing? Which Jason was real? It was like looking at a fun-house hall of mirrors, not knowing if what she saw could be believed or not.

"Hey, we might have a lead."

Kathleen spun. "What?"

"Email from Whitlock." Altee leaned closer to the screen. "Ballistics are back on the bullets Williams took out of the boys' bodies. Forty-caliber hollowpoints."

"Well, that explains the amount of damage."

"Those bullets didn't come from that rifle or the throwaway. It gets better." The excitement in Altee's voice sent tingles along Kathleen's nerve endings. "There's a match in the database."

"To a weapon?"

"No. To another case. Unsolved homicide, but it's definitely the same gun." Altee paused, dark gaze scanning the message. "You are *not* going to believe this."

"What?"

"It's the skeleton. The partial remains Dale Jenkins found on his farm two years ago."

"Botine was the agent on that. He should still have the file."

"It's a Chandler County case, too. We should call Calvert."

"Hmmm." Kathleen flipped through her notes. "Jim Ed's duty pistol is a nine millimeter. No forty-caliber registered to him, but the man is a gun fanatic. He might have one that's not registered."

"Think we could convince Judge Holton to give us a search warrant based on that?"

Kathleen's unladylike snort would have horrified her mother. "I hate to say it and cast aspersions on His Honor, but we could probably get a warrant just by mentioning whose house we're planning to search."

Altee grinned. "Let's go to the courthouse."

ଔଓ

Jason reeled a fresh report into the ancient electric typewriter and began the laborious task of getting the lines aligned to Thatcher's expectations. Why the hell wouldn't Thatcher update to a computerized system? Glancing at his notes, he started filling in the stolen property report. He stifled a yawn and glanced at the paper. With a muttered curse, he ripped it from the typewriter.

He'd typed Kathleen's phone number on the line for the date. The number was stuck in his head, probably because he hadn't allowed himself to dial it last night. Instead, he'd taken the phone out of the room and gone back to bed, letting Johnny Cash soothe him to sleep.

He'd dreamed of her, of kissing her, of those white sheets on her bed.

A brisk run, a cold shower and the sheer boredom of patrolling Haynes County hadn't put her out of his mind. The entire time Bobby Gene Butler fussed about someone breaking into his junkyard and stealing hubcaps, a part of Jason's mind relived kissing her. He got semi-hard every time he remembered that little moan she made in her throat. What would making love to her be like?

The squad room door slammed against the wall. Jason jumped and looked around.

Jim Ed, his face red, pointed at him. “Come with me.”

Fear slithered down his back. He gestured at the report in the typewriter. “I’ve got to—”

“Leave that shit and come on.”

He followed his cousin to the parking lot and Jim Ed’s unit. Latching his seat belt, he glanced at the other man’s tight jaw. “What’s going on?”

A muscle flicking in his cheek, Jim Ed slammed the car into reverse and wheeled around the parking lot. “I gave you an opportunity to get her under control. You screwed that up.”

Icy fingers grabbed his gut. “Would you just tell me what’s going on?”

“Your girlfriend and her partner are searching my house and they brought that bastard Calvert with them.”

Oh, crap. “It’s been two days, man. What am I supposed to do in two days?”

“Well, I’ll take care of it now.”

Double crap. “Listen, Jim Ed, you have to think about this. Think about who she is—”

“I don’t give a good goddamn who she is. I’m not letting the bitch ruin everything.”

The unit ate the miles between the jail and Jim Ed’s home. Trees and power poles blurred, and Jason clutched the armrest, trying to get a grasp on the whole situation. Kathleen refused to back down and now was invading Jim Ed’s private little kingdom. He wasn’t worried his cousin would harm her at the house—Jim Ed had more subtlety. Later worried him, the time when no one was around. He needed to find a way to lessen her vulnerability.

Jim Ed turned into his drive, barely slowing, and the car bottomed out on a rut with a grinding protest. Unmarked cars and a couple of Chandler County units fanned out on the yard. Before coming to a complete halt, Jim Ed shoved the gear into park. He jumped out of the vehicle and strode across the yard.

Jason scrambled after him, heart thudding against his ribs, anxiety twisting his gut. The front door opened and Stacy met them on the porch, her face pale.

She reached for her husband's arm. "Oh, Lord, Jimmy. They're searching the house. Kathleen Palmer said something about a murder. Why are they here?"

His face set, Jim Ed shook off her hand. "Stay here."

"But—"

"Stay here."

Jason followed him into the house. The image of Stacy's fear-filled blue eyes haunted him. The foyer was empty, but voices echoed from several rooms. He zoned in on Kathleen's immediately.

"Remember, everything you move gets returned to its proper place. We are not here to demolish someone's home."

Jim Ed made an abrupt turn and strode toward the family room on the left end of the house. GBI agents swarmed the large multi-purpose area. Altee and Kathleen stood in the middle and watched the other officers' every move.

The flush on Jim Ed's face deepened. "What the hell are you doing in my house?"

Altee handed him a folded paper. "Executing a search warrant."

"For what?" Jim Ed crumpled the warrant without looking at it.

Kathleen eyed him. "Specifically, the forty-caliber handgun used to murder Heath Brannon, Connor White and an unidentified male whose skeletal remains were discovered in Chandler County."

"You're crazy." Breathing hard, Jim Ed took a step forward. Jason tensed. "You can't do this. This is *my* house and—"

"Agent Ford." Kathleen glanced at the clean-cut young man who stepped forward. "Escort Mr. Reese from the premises, please. Make sure he remains outside for the duration." Her expressionless gaze flickered in Jason's direction. "Deputy Harding, too."

Kathleen waited until the three men were out of the room to release a pent-up breath. Looking at Reese's enraged face, she could all too easily imagine the man doing murder. "He has serious control issues."

"Tell me about it." Altee glanced around the large room and pulled Kathleen toward the French doors. They stepped onto the deck. Altee gestured toward the manicured lawn. Nothing disturbed the garden view. No bats, balls or bicycles. Not even a swing set. A lattice fence shielded a dog kennel from sight. "Don't these people have kids?"

"Four."

"Something strike you as odd about this place then?"

"Yeah. No clutter." Not even upstairs in the children's bedrooms. She'd peeked in earlier, after she and Tick searched the master suite. The magazine-perfect rooms showed no signs of being lived in. All the toys were in place, no shoes or clothing littered the floor. And even though Stacy Reese didn't work outside the home, Kathleen didn't see anyone with children being *that* good of a housekeeper.

"Can't you just see him standing over them, making sure they put everything in the right place?" Altee nudged her shoulder. "Notice he had your boy with him?"

"He's not my boy." First, he definitely wasn't hers. Second, she wouldn't define anyone who kissed the way he did a *boy*. When she'd touched him, muscles had flexed under warm skin, and the length of his body against hers had been firm and tight. She doubted the guy had an ounce of fat anywhere.

"Hey." The snapping of Altee's fingers brought her back to reality. Altee regarded her with a long-suffering expression. "Stop fantasizing and focus on the task at hand."

Heat flashed up her neck and over her cheeks. "I wasn't—"

"Lying is a sin, Kath. You had sex written all over your face. So when did you kiss him and not tell me about it?"

"Altee, go search something, would you?"

"Girl, you know what you need to be searching? Your soul, figuring out whether or not you've got the objectivity to stay on this case."

She spun and walked back into the house, leaving Kathleen to stare after her. Kathleen tugged at her hair and closed her eyes, concentrating on taking even breaths to still the sudden panic clutching her chest. Lord help her, Altee was right. The fascination with Jason had gone too far and, if she didn't get a handle on it quick, threatened to blow a Providence Canyon-sized hole in her career.

She couldn't let that happen. *Agent* wasn't just her title. It was the core of her being, who she was, the way she defined herself. She didn't have anything else. No room for failure existed here.

Taking one last calming breath, she opened her eyes. The only option was not seeing him again, except possibly in cuffs. He refused to walk away from Haynes County and what it represented. He'd chosen the money and family loyalty over her and any possible relationship they might forge. She wasn't enough. Kathleen smothered the pain that realization sent darting through her chest.

Stop it. It wasn't like she'd even known him long. And this wasn't the first time she'd been found wanting by a man.

But it would be the last. Jason Harding wouldn't get a second chance to choose.

ও৪ঌ

Kathleen slumped in a chair on Tick Calvert's deck and let the murmur of the river wash over her. Disappointment and defeat hung in the air.

"I would say I can't believe we didn't find anything, but when it comes to that oily son of a bitch, I'll believe anything." Altee sipped a glass of iced tea.

At the grill, Tick flipped burgers. He bounced on his heels, bare toes curling into the wood. "I could have lived without that biscuit-eating grin he gave me when we were leaving, too. He knew we wouldn't find that damn gun."

"He didn't like us in his space, though, did he?" Kathleen tilted her head back, watching the low sun sparkle through tall pines. Remembering the anger and hatred in Jim Ed's eyes, she shivered. His last words—*You'll regret this, Palmer*—pounded in her head. He hadn't shouted, had been calm and cold, almost whispering. Somehow, she'd feel safer if he'd ranted.

Silent and expressionless, Jason had stood by him.

"You know, it might not be such a bad idea for you two to bunk together for a while." Spatula in one hand and tea glass in the other, Tick nudged Altee's feet out of the way and sat on the edge of her lounge chair. "Alternate houses or something. You live close enough together for it not to be a hassle."

Altee frowned. "I really wish you hadn't said that. I was trying to convince myself there was nothing to be afraid of."

"We're going to end up shelving this case." Distaste curled through Kathleen. Damn it, why did they keep getting away with their crimes? It sickened her. And Jason's involvement made the nausea worse. "Just like all the others."

"There's always Harding. We haven't searched his place. Maybe Reese gave him the gun for safekeeping." Altee's voice was quiet and Kathleen shot her a quick look, the queasiness worsening. She remembered the roll of bills in his hand the night before. Was that where the money had come from? A reward for loyalty and hiding evidence?

"Well, you can bet one thing—if Reese had the gun, it's gone now that he knows we're looking for it." Tick twirled the spatula between his fingers like a baton. "You'd better find another way to tie him to those deaths."

"Right." Kathleen raked her fingers through her already disheveled hair. "We'd have an easier time finding a Sunday when Miles Shiver didn't sleep through Brother Ray's sermon."

The phone rang, audible through the screen door, and Tick tossed his spatula at Altee. "Flip those for me, Price, while I get that."

The screen door slapped shut behind him. Altee moved to the grill and Kathleen shaded her eyes with a hand, watching a lizard flit along the edge of the deck. Tension thudded at her temples. She should have gone to law school like her daddy wanted. She could have gone into corporate law...

"Kathleen, get in the truck." The door flapped open and slammed against the wall. Tick hopped on one foot, tugging on thick work boots. His dark hair stuck out from under the edge of his volunteer firefighter's cap. "Price, you too."

Unease jerked in Kathleen's stomach. She sat up and grabbed for her shoes. "What's wrong?"

"That was dispatch." Tick shut off the propane to the grill. "Your mama and daddy's house is on fire."

ഗ്രൈ

Smoke rolled over the roof, rising into a black column against the blue afternoon sky. Flames licked at the corners of windows, taking delicate nibbles before devouring the surrounding wood. One arm around her mother's shaking shoulders, Kathleen stood on the cracked sidewalk and watched the destruction of her childhood home.

His silver head bowed, her father stood near the corner, talking to Sheriff Reed. The fire inspector was on site, and she'd heard snatches of conversation about arson and accelerants. Brilliant red trucks from three departments blocked the street and hoses snaked across the green lawn, her daddy's pride. Voices yelled instructions and occasional curses against a backdrop of hissing, popping flames.

A rage to match those flames burned in Kathleen's heart. So this was Jim Ed's method of making her regret the legal invasion of his sanctum. Not her home, the small house on the lake, but her parents'. Showing her how easily he could get to those she loved.

One of the trucks belonged to the Haynes County volunteer fire department. Jim Ed manned a hose and she'd seen the flash of Jason's sun-lightened hair earlier. The fury burned hotter. How dare he show up here, when for all she knew, he'd helped start the blaze. Maybe he'd added a few more hundreds to his bankroll.

"Hey, thought you might need this." Altee appeared at her elbow, holding two paper cups of water.

"Thanks." Kathleen flashed the semblance of a smile and took one of the cups, pressing it into her mother's trembling hands. The pale skin with its blue veins and age spots had never looked so fragile. She glanced back at the house, then her mother's stricken face. "Mama, come on. Let's walk next door to Mr. Virgil's office so you can sit down."

Her mama's spine stiffened. "I'm fine."

With a triumphant roar, the fire flared up and the roof crashed in, tumbling three stories in a shower of sparks. The firefighters stumbled back, cursing. Kathleen gasped. Moaning, her mother fainted.

"Mama!" Kathleen dropped the other cup and scrambled to support her mama's weight. *Oh, God, please be all right. Mama, please.* They slid to the ground, her mother's head pillowed on Kathleen's thighs. She glanced around, seeking her father. "Daddy!"

"I'll radio for the medics." Altee sprinted off.

"What happened?" Fear roughened her father's voice. He knelt by them, reaching for his wife's hand. His fingers slid over her wrist. "Her pulse is strong, thank God. Elizabeth? Open your eyes, darling."

"She just fell." Kathleen brushed damp hair away from her mama's brow and loosened the collar of her white silk blouse, spotted from falling ashes.

"Kathy, let's get her over to Virgil's. We can put her on the couch there, get her out of this heat."

She shook her head. “Daddy, you can’t lift her. You just had hernia surgery not a month ago—”

“Let me.” Grim face streaked with soot, Jason knelt by her side. Kathleen glared and opened her mouth to tell him to go to hell.

“Thank you, young man.” Her father’s relieved voice forestalled her, and Kathleen suffered Jason’s help in getting her mother to the small restored house next door that housed Virgil Holton’s law offices. With her mama settled on the couch, the arriving medics took over and shooed everyone but Kathleen’s daddy from the room.

The door closed in her face and Kathleen turned on Jason, her fury out of control. “How much did he pay you for this? Did you strike the match yourself?”

“He didn’t pay me a damn thing. I had nothing to do with starting that fire.”

“You bastard.”

He shook his head. “Kathleen, you don’t—”

“You did this.” Her voice rose with wild anger and she advanced on him, her hands clenched into tight fists. Her fingernails cut into her palms, nothing to the pain cutting into her heart. “You did this!”

He reached for her, hands gentle on her arms. “I didn’t—”

“You did.” She shoved him away, the urge to strike him unbearable. “If not personally, then by refusing to help me, to tell me what happened.”

“I can’t.”

“God, stop saying that!” She did hit out at him then, her palms slamming against his chest, shoving him away again. “That’s not true. You have choices, Harding.”

He grabbed her wrists, holding her forearms against his chest in a firm yet gentle grasp. She struggled against him, hating his touch.

The scent of smoke emanated from him, body heat branding her. "You don't understand, Kathleen. I can't help you."

"I understand plenty." She choked on sudden sobs, tears spilling over her lashes. God, she'd wanted him to be different, to be something other than the tarnished knight he appeared to be. "I understand you're just another one of them. You're just like all the rest."

"You don't believe that."

"You're no better than your cousin."

He let her go, stepping back as though under the force of a blow. She glared at him, her anger a fierce pulsing in her veins. She flung a shaking hand toward the windows and the devastation beyond. "Look what you did. Look at my mama. She had nothing but praise for you, and *look what you did!*"

Face pale under its covering of soot, he stared at her. He swallowed, the muscles contracting underneath his skin. "Sugar, I swear it's not what you think."

The endearment and the intensity of his voice were her undoing. She couldn't stand it, couldn't bear to have him stand in front of her, lying, when she'd been so prepared to believe in him. "What else am I supposed to think? You've given me no reason to think otherwise. Don't you understand that not stopping it makes you as guilty as they are? You might as well have blown those boys' brains out yourself. Or did you? Were you there with him when he pulled the trigger? Did you see how scared they were? Hear them beg—"

"Stop." Strong hands wrapped around her upper arms from behind and pulled her back against a tall, lean form. Tick spoke close to her ear. "Damn it, that's enough."

Exhausted, she sagged against his hold and stared at Jason. Her chest heaved, the absence of adrenaline leaving her body drained. She shook her head, rolling against Tick's collarbone. "I hate you."

Jason blanched.

The tears flowed harder and she crumpled, her hands over her face. His hold easing, Tick turned her against him. She clutched at his shirt, sobbing, unfurled dreams she'd not allowed herself to want disappearing like the smoke outside drifting into the sky.

Tick's rough breath shook her body. "You'd better go, Harding."

Heavy footsteps on the hardwood floor and the soft click of a closing door signaled his departure. She struggled for control. She hadn't felt pain like this since the morning she went to get Everett from his crib and discovered his lifeless body.

No. That wasn't true. Because if that were true, then Jason Harding was important. From this point on, Harding was nothing.

She deserved this pain for hoping for something outside the narrow confines of her life—work, friends, her parents. Falling in love, wanting commitment and a family of her own meant nothing but pain. She knew that, had learned that lesson all too well.

Why had Jason been the one to shake her heart awake from its long slumber? Why not the man currently holding her, stroking her hair, whispering the same soothing nonsense she'd heard him use with his three-year-old niece? Why not Sheriff

Stanton Reed or the chicken farmer or any of the other good, decent men she knew?

She heaved a shuddering sigh, her forehead against Tick's chest. Losing Everett had ended her marriage and put her heart into a deep, painless sleep. It wouldn't slumber this time. Instead, Jason's betrayal would be its death knell.

ઉ৪ઊ

Jason strode across the Palmers' yard, anger and hurt jerking beneath his skin. Faced with her accusations, he'd wanted to spill the truth, force her to believe in him. Instead, he'd had to leave her in Calvert's arms, and the image lingered in his brain, taunting him with what he'd never have—the right to hold and comfort Kathleen.

In the waning light, the wreckage of the house smoldered, firefighters hosing down the occasional flare. The devastation mocked him, the death of something fine and pure. Whatever chance he'd had with Kathleen was gone. Anything she felt for him was gone and, by the time he finally broke through the wall of corruption in Haynes County and could reveal his true self, it would be too late.

In the street, Jim Ed helped roll up the hoses. He glanced up at Jason's approach and grinned. Malevolent joy glittered in his eyes and Jason's stomach turned. Why had he ever conceived of loyalty to this man? Kathleen was right—Jim Ed's only loyalty was to himself.

Jason met his cousin's gaze and forced a grin in return. His determination to take down the corruption drew strength from his pain and loss. He wouldn't have Kathleen, but he could rid a certain kingdom of its dark elements. He could help bring back Camelot.

He could do that much. He knew it as certainly as he knew one other fact—he would do whatever it took to keep Kathleen safe from Jim Ed.

Whatever it took.

Chapter Eight

Kathleen left the Wagoneer parked outside the tall iron fence enclosing the Morningside Cemetery. The grounds sprawled over a hill and tiny valley, canopied by ancient oak and pine trees dripping with moss.

Sunglasses shaded her stinging eyes from the just-rising sun. She followed one of the trodden dirt paths, surrounded by family plots, marble headstones and the occasional memorial statue. Her throat ached, from the smoke inhaled the day before and the tears shed during the night. Coming here this morning, as she had for fourteen years on this date, seemed poignantly apt.

She'd buried all of her adolescent dreams of love and family with her son. She should have left them entombed. Today she'd put them back where they belonged.

Birds twittered in the branches above and a squirrel scampered along a wrought-iron fence. The dirt and scattered gravel crunched beneath her tennis shoes. She tucked her hands in the pockets of her faded jeans and drew in long breaths of the damp morning air. Her chest ached. Just the exertion of climbing the hill. That was all. Not because she still fought the ravaging sobs that threatened.

She wouldn't report for work today and smother her pain in the minutiae of investigation as she always had before on the anniversary of Everett's birth. No, today she would meet her father at what had been their home, talk with the insurance adjusters and pick through the wreckage to see what could be salvaged.

Near the top of the hill lay the Palmer family plot, her baby cradled among generations of Palmers. Unlike many of the plots covered with protective gravel, lush green grass blanketed the graves in her family section. The waist-high iron gate creaked when she opened it.

Everett's grave occupied one small corner of the parcel. A baseball in a dew-dappled plastic cube rested next to his headstone, and she touched it, imagining Tom placing it here. Day-old flowers from her father's garden wilted in a glass vase.

A bench stood waiting nearby, but she abandoned it to kneel on the damp grass next to the headstone. She traced the name etched into the pure white marble.

Thomas Everett McMillian IV.

Tears hovered on her lashes and she let them fall free. No need to pretend here. Her fingers drifted over the dates of his birth and death, not quite three months apart.

"Hey, Ev." Her voice emerged raw and tear-clogged. "It's Mama. You know what? You'd be fifteen today. Getting your learner's permit, probably pestering me to let you drive on the way to school. Playing baseball, I know, because your dad is so crazy about the sport. Getting ready to finish your first year of high school."

If I hadn't screwed up. If I'd gotten up when I heard you cry. If I hadn't gone back to sleep. Oh, Ev, I'm sorry, sorry you missed out on so much because I wanted another hour of sleep.

Fingers pressed to his name, she cried for all she'd lost, for all he'd never gotten to be or do. For the destruction her parents faced. And for the crushing disappointment her fascination with Jason had turned out to be.

Angrily, she brushed the tears away, refusing to cry over him anymore. She had no one to blame but herself. From the beginning she'd known who he was and couldn't cry foul when she discovered what he truly was. *Just another one of them.*

Down the hill footsteps crunched on loose gravel and indistinct male voices drifted with the morning breeze. She wiped her wet cheeks. Who else was out this early? When she visited the cemetery, she usually ran into a couple of the county's elderly widows, but that was always well after nine. It was barely seven now.

She glanced down the hill in the direction of the voices. A tall oak shaded the plots at the base of the hill and Tick Calvert, clad in khakis and a sheriff's department polo, leaned one arm against the sturdy trunk. He frowned, gesturing with his free hand.

Kathleen narrowed her eyes. He stood near his father's grave and paused, the other voice filling in the gap. The direction of the breeze had changed and the tone of the other man's voice carried better.

A shiver ran through her. Oh, Lord. Her entire being recognized that voice.

She shifted her position to gain a better glimpse of the area below. Gray sweat pants and a perspiration-dampened T-shirt, both emblazoned with ARMY in big, block letters. Brown hair, streaked by the sun. A mouth, drawn in a tight line now, that had moved on hers with passion and heat.

Jason Harding. What the hell was Tick doing with Jason?

She watched, the certainty settling over her that this was no chance meeting. If Jason, out for a run, had come across Tick visiting his father's grave, they'd have passed a few words and gone their separate ways. What she witnessed now was an intense conversation.

As he talked, she watched Jason's mouth move. He spoke quickly, brows drawn together in a tense line. As if aware of her scrutiny, he turned his head, searching the hill. Kathleen pressed against the fence, holding her breath.

What was going on?

"So you were with him all afternoon?" Calvert lit a cigarette and tucked his lighter back into his pocket.

Jason shrugged. "Yeah. He was in a snit because things were out of place in the house after the search. We spent the afternoon putting them back, until we got the fire dispatch."

"Did he make any calls? Take any?" Calvert took a drag and blew out a slow stream of smoke.

"I've already told you he didn't." Frustration crawled along his skin. "I'm telling you, I don't see how he ordered it. He was there all afternoon, and I was with him."

Doubt hovered in the look Calvert shot his way. "The whole time?"

Hadn't he already answered that question four times? "Yeah."

Calvert scuffed a shoe in the dust. "What about Stacy?"

"She left to pick up the kids from school."

"When?"

"About two-forty-five."

"Son of a gun."

"You think he used *Stacy* to order the fire?"

"Yeah, I do."

"Stacy? Have you gone crazy? She's like the poster girl for the perfect soccer mom—"

"She's also lived with the man for sixteen years and he controls every aspect of her life. She's never worked outside the home, he gives her an allowance, tells her where to go, what to wear, who she can associate with."

"How do you know all that?" Jason frowned. "Wait, let me guess. FBI surveillance."

"No. Quilting circle at my mama's church. It's amazing what elderly women will tell you when they've known you since you were in diapers."

Jason chuckled. "Yeah. But Stacy? You really think she knows what he's doing?"

"I'm pretty darn sure she doesn't ask where the money comes from to pay for that house and her clothes and the new car he buys her every other year. Does she know she ordered an act of arson? Probably not. He probably had her stop off at the station with a message."

"So it could be any of them." Jason rubbed a hand over his eyes and pinched the bridge of his nose. It was one thing to keep an eye on Jim Ed, something else again to keep tabs on twelve other men.

A grimace twisted Calvert's mouth. "That's assuming it's someone in the department and not in Reese's circle of friends. I'll get Price started on running down alibis today. You can probably plan on being pulled in for questioning in the next couple of days."

Jason nodded and glanced away, his gaze trailing up the hill. Sunlight glinted off pale marble. That last image of Kathleen wrapped in Calvert's arms pulsed in his head.

He cleared his throat. "How's Kathleen?"

"She'll be fine." Calvert's voice was even. "She's a strong woman and she's been through worse."

That strong woman who'd been through worse had been devastated the day before. Devastated and ready to believe he was to blame. Her voice rang in his head. *I hate you.* He'd fallen into a fitful sleep with the words echoing in his brain and woken to their mocking presence this morning as well.

Calvert glanced at his watch. "Listen, Harding, when this is all over, she'll understand."

"Yeah." With the memory of her tear-filled gaze still haunting him, he couldn't dredge up any optimism. When this was all over. Right. As far as he and Kathleen were concerned, it was already over.

ଔ

Kathleen leaned against her shovel and wiped her wrist across her gritty forehead. Heat still rose from the ashes, but she and her father moved through the wreckage with care, seeking anything not destroyed by the flames. They'd found precious little other than his fireproof safe.

She rolled aching shoulders and stared at the thick layers of gray and black ash. Was it really worth it? Worth the destruction and threats? The constant worry? Would it be better to simply back down, let the case die the way so many others involving Haynes County had? She nudged a wire coil with the toe of her heavy boot.

Two mothers had buried their sons this week. Her answer lay in that. She couldn't turn her back and walk away. If nothing else, those mothers deserved a sense of justice. To see the person who'd taken their children put into the deepest, darkest hole the state of Georgia could find.

Her job was to make sure Tom could put that person there.

And if more than one person was responsible, so be it.

Even if that other person was Jason Harding.

Or Tick Calvert.

All morning, turning over layer after layer of soot, ash and debris, she'd turned over layer after layer of knowledge in her mind.

Jason and Jim Ed the first to arrive on scene.

Tick arriving moments later.

Neither Jason nor Tick seeing anything. Tick refusing to back up Jason's story, but not tearing it down either.

Jason with a pocketful of money.

A background making him perfect for the seduction of money and power.

Tick's squeaky-clean reputation.

The two of them together that morning, carrying on a conversation that seemed more than idle chitchat or a chance meeting.

None of it came together into a cohesive picture. Instead, she was left with something like an out-of-focus movie—a blurred, moving image that wouldn't stay still long enough for her to get a grasp of what she was seeing. Fuzzy phantasms, letting her mind play tricks, letting her see only what she wished to see.

Like a way to remove Jason from suspicion.

Right back where she started—wanting him, wanting to believe he was something other than what he was.

Surrounded by the results of his treachery and she still wanted to believe in him.

“You about had enough, baby girl?” Her daddy’s weary voice brought tears pricking at her eyelids.

Enough? He had no idea.

She brushed her bangs, sticky with sweat, away from her face and looked down at the ashes so she wouldn’t have to see the pain and defeat in his strong face. “I’m so sorry, Daddy.”

“What for?” His arm came around her shoulder, a warm, comforting weight. He pulled her tight against him for a moment, and smoke, stale sweat and Old Spice filled her nose.

“This.” She gestured at the mess. “Oh, Daddy, you know this is because of me.”

He hugged her tighter. “I wouldn’t have it any other way.”

Irritated, she tugged away, feeling instantly bereft. “What are you talking about?”

“Sometimes we suffer for our principles, Kathleen. And sometimes others suffer in our place. If you’re sticking to the values your mother and I tried to impart, how can we complain if they come home to roost?”

“They burned down your home! Because of me. How can you—”

“And they took Lamar Calvert’s life and left Lenora to raise those five children alone. They’ve taken and beaten and destroyed for years, and as hard as Lamar and Virgil and I...and countless others...tried, we couldn’t make a dent. You and Altee have got Jim Ed Reese running scared enough that he’d do this.” His face hard, he waved a hand at the partial remains of the fireplace. “Kathleen Elizabeth, your mama and I are so damned proud of you we can hardly stand it.”

“You pick some mighty strange things to be proud of.”

He chuckled and wrapped her in a quick, tight hug. “Go home. Get clean and dolled up for tonight.”

Tonight? The Sheriff's Association dinner. One of the biggest political functions of the year. She groaned. "Oh, Daddy. I really just want to go home and stay there."

She'd take a shower and pull out the box hidden in the top of her closet, unpack the photos of Everett, hold his tiny clothes and pretend she could still smell his precious baby scent, feel the incredible softness of his knees and the backs of his hands.

She sighed. "And it would be good for you and Mama to get some rest, too."

"I won't run, Kathy. Elizabeth and I will be there, and I expect to see your pretty face as well." He smiled and chucked her chin. "Besides, if you don't show up, who will Tick dance with?"

"Any blonde in the room who's under twenty-five and not the brightest bulb in the socket." Feeling like a dog being led to the veterinarian's office, she allowed him to push her toward her Wagoneer.

He chuckled. "Go on. We'll see you tonight."

She slid behind the wheel and gave him a wobbly smile. Okay, she could do this. She could put on a dress and heels and make her daddy proud. Even if it was the one day a year she allowed herself to give in to the never-ending sense of grief and loss. Even if Thatcher and Jim Ed showed up to gloat. She could handle them.

If Jason showed up? Now that could be a problem. She wasn't ready to handle him.

ઉજ઼

Altee leaned forward, adjusting her breasts into the cups of a pale pink strapless bra. "You saw him with *who*?"

"Tick." Kathleen twisted sideways, studying her reflection in the mirror. The lavender silk clung to curves she'd forgotten she had and the low back dipped to show off the dimple at the base of her spine. Behind her, dresses in a rainbow of colors spilled off the bed. "This thing is indecent. You didn't really wear it to your cousin's wedding."

"I wore it *in* Layla's wedding. Thought the church roof was gonna fall in on us, too." Altee eased an ivory slip dress over her head, the beaded detail shimmering with each movement. "It looks good on you. Better than it did on me. Are you sure it was Calvert?"

"I'm sure." Facing the mirror again, Kathleen lifted an eyebrow at her reflection. Her bra pushed her breasts together to create a rounded cleavage that rivaled the height of Stone Mountain over Atlanta. An image invaded her brain, Jason's mouth moving along the shadowy curve, and she closed her eyes, suppressing a strangled moan. Why couldn't she forget him?

"Okay, that just doesn't make sense."

"Tell me about it."

"Calvert, who wouldn't spit on a Haynes County deputy if he saw one on fire, hanging out and talking with Harding? Kath, are you sure?"

Kathleen grimaced at her. "Altee, I'm sure. It was Tick. And Jason. Together."

"Well, you have only a few scenarios to consider then. One, Calvert's turned corrupt. Two, Harding isn't the corrupt son of gun we think he is. Or three, that rumor Lynn Harris is doing her damnedest to spread around about Calvert being gay is true, and Harding is his new boy toy."

"I think we can rule out Tick being gay. That's pretty much Lynn's sour grapes because she couldn't break his celibate streak." Kathleen glanced back at the mirror. Excited color flickered across her cheekbones. Hearing Altee voice the possibility she'd refused to consider made it seem more real. The intensity with which she wanted it to be real terrified her.

"And if Mr. Fidelity, Bravery and Integrity has gone bad, then I'm turning white." Altee perched on the foot of the bed to slide on impossibly spiked heels. "So I think we can safely consider the possibility that your boy isn't who he appears to be."

I can't help you, Kathleen. His tortured words returned to her. "He said he couldn't help me. Not that he wouldn't. He said *can't.* His agenda could be separate, but parallel to ours."

"So maybe you were right and he's not involved. Maybe he's a knight in shining armor the Bureau's OCD sent down here. It makes a weird kind of sense. You'd have to have someone local, someone with close ties, to get in there." Altee's voice turned wry. "Of course, we also have to consider the possibility that he's exactly who he appears to be. It's not like you can just walk up and ask him."

"It's not like we can just ask Tick either."

"Why not?"

"Because. He'll lie."

"Oh, sure. We're talking about the boy who takes his mama to church *every* Sunday."

"We're talking about the boy who worked in the FBI's Organized Crime Division for ten years, including a couple of undercover operations. Trust me. He'll lie."

Kathleen picked up a shoebox and removed a pair of strappy, rhinestone-dotted high heels from a protective layer of tissue. She leaned over to fasten them onto her feet, the flirty hem of the dress brushing her skin like a phantom lover's fingers.

"Kath?"

She smoothed the strap into place above her ankle and lifted her head. "What?"

"What if we didn't ask him?"

"Meaning?"

"What if we fudge a little? Use Calvert's background against him."

Kathleen laughed, intrigued. "Just spell it out, Altee."

"He's still a Fed at heart, even if he is wearing a six-pointed star now. What's the one thing a Fibbie hates most?"

"Having his territory threatened."

"So let's threaten it a little. Tell him we're working an undercover angle, about to get someone inside Haynes County. If we're right and Harding is a Fed, you can bet we'll be in some high-ranking Fed's office within the week. They won't let us intrude on their investigation, if that's what's really going on."

"Exactly." Kathleen laughed. "Lord, you're devious. I like the way you think."

"Think it'll work?"

"Oh, hell. As crazy as this idea is, it just might."

"C'mon." Altee grinned and reached for her purse and gauzy shawl. "Let's go stir up some trouble."

ᦳ

Music and laughter blended with the scents of a warm Georgia evening drifting in through the open French doors. Seated at a large round table in a corner, Jason counted heads and figured the estimated donation the Sheriff's Association would make to the local women's crisis center. Once circumstances and the Federal Bureau of Investigation allowed him to have his real life back, he'd send them a check, too.

People packed the historic Radium Springs Casino's ballroom—cops, their wives and girlfriends, local politicians, single women looking to be the wife or girlfriend of a cop or local politician. Conversation swirled around the tables decked with white cloths, floating candles and fresh flowers.

Earlier, he'd been surprised when Tori Calvert delivered the evening's opening remarks. She couldn't be more than twenty-four or twenty-five, too young to be the director of the women's center. Muttering beneath his breath, Jim Ed had refused to join in the wild applause that greeted her.

Calvert was here, too, sharing a table with his sister, the sheriff of Chandler County and several others, including Altee and Kathleen. Jason struggled to keep his gaze from straying to her. He'd thought she was beautiful in her GBI polo and khakis or the casual denim and blouse outfit. Tonight, wearing a walking fantasy of a lavender dress, she blew his mind.

She laughed at some remark of Calvert's and leaned closer to reply, her hand on his arm. Jason's chest tightened. He had *never* made her laugh. She'd smiled once or twice during the dinner they'd shared, but he'd never heard her real laugh, the one Calvert coaxed forth with such ease. Damn it, he wasn't even near enough now to hear it.

"Close your trap. You'll catch flies." Returning to the table, Jim Ed slapped him on the back. Stacy stood a few tables away, talking with animated gestures to the women seated with a few of Haynes County's finest. The slim red dress she wore highlighted a too-thin figure. Jim Ed slumped into a chair and shot a malevolent glare at Calvert's table. "Looks like Calvert's moved in on your woman."

Jason aligned his remaining silverware to military precision. "They're sitting together. Doesn't mean anything."

"His hand's under the table. Bet that doesn't mean anything, either." Jim Ed nudged him in the ribs, hard, then stretched an arm along the back of Stacy's vacant chair. "Did you get that far?"

Anger burned an acidic trail down his throat and into his gut. He gritted his teeth, molars grinding until his jaw ached. "She thinks I started that damn fire. How far do you think I got?"

"Forget her. You've got better things waiting for you."

"Like what?" Anticipation made a dent in the anger and he darted a look at his cousin.

"Sheriff's got some situations he needs handled. Light work, mostly. Thought you could help out with that. Kinda supplement your income, you know?"

"Yeah. Sounds good."

"We thought you might appreciate it."

"So what—"

"We'll talk later."

Stacy approached the table and Jim Ed straightened. A wide smile lit her face and she laughed, tugging at his hand. "Come on, honey, and dance with me."

"Baby, I'm about danced out. Maybe later."

Her full mouth made a pretty little moue. "Then I'll dance with Jason."

He tensed, but Jim Ed chuckled and nudged him again. "Go dance with her, cousin. Keep her off my back for a while."

Faking a smile, Jason pushed back his chair and took Stacy's outstretched hand. He really didn't want to do this—the only woman he wanted in his arms hadn't looked his way all night.

The band covered an old Patsy Cline number and Stacy went into his arms easily, her hand small and fragile in his. She tipped her head back to look up at him, her smile brittle and too bright. "I'm so glad you came home, Jason. Jim Ed is thrilled to have you here. Ever since Billy...well, he's missed having family, you know? And he's crazy about you, always talking about stuff you did together as boys."

"I appreciate him helping me get on with the department." Jason moved her around the floor and refused to look over her shoulder at Kathleen.

"He really needs somebody he can trust." She glanced down, blinking, black lashes brushing her cheeks. Her chin trembled. "I worry about him."

He couldn't handle this. He'd spent weeks letting the profiler from the Bureau's Behavioral Science Unit get inside his head, prepare him to betray his cousin. The facts had been black and white at the time—if Jim Ed was breaking the law, he had to pay the consequences.

The gray area was turning out to be Jim Ed's family.

If Jim Ed gave a damn about them, he wouldn't be doing what he's doing. Remember Kathleen.

That wasn't hard. His mind continued to dredge up the memory of her angry words and hatred-filled eyes. *I hate you.*

A flash of lavender caught his attention and he watched Kathleen walk out into the stairwell. The urge to follow her was a physical ache.

"Hey." Stacy patted his cheek. The emotional distress had disappeared from her heart-shaped face, the pretty mask back in place. "Earth to Jason. Where'd you go?"

He grimaced. “Sorry. I was thinking.”

“My friend Mandy wants to meet you. I’ll introduce y’all later. She’s real cute. She works over at the poultry plant.”

He let her prattle on, his gaze sweeping over their table. Jim Ed’s chair sat empty. A chill gripped the base of his spine.

He scanned the room. No Jim Ed. The ice spread into his gut.

Kathleen wasn’t in the room.

And neither was Jim Ed.

Chapter Nine

His footsteps muffled by the ornate carpet, Jason bounded down the stairs to the main level of the old casino. Massive crystal chandeliers dappled light over polished wood floors. A handful of couples seeking privacy occupied the dim dining room, but he didn't see Kathleen's distinctive copper hair or Jim Ed's hulking shoulders.

In his throat, his pulse thudded an uncomfortable tattoo. He loosened his tie and popped free the top button of his too-starched shirt. Where was she?

The rational part of his mind whispered he was overreacting. She could be anywhere—the ladies room, taking a breather from the noise upstairs, on her way home. And he acted like she was in imminent danger.

His gut screamed she was.

He'd seen guys listen to their rational minds and get blown away. He'd seen just as many guys stop because a gut instinct told them to—and the action saved their lives.

He needed to find Kathleen *now*.

A server wandered by, bearing a tray of tiny quiches. Jason stopped him. "Have you seen a redhead, lavender dress, average height?"

The kid jerked his head toward the patio. "Just went outside."

"Thanks." He strode to the French doors and stepped onto the marble patio to find it empty. Party noise floated down from the ballroom above, and he walked to the elaborate balustrade, his gaze scanning the darkness beyond the springs.

Low lights illuminated the footbridge leading from the patio to the bank of the cool blue springs. On the bank, tall trees stood like sentinels, darker than the navy sky. A slip of lavender flashed against that darkness and disappeared.

Jason jogged across the footbridge, his ears attuned to any noise. Soft footsteps slithered against pine straw and he followed, tracking by sound, waiting for his eyes to grow accustomed to the lack of light. Only one set of steps. If Jim Ed was out here, he wasn't moving.

To his left, the river murmured and he knew she wouldn't go far. Only someone without good sense would go traipsing too close to the treacherous Flint River in the dark.

Sure enough, her footsteps stopped a few yards ahead. Jason tucked his hands in his pockets and began whistling "Boy Named Sue". Coming upon her by surprise in the dark didn't seem right, especially under the circumstances.

Pine straw rustled. "Jason?"

A nervous note quavered in her voice. Anger burned his gut. She shouldn't have to be afraid. She was doing the right thing, and she shouldn't have to be afraid.

"Yeah," he said, almost whispering. "It's me."

"What are you doing out here?"

"Looking for you." He could just make out her face in the darkness, but couldn't see enough of her eyes to read her mood. Filtered starlight danced off the shimmery satin of her dress.

She shook her head, the diamonds in her ears glinting. "Why?"

"I wanted to make sure you were all right."

"I'm fine." Her voice trembled, still sounding uncertain.

Silence stretched between them. Her scent wrapped around him, not the clean Ivory that had invaded his fantasies, but a blend of mimosa and roses, a scent invoking the sensual warmth of a Georgia summer night.

He wanted more than her scent—he wanted arms, legs, all of her wrapped around his body. He wanted to lose himself in her, until there was nothing left but the reality of them together.

I hate you.

He rubbed his jaw, wishing he could see her face more clearly. He took a step forward. "Kathleen, about yesterday—"

"Tell me you didn't have anything to do with it. Any of it." Desperation roughened her voice.

Another step. "I didn't have anything to do with it." A step closer and he could hear her breathing. "Not the fire." Closer still, and satin rustled against starched cotton. His hands cupped her face. "Not those boys' deaths. None of it. I swear."

"Don't swear."

His fingers traced the warm curve of her cheek. He lowered his head, his lips brushing hers. "It's true. I promise."

Her breath moved against his mouth, a sweet, minty rush. Gentle fingers sank into his hair. "Don't promise."

"Then what do you want me to do?" With each syllable, their mouths touched.

"Just kiss me."

Lips tangled, opened, meshed. Heat seared along his nerves, spreading throughout his body, settling in his groin. A tiny moan vibrated in her throat, sending a shiver through him.

With her arms around his neck, she stroked her fingers through his hair, over his nape, across his shoulders, and pleasure shot out from each simple caress.

His hands slid over her shoulders and down the sweep of her back, memorizing the feel of her skin. She made that growling little moan again and pulled him closer, the swells of her breasts pressed to his chest. Kissing her was better than any sex he'd had in his life. He could stand here all night, with her hands on him, her tongue making maddening little forays into his mouth, her curves accepting his planes and angles.

I hate you.

"Kathleen." He kissed along her jaw to her throat. "Say you didn't mean it."

"What?" Her head fell back, offering him access to the scented hollow at her collarbone. Never again could he look at a lacy pink mimosa blossom without thinking of her. She'd marked him for life with that scent.

"About hating me." He murmured the word against her shoulder, caressing the line of her waist and ribcage. "Tell me you didn't mean it."

"I don't hate you." He curved his hands around the sides of her breasts, and she gasped. The soft sound of her arousal jerked through his erection.

He sought her mouth again, tasting, nibbling, devouring. She touched him, shaping his pecs, tracing the line of his abs, driving him crazy. Fingers flexed against his chest and she whispered into his mouth. "You're hard. Everywhere."

The only sound he could manage was a shaky chuckle. He slid his fingers over her hips to cup her buttocks and pulled her closer. He rubbed against her, a delicious, frustrating friction, and she gasped again.

He teased her ear with his lips, her skin a wild mix of salty and sweet. "Sugar, you have no idea how long I've been hard for you."

With her arms twined around his neck once more, she played with his hair. "Why do you call me that?"

"Because you're pure sweetness." He nuzzled her temple and felt her smile against his cheek. "And you melt in my mouth."

She laughed, the soft, velvety sound falling on him like rain on a parched cornfield. He wanted to stay here forever, in her arms, with nothing but the dark, the scent of pines and the sighing river around them. He wanted to forget the real world and what awaited him.

Reality came in the form of Price's voice, calling from the footbridge area. "Kathleen! Kath, are you out here?"

Kathleen jerked in his arms and pulled away. She smoothed her dress and ran a thumb along the curve of her mouth. She glanced at him, her eyes still unreadable in the dark.

"I should go."

"Yeah."

The chasm widened between them again.

"Kathleen!"

"I'm coming." She moved by him, but Jason reached for her arm.

He drew her to him, his mouth near her ear. "Be careful, Kathleen." He forced himself to let go and she hurried away.

He followed, their voices wafting to him. Price scolded like a frantic mother. "Where have you *been*? I've looked everywhere."

"I just needed some air."

"Air."

"Yes. Air. You know, oxygen."

A long pause passed before Price spoke again. "Well, come on. Calvert has this wild idea that we should drive to the coast for breakfast. I'm telling you, the white boy can dance, but he has no life. No wonder you two get along so well."

"Don't start that again. I told you..."

Jason let the distance grow and the voices drifted away. He'd been so focused on Kathleen he'd forgotten his purpose in going after her. He'd found her.

But where the hell had Jim Ed gone?

"Air, huh?" Altee held out Kathleen's tiny, beaded clutch. Kathleen, aware of her partner's searching gaze, took the purse without comment. Altee shook her head, earrings swinging against her neck. "Must be some damn fine air to put that look on your face."

"Not now, please." Not while his touch, his kiss, still thrummed through her body. Not when she wanted to walk back into those woods and into his arms. Not when her lower abdomen and the cleft of her thighs ached with liquid desire.

"I'm just—"

"Don't."

The music and laughter grew louder as they approached the casino. Tick waited for them in the lobby and Kathleen caught the sharp glance he darted at her face. The urge to find a mirror overwhelmed her, but she didn't really need one. Heat flushed her cheeks, and her lips felt lush and swollen. She had to look thoroughly kissed.

Tick pushed away from the pillar he lounged against. "Ready to go?"

Kathleen lifted an eyebrow. “You really want to drive all the way to Carabelle-St. Marks? On a Thursday night?”

“Why not?” A lazy shrug accompanied his grin. “We can watch the sun come up and still make it back to work on time.”

“I can do that on my deck.”

“Ah, but not with pancakes from Captain Jack’s.” He pushed the door open and held it for both women. As they moved to the parking lot, he draped an arm over their shoulders. “Price tells me y’all think you’re going to get someone inside Haynes County.”

At his casual tone, Kathleen hid a grin of her own. “Looks that way. Just think about what we could do with someone undercover.”

“Yeah.” Tick lifted his arm from her shoulder and rubbed at his mouth. “That would be great.”

Kathleen shared a quick look with her partner, a smile quirking at Altee’s lips. “Of course, you’d need someone who already had some type of tie to…”

The sight of her beloved Wagoneer killed the sentence in her throat. The trio jerked to a stop.

“Oh, my God,” Altee whispered.

Someone had slashed the tires. Glass from the shattered windshield glittered on the hood and dash. Long gashes gouged the paint.

Fury exploded in a red, stabbing pain behind her eyes. She fought it back. Yesterday’s loss of control, shouting at Jason, had been enough. Couples and small groups of revelers trickled into the parking lot. She wouldn’t create a scene here.

A hand at her throat, she turned to look up at Tick. “Is there any point in even filing a report?”

He grimaced. “For your insurance.”

She shook her head, staring at the destruction. “I don’t believe this.”

Altee wrapped an arm around her shoulders. “Yeah, you do.”

Fear nudged the fury aside. She didn’t want to be afraid, but the attacks didn’t have a rhyme or reason to them. The snake, her parents’ home, now this. What was next? Damn it, how far would they go to maintain their balance of power?

She looked up to find Tick’s inscrutable gaze on her again while he used his cell phone to contact Chandler dispatch, requesting a tow truck, and a memory flashed across her mind—a younger, boyishly thin Tick thrust into manhood too soon, standing over his father’s open grave, that same unreadable look on his face.

They were willing to kill. That was how far they would go.

Again, fear she didn’t want to acknowledge curled through her. Would they go after her? Her family? Altee?

“Stop it,” Altee murmured in her ear. “You’re giving them what they want. Shake off the fear.”

“Aren’t you scared?”

“Witless, but we’re not letting them know it.”

Tick snapped his cell phone closed and tucked it into his jacket pocket. “Bobby Gene will be here in a few minutes. He’ll tow it over to Lawson’s Automotive for you.”

“Thanks.” She forced a smile, but over his shoulder, her gaze clashed with Jim Ed Reese’s. His arm around Stacy’s waist, he strolled to his shining white pickup, grinning at Kathleen the whole way.

She narrowed her eyes, fury pricking at her skin. *Bastard.* She swallowed the urge to scream at him. *Don’t let him know it.*

Making herself assume a relaxed stance, she pulled her gaze from his mocking green eyes. Eyes the same shade as Jason's, but never had Jason's been that cold, filled with malicious satisfaction.

The memory of desire lighting Jason's eyes poured molten fire through her veins, warming her.

She and Altee had to be right. There was no way Jason Harding was cut of the same cloth as his cousin. Jason wouldn't do something like this.

They had to be right. They *had* to be.

ℭℜ

"Are you sure you don't want me to stay?" Genuine worry lingered in Altee's big doe eyes.

"I'll be fine. Go home." Kathleen flashed a grin that made her weary face ache.

"You know I can be here like that." Altee snapped her fingers, the low light in Kathleen's living room glittering off polished nails. "You call me if anything happens. You hear me?"

"You're worse than my mother. Heck, you're worse than Tick, the biggest mother hen known to man. I'll be *fine*."

She gave her partner a light push toward the French doors. Altee twisted to look at her. "Are you sure?"

"I'm sure. Go *home*, Altee. And call me when you get there."

"Now who's being a mother hen?"

A few minutes later, with Altee gone, Kathleen threw the locks and surveyed her living room. Everything remained in place, but unease lurked in the house's shadows. She wrapped her arms around her stomach.

"You're not doing this. You're not letting them take over your life." Saying the words aloud made her feel better.

Leaving the lights on, she walked down the hall to her bedroom. The strappy sandals returned to their bed of tissue and Altee's indecent dream of a dress to its padded hanger. In her underwear, she went into the bathroom and turned on the shower, steam rising to dance around the edges of the room.

The phone rang in the bedroom and she hurried to pick up. Altee's indulgent voice rang across the line. "I'm home, Mom. Everything's fine on my side of the lake."

"Same here."

"Be careful, Kath."

"You, too. See you in the morning."

After replacing the receiver, Kathleen padded back to the bathroom. Relaxing, she dropped her panties in the hamper and stepped into the shower. Hot water streamed over her body, sensitized skin tingling under the spray. She reached for her loofah and the white cake of Ivory.

Suds clung to curves, the sharp, clean smell of the soap tickling her nose. The familiar scent triggered a recent memory—the same fragrance on Jason's warm skin. He hadn't smelled of Ivory the time she'd kissed him in the Winn Dixie parking lot.

He used the same brand of soap she did now. A coincidence, since every grocery store in town ran it on special at least once a month. But the idea consumed her, of him in the shower, thinking of her, lathering those hard, defined muscles she'd stroked through his shirt. A sharp ache settled between her thighs and begged for relief. A swift, self-induced climax wasn't going to offer any real satisfaction, though.

No, the relief she sought would come only from having that muscular body on hers, his hands and mouth against her skin.

A moan slid past her lips and she sagged against the shower wall, the loofah twisted in her hands.

She didn't care *who* he was, undercover officer or corrupt-as-hell Haynes County deputy. She wanted him with a fierceness she'd never experienced in her life, a pulsing spreading from her core and out through her entire being.

The knocking permeated her consciousness and she jerked out of the erotic haze. Icy fear slithered after the desire, smothering it. She turned off the water and reached for her towel, listening. With as little noise as possible, she toweled off and wrapped her robe around her still-damp body.

The pounding continued at her French doors. Her heart echoed the cadence. She edged toward her room, wanting her gun and the phone.

"Kathleen?" Jason's deep voice filtered down the hall. The wanting flared again, melting the fear.

Another anxiety reared. If she opened that door, she wouldn't be able to keep her hands off him. She stuck her head into the hallway, his shadowy outline visible at the door. "Just a second."

She avoided looking at the bed and grabbed clothing from her bureau—panties, faded jeans, a white T-shirt. Her fantasy lingered and she shuddered while rubbing moisture from her hair, a sharp stab of desire hitting her. She didn't need clothes. She needed a freakin' suit of armor or one of those iron chastity belts. Something to protect her from her own wanting.

Dressed, she padded to the door. She smoothed back her hair, tucking longer strands behind her ears. With a deep breath to calm the jittery nerves galloping in her stomach, she opened the door. His dark suit was gone, replaced by jeans and a sage green polo shirt, his hair damp from a recent shower. He smelled clean and she curved a hand around the doorframe to keep from grabbing him.

"Hey."

He didn't smile. "Hey."

She turned away, needing distance from the temptation he embodied. The door open, she walked into the living room. "I suppose you know all about my truck."

"I heard."

At his wry tone, she glanced over her shoulder. He stood just inside, still only a few feet away, his stance deceptively relaxed, thumbs hooked in his pockets. Muscles tensed at his neck and shoulders.

When she didn't say anything, he ran a hand over his nape. Golden-tipped spikes stood out from his scalp. "I keep telling myself this is a bad idea. I should stay away from you."

"But?"

"But I can't."

Her breath rushed out in a whoosh. Had she been holding it? Her burning lungs seemed to think so. She touched her throat and remembered his mouth there.

Her gaze locked with his. "It's a really bad idea."

His eyes darkened to the murky green of Lake Blackshear during a heavy storm. "Kathleen—"

"But I don't want you to stay away. It's crazy. Do you know how crazy this is?"

"Yeah." A slow grin curved his mouth and she knew he wasn't thinking of the obvious dangers, but something deeper, more physical. "I don't care."

He reached out and snagged her wrist, pulling her against him. She flattened her hands against his chest. "Don't kiss me."

One of his eyebrows lifted. "What?"

She flexed her fingers against him, wringing a muffled groan from his throat. "If you do, I won't want you to stop. And I'm not ready to go any further. Not yet."

His lashes dipped, a frown drawing his eyebrows together. He lowered his head and tense anticipation gathered in her muscles. He was going to kiss her anyway.

He rested his forehead against hers, his ragged breathing audible. She inhaled sharply, struggling for composure, and her already-tingling breasts, bare under the thin cotton of her T-shirt, brushed his chest. He jerked in reaction and liquid heat poured through her.

"Damn it, Kathleen." He bit the words out through clenched teeth. "It's not just crazy. *I'm* crazy. I want *you*. Understand?"

His heart thudded against her hands. What would it hurt, to pull him into her room, open herself to him? No one had to know and she was a big girl. She could handle the consequences.

All she had to do was tilt her head and his mouth would be on hers. One little movement. So much pleasure to be had.

She couldn't do it.

There remained too many truths about him she didn't have. Reluctance dragged at her movements, but she let her hands fall from his chest and stepped away. Afraid those passion-dark eyes would draw her in again, she looked at her bare feet and tugged hard at her hair.

"I shouldn't have come here tonight." Frustration lurked in the tight words. "I won't do it again."

Her head jerked up, her gaze flying to his. "Don't go."

Surprise flared in his eyes. "What?"

"Don't go. I-I want you to stay." She swallowed against the sudden dryness of her mouth and throat. With a shaky smile, she tilted her head toward the kitchen. "I'll get us something to drink and meet you on the deck."

She spun on her heel and walked into the kitchen. The refrigerator's cool air was a welcome relief to her heated cheeks. She grabbed the two longnecks, straightened, and slammed the refrigerator door. Turning, she collided with the solid firmness of Jason's chest. A tremulous laugh burst from her lips and she fumbled the bottles.

"God, Jason, don't sneak up on me like that. I thought you were outside—"

His mouth covered hers, his fingers wrapping hers on the icy bottles. Shock and desire held her still while his tongue made a long, lazy foray into her mouth. He stepped back, one of the bottles in hand. She stared at him and touched a finger to her parted lips.

The cap popped off his bottle with a muffled hiss and he took a long draw, the muscles in his throat working. How many other men had she watched swig a beer? Not one of them had affected her this way, making her want to run her fingers, her lips, her tongue over those muscles.

She had to get him out of the house, where her bedroom was a constant temptation.

"Jason." Her voice trembled and she laughed, resting her own bottle against her flushed face. "Let's go outside and talk."

A cynical smile quirked at his mouth. "Anything you want, Kathleen."

Anything she wanted? Oh, if he only had a clue. Shaking off the feeling of a lost opportunity, she led the way outside to a warm, star-filled night.

Chapter Ten

"Why the GBI?" Jason's quiet voice floated on the humid air. They sat on the covered end of Kathleen's deck, the ceiling fan turning in lazy circles. Below them, frogs croaked a slow chorus along the lake's edge.

Kathleen shrugged and looked away from his intent gaze. "It was something no one expected me to do."

Seated on the steps, he leaned his head against the railing and tipped his bottle up, the same beer he'd been nursing all night. "That was important?"

"It was." She stared into the distance, the lake dark and mysterious under a layer of night. With a sigh, she turned back to him. "I'd always done what everyone expected of me and I'd always messed it up. I thought I'd try the last thing anyone expected me to do and maybe I'd get it right."

He lifted an eyebrow. "I can't imagine you screwing anything up. But your plan worked, huh? You've done well. You're a respected senior agent. I bet your daddy's proud."

How had they gotten from passion to a dissection of her life? The need had retreated to simmer over the last couple of hours, while they talked about the minutiae of their lives—likes in movies, hobbies, books. Now with the conversation drifting into personal territory...maybe sleeping with him would have been safer.

She glanced away again. “He says he is.”

“You don’t think so.”

“Do we have to talk about this now?” Agitation jerked under her skin. She rose from the lounge chair and walked to the far edge of the deck, her fingernails digging into the wood railing. “What about you? Why the army? Why not a drama scholarship?”

“Scholarships don’t pay everything.” His wry tone didn’t quite cover the edge of bitterness. “I was tired of always feeling like I owed someone. With the army, I was doing something for someone else and getting paid for it, plus college on the GI Bill.”

Kathleen frowned, glad he couldn’t see her face. College? His background file had not shown a completed degree. Or had she overlooked that detail? Her certainty that he was not what he seemed kicked up a notch. Her level of relief over that certainty was scary.

Cloth rustled behind her. “Where’d you go?” he whispered, his arms coming around her, hands covering hers on the railing. Body heat seared her back and his groin brushed against her bottom. Warmth flushed her neck and face.

He made her want him so easily. She shook her head, his chin brushing her hair. “Nowhere.”

“Enough about work.” He nuzzled the curve of her ear. “Tell me about the real Kathleen Palmer.”

Her stomach clenched, nerves this time rather than desire. “Then I’d have to tell you about work,” she said, struggling to keep her voice even. “Tell me about the real Jason Harding.”

“Not much to tell.” Distance invaded his voice, and she shivered despite the muggy air and the combined heat of their bodies.

"Jason." She turned in his arms, but he was already pulling free.

"I've got to go. I'm supposed to be on duty at seven." He glanced down, then back at her. "Oh, hell."

He took one step forward, wrapped his hand around her nape and pulled her forward to cover her lips with his. Startled, Kathleen didn't have time to react before he stepped back again. He shook his head, not smiling.

"I told you I couldn't stay away."

"And I told you I didn't want you to."

Now a slight smile flirted around his mouth. "Good. But I really do have to go."

She caught his hand. He lifted an eyebrow at her in silent inquiry. "Come over when you get off duty. I'll cook. And I won't cancel on you this time."

ଔଓ

Wearing a uniform and badge, Jason committed a felony. Actually, a series of felony offenses. He scowled at the yellow lines bisecting the rural highway. His "light work" had begun. After completing his regular shift, he was making "public relations" visits on a "special patrol route".

Uh-huh.

Somehow he doubted the real world's definition of public relations involved collecting protection money and payoffs from small-time dealers and gambling operations. Paper bags, envelopes, even a Bible with money pressed between the pages.

He would receive a cut of that cash and he had to act happy about it. The thought made him sick to his stomach. He might have to take the money, but he didn't have to spend it.

Yeah, he did. That was the whole point—to look genuine, even if it meant going against everything he'd been taught, everything he believed in.

And this was penny-ante stuff. Not the big deal the Bureau sought. At this rate, he wouldn't have enough information to satisfy the FBI until he was old enough for mandatory retirement. Kind of like getting Kathleen to believe in him. He'd be out of the game before she let go of her invisible armor.

The damn charade made it impossible for her to trust him. The irony was the game bringing her into his life in the first place. Dangle just what he wanted in front of him and make it impossible to reach for it.

Hell, he knew *exactly* how Lancelot felt the first time the soon-to-be-fallen knight saw Guinevere. The closer he got to the woman Kathleen had become, he more he forgot about the ideal she'd been. He wanted to peel the layers away, find out what made her who she was. The irony in that desire brought his brows together.

He swung the car onto Smokehouse Road. Potholes rutted the surface and the yellow lines had faded into near nothingness. Road maintenance wasn't a high priority for the Haynes County Commission.

Four miles down the road, he steered into a long, narrow dirt drive. Trees arched overhead, shutting out the sunlight, and the occasional bush reached out to screech twigs along the side of the unit. The car bounced over a washout and he winced at the jarring his spine took.

The driveway opened into an overgrown yard. A small doublewide trailer sat between large oak trees. Someone had tried to turn the place into a home—plants struggled for life amid the choking weeds, rickety wicker porch furniture graced the tacked-on porch and a faded "welcome" flag fluttered from the end of the trailer. Memories of his mother's attempts to brighten their tiny mobile home flitted across his mind.

Shaking off the depression, he called in his location and stepped from the car. A tricycle lay overturned on the makeshift brick patio in front of the porch and a doll lay forgotten under a shrub.

Great. He was putting the shakedown on somebody's daddy. The depression tried to grab him again.

Halfway up the porch steps, he remembered the handheld radio lying on the seat. Damn it, he couldn't get used to carrying that thing.

He rapped on the front door and waited, his gaze sweeping over the tree line behind the house. Wonder how many marijuana plants the thick woods concealed? Great place for a meth lab, too.

The door swung open and he had to look up at the massive man in the doorway. Long, dark hair hung over huge shoulders and the guy's beard brushed the lightning-and-skull design on his black T-shirt. "What d'ya want?"

Oh, hell. The behemoth wasn't expecting him. Someone had informed all of his other stops to be prepared for him today. This guy had been left out of the loop, and from the thunderous expression tying his thick eyebrows together, that wasn't a good thing.

Jason tensed, watching the man's wild, bloodshot eyes. "Sheriff Thatcher sent me."

"Yeah?"

"Yes." Jason shot a glance at the steps and the distance to his unit, his instincts screaming at him to just get out of the situation. The last time he'd seen eyes like that was the crazy private who'd attacked Bull Jones after a night drinking. Bull outweighed the kid by thirty pounds, but had ended up in the emergency room with two cracked ribs and a broken nose.

"What's the sumbitch want?" The words wafted on a wave of Jack Daniels-scented breath.

Jason edged toward the steps, trying to maintain a calm, authoritative stance at the same time. "Listen, sir, I'm sorry I disturbed you. I'll have the sheriff contact you—"

"Man, what are you *really* doing here?" Bearded Behemoth demanded, stepping forward. The door slammed shut behind him.

Jason took another sliding step.

"Who are you? You're not one of Thatcher's boys. I ain't seen you before. You're a freaking Fed, ain't you?"

Behemoth reached into his back pocket and sunlight flashed on a blade.

Oh, holy shit. Only eight feet or so between him and that knife.

A suspect with a knife can be lethal at twenty-two feet. At that range lethal force is justified.

His Quantico instructor's voice invaded his head, drowning out Behemoth's continued ranting. He'd screwed up, walked into this situation with deadly complacency.

The realizations raced through his mind in nanoseconds, his instincts guiding his actions, his hand already reaching for the pepper spray at his waist.

With a snarl, Behemoth rushed him, slashing wildly.

Jason staggered back and fired the canister, enveloping them both in the fiery spray.

The other man kept coming and Jason was still spraying when they crashed through the porch railing and onto the brick patio below.

The shock of impact jerked through Jason's spine, the breath whooshing from his lungs. Choking and coughing, he struggled to extricate himself from Behemoth's weight. The man crawled away, screaming and clawing at his eyes.

The knife lay abandoned on the brick.

Tears streaming down his face, Jason scrambled to his feet, kicked the knife into the bushes and pulled his cuffs from his belt. Trying to catch his breath, he ignored the burning of his skin and went after Behemoth. He pushed his knee into the other man's back, shoving him onto his stomach.

Jason choked, his voice emerging a hoarse croak. "Hands behind your head!"

Sobbing now, the man complied, mumbling and crying. Jason cuffed one wrist, yanked it down and followed with the other. He pulled the man to his feet and used a pressure grip to guide him to the car.

Eyes stinging, Jason performed a swift, thorough search and deposited Behemoth in the backseat. His chest heaved with exertion, his lungs starving for oxygen. He collapsed into the driver's seat and reached for the radio's handset. "H13 to Haynes."

"Go ahead, H13."

Agony seared his lungs and settled in his side. He gripped the muscles, trying to squash the stitch. Fluid gushed over his fingers. Disbelieving, he stared at the blood coating his hand.

"Haynes, request H2 at 147 Smokehouse Road. Officer injured."

"10-4, H13. Request an ambulance?"

"Negative, Haynes. Just H2."

He slumped against the seat and clutched his side, eyes closed. Scant minutes passed, filled with burning skin, searing pain and Behemoth's mindless ramblings.

A siren chirped once and he opened his eyes to blue lights flashing behind his unit. Jim Ed approached and pulled the door open. "Hell, boy, what happened to you?"

Jason stumbled to his feet and nodded at his cousin, accompanied by Sheriff Thatcher. He jerked his head toward the backseat, where Behemoth moaned about his face. "Someone forgot to let him know I was coming."

Thatcher shook his head, brows drawn together in disgust. "Take the boy to the hospital and get him stitched up, Jim Ed. I'll stay here and clear things up with Johnny."

ଔ୬

"That vest saved your life." The physician's assistant probed at Jason's side again, her slender mahogany fingers wringing a pained gasp from him. He swallowed a curse and she smiled. "Sure you don't want something more than a local?"

"I'm sure." Jason pushed the words out between clenched teeth. Jim Ed leaned against the wall of the ER, watching, and Jason couldn't risk a stronger medication loosening his tongue.

"So tell me how this happened again?" The PA's lyrical voice held a note of tempered steel.

Jason winced against the pull of the suture material and focused on counting the dots in the acoustic ceiling tiles. "Chasing a suspect. Ran into a barbed wire fence."

"With only one barb?"

"He told you what happened." Iron laced Jim Ed's voice. "Just put in the damn stitches."

"Yes, sir."

Jason wanted to laugh at her sarcastic salute, but her other hand pierced his side with the needle again, putting all thoughts of laughter out of his mind.

The line of interrupted stitches took forever to put in, but finally, he sat on the edge of the exam table and waited for his discharge papers.

"Here." Jim Ed appeared around the curtain and tossed him a clean white undershirt. "It'll probably be a little big on you."

"Thanks." Moving with painful awkwardness, Jason tugged the shirt over his head. As predicted, it hung on his frame.

"Listen, the sheriff just called, and I've got some business to take care of. Can you find a way home?"

"Yeah." Jason touched his cheek, the skin still irritated and tender. "I could probably call Kathleen."

"Guess you're poaching on Calvert's territory now, huh?" Jim Ed laughed and slapped him on the back.

Pain shot through his side, swamping the anger. Jason gritted his teeth again. "Guess so."

"So is she any good in the sack?"

"Didn't you have something to do?"

Jim Ed's laughter rumbled in the room. "Yeah, I'm out of here. I'll come by and check on you later."

Jim Ed passed the PA on his way out. She laid a sheaf of yellow and pink papers on the end of the exam table and handed Jason a prescription bottle. "You can take one of these every four to six hours for pain. Keep that wound clean and dry, and see your doctor in seven to ten days for suture removal. Any questions?"

"No, ma'am."

"Sign here."

"Yes, ma'am." Jason signed the release forms. "Is there a pay phone I could use?"

Unsmiling, she pointed toward a phone hanging on the wall. "Dial nine for an outside line."

Stuffing his copies of the papers into his back pocket, he shuffled to the phone, each step pulling at his side. He punched in Kathleen's number and waited, his forehead against the wall.

She picked up on the third ring. "Hello?"

He let her voice wash over him before clearing his throat. "It's Jason."

A pause stretched over the line. "Are you calling to cancel this time?"

"Sort of." Food was the last thing on his mind right now, with his side aching and fire still searing his throat with every breath. "I need a ride home."

"Where are you?"

He winced at the suspicion in her voice. "Emergency room. Chandler General."

She swore softly. "I'll be there in ten minutes."

ଓଃ

"You look like hell." Kathleen held the rental car's passenger door open. Jason collapsed in the seat with a muffled groan.

"Sugar, I feel like hell."

She didn't close the door, although the urge to slam it itched along her palm. "A barbed wire fence?"

He closed his eyes. "Yeah."

"Jason." He opened one eye and Kathleen glared at him. "Layla knows what a knife wound looks like."

"Layla?"

"The physician's assistant who stitched you up. She's Altee's cousin."

His eyelid drooped shut again. "So that's why she looked familiar."

She slammed the door. Muttering curses, she walked to the driver's side and slid behind the wheel. Before starting the car, she surveyed him. "What about your face, then?"

"What about it?"

Red patches of irritation highlighted his cheekbones and surrounded his eyes. "You've been hit with pepper spray, haven't you?"

"Training."

Liar. She jerked the car into gear and shot out of the parking lot, hitting a speed bump too fast. He yelped and grabbed at his side. She glared at him. "Why wouldn't you let Layla give you something for the pain?"

"Didn't need it."

Lord, he had a stubborn streak deeper than Tick's. She hadn't seen the wound, but Layla's description had been enough. A five-inch gash, not caused by a barbed wire fence. A cut that could have been fatal if his bulletproof vest hadn't taken the brunt of it. And pepper spray. Scratches on his hands, a huge bruise on his back. What the hell had he been up to?

She slowed for a stoplight and glanced at him again. He frowned, his lips tight, the skin around them pale. Damn it, men were so stupid when it came to pain.

"She gave you a prescription painkiller, right?"

He lifted the small brown bottle and rattled the contents.

"Did you take one?"

A negative shake of his head.

"Good Lord, Harding." She pulled into the parking lot of the convenience store on the next corner. She left the car running and jogged in to purchase a bottle of water. When she returned, she dropped it in his lap.

He jerked upright. "Damn it, Kathleen."

"Take the pill."

"I don't need it."

"Take it." His eyebrows dropped into a scowl and she glowered back. "We can sit here all night, Harding."

"Fine." Still scowling, he juggled the bottles and shook a tiny white pill out in his palm. He tossed it in his mouth and chased it with water. He set the water bottle in the cupholder. "Happy now?"

"Immensely."

Silence descended on the car as she navigated out of town and onto the rural highway. The tension eased in his face, and his body relaxed into the bucket seat.

Kathleen cast quick, furtive glances at him. He could have been killed. The realization sat in her stomach like a lump of cold lead. His expressive eyes closed forever. No more opportunities to feel his touch on her skin, his mouth on hers.

Too many missed chances. Life could be gone so quickly, and she'd played it safe so long now. Maybe too long.

A shiver traveled down her spine at the thought of him gone forever, before she had the chance to experience loving him.

Loving him? Whoa, Palmer, where did that come from?

Her fingers tightened on the steering wheel. She was on the verge of falling in love with Jason Harding. Fear coursed through her, followed by determination.

She'd lived in fear far too long.

ଔ

The setting sun painted his trailer in orange and gold. Kathleen parked as close to the steps as possible and walked around to open the passenger door. His head thrown back, he slept, soft snores escaping between parted lips.

She smiled, her earlier irritation gone. He was here, warm and alive. She nudged his knee. "Jason. We're home."

He opened bleary eyes and stared at the trailer. "Kathleen? What are you doing here?"

"Taking care of you." She brushed his ruffled hair back from his forehead.

His eyes drifted closed again. "Good."

The lazy satisfaction in his voice made her laugh. "Come on. You can't sleep in the car."

Moving with drugged slowness, he sat up and swung his legs out. Hands between his knees, he shook his head, like a dog shaking off water. He reached out for the car door.

"Here. Let me help." Kathleen slid her hand under his arm and pulled him to his feet. He swayed and she wrapped an arm around his waist, careful to avoid his wound.

The steps creaked under their weight. She pulled the screen door open. "Where are your keys?"

"S'not locked," he mumbled into her hair. He chuckled. "Nothing to steal."

Still supporting him, she pushed the door open and fumbled for a light switch. A ceiling fan creaked to life and light spilled over a tiny combination living room-kitchen area. The musty scent of a long-abandoned house washed over her.

Standing just inside the door, her arm around his waist, she studied his home for the first time. The room was military spotless and Spartan. A small television sat on a table, a single couch in the room. No pictures, no books, nothing to indicate who lived here.

Her heart stuttered at the thought of him coming home to this emptiness every night.

He muttered something under his breath and rubbed his face against her hair. Kathleen smiled, warmed by the affectionate gesture. “Let’s get you to bed. Where’s your room?”

“First room. Left.” He pointed toward the narrow hall, a half-hearted gesture. She turned that way and he stumbled, cursing. “S’why I don’t drink hard liquor or take pain meds. Hits me too hard.”

“Come on.” Through his T-shirt, she stroked his ribs above the bandage, loving the solid strength of his body against hers.

As bare as the rest of the house, his room held nothing besides a double bed, a small table, and his alarm clock. She lowered him to sit on beige sheets patterned with cabins and bears.

His motions uncoordinated, he tugged at the shirt, trying to pull it over his head. Kathleen grasped the hem and helped him. The white bandage stood out in stark contrast to his tanned skin, and the muscled indention of his abs dried her mouth. Her fingers itched to trace those muscles, tangle in the hair on his chest, stroke over his shoulders and arms.

He fumbled with his belt. Heat flashed through her. Oh, Lord. She wanted him, aching and ready all at once, and he was out of his mind with pain meds.

"Here." She brushed his clumsy hands out of the way and unfastened his belt, her face burning the entire time.

"Got it." He managed the button and zipper, pushing the brown uniform slacks down. Snug gray boxer-briefs hugged his thighs. He fell back on the pillows and groaned, one hand going to clasp his side.

Kathleen pulled his shoes and socks off, followed by the slacks. She avoided looking at what else his boxer-briefs hugged. Wanting pounded with her pulse and she fought the urge to climb into bed with him.

Oh, she'd definitely gone too long without sex. She was tempted to take advantage of a drugged, injured man. Altee would die laughing.

No, she wouldn't, because of who this drugged, injured man was.

With a restless movement, he pulled the sheet to his waist. He opened one eye and smiled an adorable goofy smile, crooking a finger at her. "C'mere, sugar."

Desire tugging at her stomach, she leaned over him. "Call all the girls that, do you?"

"Just you." He grasped her wrist, his grip surprising in its strength, and pulled her down beside him. His arm draped over her waist, the length of his body pressed to hers. "S'better."

Kathleen tensed, fighting the urges sweeping her body. "Jason…"

His fingers slipped under the edge of her shirt and he rested his face against her throat. He sighed, a rush of hot breath against her skin. "S'not like this."

She gave in and stroked her hand down his side, muscles hard under her palm. "What?"

His mouth moved against her. A smile. "Wanna make love on pretty white sheets."

He meant *her* sheets. His tanned skin against all that white, his body making her writhe on soft Egyptian cotton. That image slammed into her, heat spearing out from her belly. She laughed, trying to gain control of desires that didn't want to be corralled. "Right now, you're not going to make love to me on these sheets either, Deputy Harding."

He stiffened and rolled away, eyes closed, a frown tightening his face. "Not deputy. Agent."

She stilled, breath freezing in her lungs. "What?"

A self-satisfied grin curved the edges of his mouth and he sighed again. "Calvert's not th' only one." He threw an arm over his eyes, his body appearing boneless, and he lifted his free hand to his lips in a shushing motion. "Sshh. Don't tell, 'kay?"

Kathleen struggled free of his hold and sat up. Hope trembled in her throat. "Jason. What are you talking about?"

A soft snore interrupted her. Frustrated, Kathleen lay down beside him. He needed the rest.

And they'd have plenty of time for a little game of truth and consequences later.

Chapter Eleven

The scent of Ivory surrounded him. Warm caresses drifted over his chest and shoulders, and a hot mouth teased his ear. His hands roamed, finding silky skin under a cotton shirt. His fingers curved over high, firm breasts, nipples hard against his palms, and the mouth at his ear moved, a throaty moan zinging over his nerves, adding to the pressure at his groin.

Long legs intertwined with his and he tilted his hips, pressing his aching erection against the heat settled tightly over him.

He nuzzled at her neck, pushing soft cotton up and out of the way, baring her breasts. When he didn't encounter a bra, he growled his approval and nibbled along the curves. He brushed his mouth against a nipple, a butterfly caress.

She jerked, tangling her fingers in his hair. "Oh, Jason."

His eyes snapped open, awareness returning in a rush. Darkness shrouded the room, but there was no doubt where he was or who was in his arms. *Kathleen.* In his bed. Touching him, writhing against him, pressing against his arousal.

Talk about a dream come true.

She wore way too many clothes. He stroked from her torso to her hips, oft-washed denim soft under his fingers. He pulled her closer against him, the thick cotton fabric doing little to weaken the heat pulsing against him.

The tip of his tongue stroked the line of her cleavage. The tang of soap rested on his mouth, made sweeter by her skin's smoothness. He sucked her other nipple, rolling the stony bud into his mouth.

Her fingers dug into his hair, nails scoring his scalp, and her hips pushed harder against him. Sharp pain stabbed at his side and his bruised back ached, but he wasn't moving for hell. Not with the hottest, sweetest woman he'd ever known in his arms, moaning and surging against him like he was going to make her climax from a little foreplay.

She rubbed against him again and he groaned at the pleasure spreading out along his veins. He ached to be inside her, to have the wet silk of her body closing around him. Her nipple slipped from his lips and he buried his mouth between her breasts.

"Keep that up, sugar, and I won't last."

"There's something to be said for hot and fast," she said, pushing him to his back and sitting up to pull the camisole top over her head. Filtered moonlight silvered her curves.

Still wearing her jeans, she straddled his thighs, her hands stroking his ribs and stomach. She brushed the bandage with gentle fingers. "Maybe we shouldn't—"

"Yeah, we should." Knees cradling her bottom, he sat up, his side screaming at him to stop. He ignored it, more focused on other parts of his anatomy demanding release. That part of his body nestled nicely between her thighs. He brushed his nose against hers and kissed her.

"You're hurt." Her tongue danced at the corner of his mouth. "And under the influence. I feel like I'm taking advantage of you."

"I'll hurt worse if you don't. The drugs have worn off. And I hope to hell you *really* take advantage of me."

She laughed, the sound shimmering through him. Her hands roved over his torso, shaping muscles, and her pelvis tilted into his. "Mmm. You feel so good."

He grabbed her hips, holding her to him. "Shimmy out of those jeans," he whispered near her ear, "and I'll show you how good."

"Convince me."

She was a tease and he loved it. He trailed his mouth down her neck, sucking at the curve of her shoulder. He rubbed the back of his hand across her stomach. Muscles jumped against his touch and he chuckled, skimming a finger along her waistband, relishing the softness of her skin.

Her response to him fired his desire, made him want to linger over her. He'd waited forever to have her in his arms and he never wanted it to end.

Her scent, warm and clean, wrapped around him. While he unbuttoned her jeans and slid down the zipper, he peppered light kisses over the swell of her breast. He encountered tiny silk panties over pulsing heat and she gasped into his hair. Her grip tightened on his shoulders, nails biting into his skin.

He cupped her, stroking, teasing, testing. She moaned, breath coming hard and fast, her hips pushing into his hand. "Wait. It's been a while, and—"

"Want me to stop?" He muttered the words against her throat, his own body aching in response to the building tension in hers. He steeled himself to let her go, if that's what she desired.

"Yes. No." Her head lolled back and he grazed her neck with his teeth, wringing another smothered sigh from her lips. "I want you."

"Sugar, I'm yours."

Denim rubbed against his thighs, her movements increasing in tempo and intensity. The delicious friction urged him to thrust against her and he slid his fingers beneath the hem of that little silk triangle.

"Jason." The breathy way she said his name threatened to send him over the edge. "I can't...you have to..."

Her words morphed into a strangled cry, her wet core contracting around his fingers. Her climax trembled in his own body, supreme satisfaction thrumming through him. He kissed her, swallowing another moan, his tongue sweeping against hers.

She grabbed his wrist and pulled her mouth from his. "Too much."

He laughed and hugged her to him, reaching to brush back her damp hair. She buried her face against his neck, her voice muffled. "Oh, God."

"What?" His lips caressed her temple.

"I'm not usually like that." Embarrassment colored her small voice. "It usually takes me forever to..."

Pure male pride made it hard to breathe. He was never letting her go. Cradling her head in his hands, he tilted her face up. Moonlight glittered in her eyes. "I like you like that, Palmer. Believe me."

He liked her like this, too, shy and her skin hot with a flush of embarrassment and lingering pleasure. Nothing like the women he'd known before, the soldier groupies who hung out in bars near the bases.

And she was incredible—hot, responsive, yielding. Who the hell had she been with for it to take forever? Whatever. He wasn't asking—he wanted her mind totally on him. On them. On what he had planned for them. Making the fantasies that had plagued him for days come true.

Those white sheets popped into his mind and he sighed, rubbing her back. "You deserve better. I wanted—"

With her mouth, she cut off his words, her tongue darting between his teeth. She kissed him until he could hardly remember his own name. "This is perfect. *You're* perfect."

His arousal jerked and she laughed, skimming her hands down to delve beneath his waistband. She scored her nails lightly across his hips and buttocks before stroking his lower abdomen, sending wilder fire to his groin.

He rolled, ignoring his protesting side, and grinned down at her in the dark. "You're starting things."

Her hands shaped his jaw. "We never finished."

"You're right."

With a chuckle, he dropped kisses along her chest and stomach. His fingers wrapped around the waistband of her jeans and tugged them down, taking the silk underwear with them. His nose brushed the soft patch of hair, and her thigh trembled when he feathered his mouth over her skin. The curve of her knee held a faint trace of salt.

He dropped the jeans on the floor and kicked off his boxer-briefs as well. With his thumb, he caressed the sole of her foot, the arch smooth. She giggled and jerked her foot away.

"Ticklish?" he murmured, moving back up her body, his hands and mouth lingering over curves and hollows.

"Are you?" Her finger ventured under his arm and he cringed, laughing and trying to capture her marauding hand. He ignored the aftershocks of pain running through his side.

His mouth covered hers and their laughter died, replaced by sighs and whispers in the dark.

No shyness lurked in her touch and his turn to moan came when slender fingers wrapped around his erection, stroking to the base and fanning out over his thighs. Fire building in his belly, he turned his attention to her breasts again. He shaped them with his hands, her skin like hot satin. The nipples hardened further against his tongue, the rippled surface a sharp contrast to the smooth curves.

She gave a long, sighing moan and moved restlessly beneath him, her damp core rubbing along his erection. "Jason?"

"Say it again," he muttered, loving the sound of his name on her lips. His teeth grazed a distended nipple before he enveloped the aureole.

She flexed strong fingers into his buttocks, bumping her pelvis against him. "Jason. I want you. Inside me."

He dropped a last caress on her left breast and slid to the end of the bed. He felt for his uniform pants, seeking his wallet. "Watch your eyes. Gotta turn on the light."

Light flooded the tiny room and he blinked. He grabbed the slacks from the floor, pulled out his wallet and extracted the condoms he'd bought earlier in the day, just in case. He tossed two on the table and pulled the wrapper free on the third. She laughed. "Feeling ambitious?"

"Ambition is my middle name," he said and glanced at the bed. His lungs shut down and the condom dropped from numb fingers.

She lay against his pillows, watching him with passion-dark eyes. The Botticelli nudes he'd seen in Europe had nothing on the vision lying in his bed.

Creamy skin and cinnamon nipples still damp from his mouth. A perfect curve to her waist that would have made Michelangelo's sculptures jealous. Fiery curls nestled between long legs.

She laughed, a quick, nervous sound, one hand covering her lower abdomen. “Quit staring, Harding.”

He shook his head and reached for the dropped condom. His fingers trembled, taking twice as long as it should to get the protection in place. “My God, you’re beautiful.”

With a sultry laugh, she crooked a finger at him. “Come show me how ambitious you are.”

“Very.” He crawled up the bed, dropping a kiss on her stomach. The muscles quivered under his lips. “Very.” Using his knee, he nudged her thighs apart, nuzzling her neck. Her thighs hugged his hips, her body arching under him. “Very ambitious.”

Her wetness welcomed him and closed around him. Entering her was like sliding into a hot, tight haven. He growled low in his throat and she wrapped her arms around his neck. He thrust, slow and deep, her moan vibrating through him. Pleasure spiked low in his gut and he ground his teeth, determined to make this the most intense experience of her life.

She was already his. For the rest of his life, her scent, her voice, the feel of her, would be imprinted on him.

Her head tilted back, his gaze on the tiny pulse thundering at the base of her neck. Her eyes closed, long lashes shadowing her cheeks. He leaned forward, bringing their bodies even closer, and brushed her parted lips with his. “Look at me.”

Those lashes trembled and lifted. He stared into brown depths flecked with gold and saw himself. Connection. He’d never in his life been this connected to anyone.

Her hips rose to meet his thrusts, her breasts rubbing his chest. She massaged his back, the occasional bite of her nails making the passion stronger. Every nerve sensitized to her, he experienced every tremor, every sigh, every moan deep within. He was lost.

She *owned* him. He was hers, body, soul, whatever she wanted, for as long as she wanted.

This was the woman for whom he'd walk any line, brave any circle of fire, do anything.

Her eyes drifted closed again, her breathing coming in short pants, her body moving faster against his. This time, the contractions of her climax started deep within, traveling all along the length of his arousal. Her nails pierced the skin of his buttocks and her long, slow moan slid over his senses, jolting pleasure through him.

He could hold on to this reality.

No lies here, just him and her and the sensations exploding between them.

He had to tell her, had to let her know how much this meant.

But the words wouldn't come. His muscles bunched, the desire taking over completely. The climax barreled over him, wringing her name from his throat. He collapsed, her arms around him.

ଔ

Kathleen lay against Jason's chest, her mind drifting in drowsy circles. She drew a pattern on his arm with one finger and tried to repress a satisfied giggle. She'd always been drawn to ambitious men and Jason's brand of ambition suited her just fine.

His arm tightened on her waist. "What's so funny?"

Sleep slurred his words and Kathleen shook her head. Exhaustion tugged at her, but she didn't want to sleep. The real world would intrude all too soon and she didn't want to waste a moment of this time with him.

She rubbed the pad of her index finger across the puckered scar on his shoulder. The rough, round mark was paler than the rest of his skin. "What is this?"

"Battle scar. Kuwait." He mumbled the words against her hair. "Not important."

Her hand slid down his side. A similar wound marred his hip. His heart thudded under her cheek and she pressed closer, aware once again of time's passage. He winced, and remembering his wounded side, she pulled away and rolled to lie on her back.

He followed, as if he couldn't bear to not touch her. He relaxed, his face nestled in the crook of her neck. Her chest squeezed and she closed her eyes, fighting the rising fear. This one night in his arms wasn't going to be enough. She wanted this, wanted him, forever.

The last time she'd tried forever didn't bear thinking about.

She stroked hesitant fingers across the thin lines on her stomach. She knew without looking they were pale and silvery. Her eyes closed, the phantom weight of a baby in her arms. Only this time, not Everett. Another baby, Jason's son. Wanting clenched her empty womb and a self-derisive laugh hurt her throat, the sound verging on a sob.

What was she thinking? Forever and babies? Never again.

Jason stirred. "What?"

She swallowed against the tightness in her throat and struggled to sit up. "I've got to go."

"What?" He pushed to a seated position and rubbed a hand over his hair. He blinked, eyes heavy with sleep. "It's the middle of the night."

"I'm going home." She scooted to the end of the bed, fighting the sudden urge to cry. Lord, her clothes were scattered everywhere. She stepped into her panties and tugged her camisole top over her head.

"Kathleen." He snagged her wrist and pulled her back onto the bed. She fell over his legs, her thighs lying atop his. "What's going on?"

The concern darkening his green eyes made the tears push harder in her throat. She shook her head and dropped her gaze. Drops of blood seeped through his bandage. "You're bleeding."

"I'll live." He caught her chin in his fingers and forced her gaze to his. "Talk to me."

"I just...I need to go home." She swallowed again and tugged away. She speared both hands through her hair. "This is too much, too fast. I don't know you, don't know anything about you—"

He captured her mouth in a long, sweet kiss. "You know what's important," he whispered against her lips. "You know what's real."

"I don't know anything anymore." That lost voice didn't belong to her. It couldn't. Feeling the worst kind of weak, she let him lower her to the bed once more.

He leaned over her, his eyes stormy and intent. "Look at me, Kathleen." She couldn't pull her gaze away. He rubbed a finger across her swollen lips. That finger traveled down her throat to lie against her pulse. "This is real, sugar. *We're* real."

The desire to believe him bordered on desperation. They stared at each other, the only sound in the tiny room their soft breathing. The emotion on his face went deeper than passion, thrilling her and scaring her to death at the same time.

She didn't want to name that emotion. It whispered of forever, happily ever after and other expectations she couldn't live up to.

Lord, don't let him see that in my eyes, too.

A truck rumbled into the yard. Jason stiffened against her, his head jerking toward the window. He pulled away. "Stay here."

"Jason—"

"Stay here. I mean it." He tugged on a pair of faded jeans and pulled his gun from the holster on his duty belt. He tucked the gun into the back waistband and walked into the hall.

Kathleen listened to his cautious footsteps in the living room. A moment later, the front door opened and closed.

"Hey, cousin." Jim Ed's voice filtered through the heavy plastic covering the bedroom window, taking the place of the missing glass. "How you feeling?"

"Sore."

"Palmer still here?"

"You see her car, don't you?"

"Where is she?"

"Asleep."

Jim Ed's all-male laughter crawled over Kathleen's skin. "Wore her out, did you?"

"Guess so." If Jim Ed's laugh had been bad, Jason's was worse, clenching her stomach, turning something beautiful ugly and sordid. "Told you I'd find a way to distract her."

Acting. Remember—he's playing a role.

Yes, but which one? Which Jason was real?

She was sure the corrupt deputy was a fraud. That left two options. An undercover agent who cared for her, but needed to convince his cousin she was nothing more than a sexual conquest. Or an undercover agent who'd do whatever it took to keep her out of his way.

No. Stop. She touched a finger to her lips, still tingling from his kisses. Her body ached, a sweet, feminine ache, from the passion and fire of his lovemaking. His throaty whispers echoed in her head. Earlier, she'd seen promises in his eyes.

No one was that good an actor.

Was he?

Conscious of the two men outside, she slid her jeans and shoes on with as little noise as possible.

"We'll deal with Johnny," Jim Ed said. "You won't have trouble out of him again. I don't know why you didn't just shoot him, though."

"Oh, I don't know. Maybe because I was breaking the law and didn't want to add murder to it?"

"The guy tried to kill you. I'd say it was justified. It's not like you ain't done it before."

Kathleen's lungs constricted.

"Maybe that's the difference between you and me. I've had enough."

"Maybe." A jovial laugh. The sound of a slap on the back. "See ya tomorrow. Keep that woman satisfied and out of our hair, you hear?"

She closed her eyes, listening, keeping her mind a deliberate blank. If she thought about it, she'd attack him as soon as he set foot back in the house.

The truck fired to life and rumbled away. The front door opened, closed. Soft footsteps ventured down the hall.

Kathleen, sitting cross-legged on his bed, opened her eyes and waited. He appeared in the doorway, his expression closed and wary. He scratched at his bare chest, and she hated herself for letting that expanse of skin send a curl of desire through her again. The ache between her legs pulsed.

She narrowed her eyes and watched him, waiting.

His chest heaved with a breath and he rubbed a hand over his nape. "Kathleen, don't look at me like that."

Fury erupted in her chest. She smothered it. "Is that what this was all about? Keeping me out of things?"

His brows lowered. "It was about us. About keeping you safe."

She laughed, a short, derisive snort. "You can't even keep yourself safe."

"Would you hear me out?"

She unfolded her legs and rose. "I've heard enough. I'm going home."

Not looking at him, she brushed by him into the hall. In that narrow space, he grabbed her arm and pulled her against him. "Not yet."

She pushed away, putting her back against the wall. Anger pulsed in her throat. "Let go."

"Damn it, Kathleen." He jerked his head toward the front of the trailer. "I don't know where he is. He could be waiting at the road. Or maybe he ditched the truck and is walking back up here. I'm not letting you go out there."

Shivers trailed over her at the pictures he created. Fighting off the fear, she tilted her head back and glared. "I don't need you to take care of me."

He traced the curve of her ear with his thumb. "Too bad. Because I really need you."

Men and sex. With an irritated huff, she closed her eyes and tried to ignore the need he created in her.

His hands slid to her shoulders and he gave her a slight shake, pulling her gaze back to his. “Kathleen, you believe me, don’t you? About us?”

“I don’t know what to believe anymore.”

“Believe this.” He brushed a gentle kiss along her jaw. “And this.” Another teasing kiss at the corner of her lips. He pressed her hand to his chest, his heart pounding against her fingers. “And this. *This* is real.”

“*This* is just sex.” She tried to push a hearty dose of disdain into the words. They emerged breathy and hesitant.

“No.” His mouth played with hers and he tugged her against him, backing toward his room. “*This* is more.”

“Jason.” Her weak protest was lost under his persuasive kiss. She stroked his neck, his shoulders, his chest. One night. What could one night hurt?

“Believe, Kathleen,” he whispered, stirring the fiery passion again with his hands and mouth. “In me. In us.”

One night. One night to allow herself to believe in a future that wouldn’t come true. The truth and its consequences could some later.

Winding her arms around his neck, she let him wrap her in beautiful lies once more.

ঙ

Kathleen located her shoe behind the bedroom door. Dust motes danced in shafts of early morning sunlight. While she tugged on her shoe, she tried not to look at Jason and failed.

Lying on his stomach, he slept with the total abandonment of a child finally succumbed to a nap after playing too hard. The urge to climb into bed with him and wake him with kisses attacked her. No. She'd promised herself one night. She had to be satisfied with that.

Even if that one night made her an official inhabitant of the too-stupid-to-live category.

Even if the unbelievable satisfaction she'd found with him made her want more, like an addict craving another fix before the original high faded.

She slipped from the room and froze once when the floor creaked a loud protest under her steps. No sound came from the bedroom, and she crept through the living room and outside. In the car, she let out a long, slow breath and fired the engine.

She eased the car down the pitted driveway, trying not to remember Jason's fears that Jim Ed might be lying in wait for her.

His scent lingered on her skin, filling the small interior space, and she sighed on a wave of reluctance and despair. She was leaving behind what she wanted most.

She wanted more, not just the physical connection, but more of what made him the man he was. She wanted to know everything—his favorite foods, why drama first piqued his interest, who'd first broken his heart, what had happened in Kuwait to leave two bullet wounds on his body.

Battle scars.

The fire had destroyed her father's Purple Heart as well as their home. Jason's background file didn't mention any awards, and if he'd been injured in battle, he should have a Purple Heart. Another hole, real proof she could hold on to.

The back roads winding from Haynes County into Chandler County held few other vehicles. She passed a tractor and, when she entered Chandler County, a sheriff's unit parked under a tree just off the road. A few minutes later, she pulled into her own driveway. The ducks chattered and fussed around the dock, and she scattered food for them.

This early on a Saturday morning, the lake lay still and deserted. Later, the surface would ripple with bass boats and jet skis.

She didn't have to work today. The idea of lying around on the dock in a bikini, napping and soaking up rays, appealed, but another duty called. Sometime today she had to drive over to Lenora Calvert's house to see her parents. Her father coped with the tragedy by throwing himself into insurance forms and cleanup efforts. Her mother remained quiet and stoic, her demeanor an eerie echo from the dark days following Everett's death.

Her fingers brushed her stomach. She'd lost a child, her parents their only grandchild. Like her mother, she'd locked him away in her heart, refused to talk about him, refused to consider ever putting herself at that kind of risk again.

Jason made her dream those dreams again—a chortling laugh, the warm curve of her baby's head beneath her chin, tiny fingers wrapped around hers. Watching the man she loved cradle the child they'd created.

"No." The raw word sent startled ducks scrambling into the water, squawking and quacking.

She wouldn't be anyone's mother again.

And she wasn't going to fall in love with Jason Harding.

Chapter Twelve

Layers of sleep slipped away. Jason rolled over, an arm over his eyes to block out the sunlight pushing into his room. Fiery pokers danced along his side, the remnants of too much physical activity. A grin quirked at his mouth, memories of that activity tumbling through his head.

Oh, man, he'd do it again in a New York minute, too, major pain or not. Warm contentment settled in his chest and, eyes closed, he reached for Kathleen.

His bed was empty. Fully awake now, he sat up and listened. Silence hovered in the trailer and he didn't bother to call her name. The quiet emptiness was familiar, but her absence intensified it.

The void settled around him, pressing in, as he walked to the bathroom, then to the kitchen.

Already, he missed the warmth of her touch, the shimmery quality of her rare laughter, the way she loved him as if her life depended on it.

She'd made love to him without knowing who he really was.

He didn't know what to make of that. The passion could have been nothing more than a strong physical attraction on her part. He didn't want to accept that, but had no choice. He wanted to believe she felt something deeper for him.

For the first time in his life, he wanted it to be more than just great sex, but about the connection he'd felt.

He needed her to know who he was. Last night, the truth had trembled on his lips and he'd bitten the words back. Too many years of following orders, too much indoctrination by the Bureau. He couldn't just spill the details without permission. Heck, he couldn't even call his superiors and ask for that permission.

But he knew someone who could.

ଔ৪ତ

Kathleen pulled into Tick Calvert's driveway and parked behind his dusty Z-71. The warm breeze swayed through the pines sheltering his white frame farmhouse. A partially finished brick pathway led to the back porch, scattered with paint cans, tools and stacks of lumber.

She stepped over a circular saw and rapped at the door. Long moments passed and she knocked again. Anger hummed under her skin, a fury that had started to brew while she showered Jason's scent from her body.

Washing away the memory of his touch had been unsuccessful. Her skin still tingled from the hot water against tender skin abraded by his stubble. A tiny love bite reddened the upper curve of her breast, hidden by the skinny T-shirt she'd tossed on with khaki shorts. He'd marked her.

In more ways than one.

He'd made her feel, forget all her ingrained rules. He made her want it all to be real.

Enough games. She could at least find out if his muttered "agent" was the truth. If it was, Tick Calvert would get an earful about not involving the GBI in what should have been a joint operation from the beginning. The Feds weren't the only ones peculiar about their territory.

"Tick!" She knocked a third time and glanced toward the river. Knowing him, he could be up early, down on the dock fishing. She walked toward the porch's edge, wishing the heavy tree line didn't keep her from seeing the water.

The door swung open. She spun and glared at Tick, clad in a pair of worn jeans. "What took you so long?"

Scratching his bare chest, he glowered, blinking bleary eyes at her. "I was asleep."

"We need to talk." She brushed by him and walked into his large keeping room kitchen, heavy with the scent of fresh-brewed coffee and new paint. He'd removed the horrid green linoleum she remembered and her tennis shoes whispered on plywood.

"Well, good morning, Mary Sunshine." He closed the door with a little more force than necessary. "I'm fine, Kath, thanks for asking. How are you?"

"Annoyed."

"What else is new? Want some coffee?"

She settled on a stool at the island and watched him move about the kitchen, muscles rippling along his lean frame as he tugged on a faded UGA T-shirt. Why couldn't she want him? He was decent, hardworking and upright, loved his mother and spoiled his nieces and nephews. Her parents thought the sun rose and set in him. His devilish grin and chocolate eyes set hearts aflutter all over southwest Georgia. Giggled whispers proclaimed him the best kisser in three counties.

And he did absolutely nothing for her.

No, she had to go and fall for a man she didn't even know, one she couldn't trust.

"Kathleen?"

Her gaze focused on Tick once more. He eyed her with a quizzical expression and set a mug of coffee before her. She grimaced. "Sorry. I zoned."

"No kidding." He pulled a frying pan from a cabinet, set it on the stove and went to the refrigerator. Juggling eggs and butter, he faced her again. "Now why are you dragging me out of bed at eight o'clock on a Saturday morning?"

She narrowed her eyes at him. "Harding's a Fed, isn't he?"

"Yeah."

"Yeah? That's all you can say?"

"You got your way, Kathleen. You lied about having someone ready to go in Haynes County and you manipulated me into getting permission to tell you about Harding. So, yeah, that's all I have to say."

Relief flooded her body, followed by a crashing wave of fury and fear. "And of course it never occurred to anyone to involve the GBI?"

"Need-to-know basis." He cracked eggs into a bowl, shoulder blades flexing while he whisked. "The boys at the OCD didn't think the GBI needed to know."

"So why tell me now?"

"Because we'd rather Harding's attachment to you was useful instead of harmful." He stacked bread in the bowl of eggs. "I'd hate to see the kid get killed because his mind's on you."

"Harding isn't attached to me."

"Lying's a sin, Kath. Remember that. The only way that boy could be more attached to you would be if I duct-taped you together."

"Define useful."

He laid the first two pieces of egg-sodden bread in the frying pan. Melted butter hissed and popped with the contact. "Communication has been a bitch. It's too easy to get caught meeting. If you're involved with Harding...that makes you the perfect go-between."

"We're not involved."

"Yeah." He shot her a disbelieving look over his shoulder. "Jim Ed thinks you are. That's what counts. And it could also solve another little problem."

"What kind of little problem?" She eyed the back of his head and tried to ignore the tempting smell of French toast. Her stomach rumbled.

Tick slid a plate in front of her and reached into a cupboard for syrup. He looked everywhere but at her and her chest clenched.

"Tick. What kind of little problem?"

He returned to the island with two forks and his own plate. He took the syrup bottle and dribbled an intricate pattern over his toast. The tight foreboding in her stomach grew with his silence.

Finally he looked up. "Harding's profile indicates loyalty is a strong motivation for him. We've played on his loyalty to his country, to the law, to right and wrong."

"You mean you've manipulated him." The thought sickened her.

"Yeah." Brows drawn together and his mouth tight, Tick didn't look too happy about the idea either. "But he's our one shot. We'll never be able to get anyone else in that department. He knows that."

"I don't see the problem." Or it was right in front of her and she didn't want to acknowledge it.

"Family is important to him."

"And Jim Ed is family. You're afraid his loyalty will shift when it gets down and dirty."

"It's a possibility."

"No, it's not." She couldn't articulate how she knew. She just did.

A grin quirked at Tick's mouth. "I didn't think so either, but I learned a while back not to argue with the Behavioral Science guys."

She fixed him with a look. "Now explain how I'm supposed to keep his loyalty from shifting."

"You already have."

"Right."

"Kath, listen. Being undercover, being someone you're not—it plays with your head. Makes you wonder where you end and where the persona really begins. A guy needs something to hang on to." He stared at a spot over her head while he talked, a faraway expression in his eyes.

What had he hung on to during that year he'd worked deep cover in Mississippi? The one that brought him back to Georgia a changed man, quieter, more withdrawn. What was this operation going to do to Jason?

What had it already done? What kind of man had he been before?

"Tick?"

His eyes regained their sharp focus and he looked at her. "You're Harding's something to hold on to."

Another expectation. Her stomach twisted and she pushed her plate away untouched. She didn't want Jason to need her, anymore than she wanted to need him. She did, though, the need going beyond the physical.

"This should work a heck of a lot better than what we had before." Tick forked up a piece of toast. "No need for sneaking around any longer. You'll need to sweep your place for bugs daily, though."

His casual approach grated. She struggled for an even tone. "You have this all worked out, don't you?"

"It's perfect. I wish we'd thought of it before."

"Glad to be of service."

He stared, another bite of syrup-laden toast halfway to his mouth. "Why are you pissed? I thought you liked Harding and would want to be in on this."

"I do."

"Then what's the problem?"

"There's not one." No problem except she'd fallen in love again and there was more than her heart on the line. If she failed, it could mean Jason's life.

ര്ജ

Jason hacked at the weeds choking his mother's roses. His side ached with each movement, but he needed something physical to do. He'd made two unsuccessful attempts to raise Calvert on the encrypted cell phone, and the urge to say the heck with rules and regulations snaked through him.

He should have told her last night, standing in the hallway. He'd known then he should toss the dictates, but he hadn't. He wanted her trust, wanted her to believe in him regardless.

The phone rang, the shrill sound carrying through the open windows. He flung the machete down into the earth, the handle standing at attention and vibrating. Each jogging step jarred his side. Inside, he grabbed the cordless phone. "Hello?"

"It's Kathleen." Her cool voice washed over him, a dip in the lake on a blazing day.

"Hey." He leaned against the counter, fingers wrapped around the phone, wishing those same fingers were against her skin.

Silence stretched along the line and he swallowed. What was he supposed to say to the woman who'd loved him like none other? The one who'd left while he slept. He said the first words that came into his mind.

"I missed you this morning."

"I'm sorry." Her soft sigh whispered against his ear. "I needed some time...to get things straight."

That didn't sound good. On the other hand, she was calling him. He tilted his head back against the cabinet. He didn't get women, and he didn't get this one in particular. But he wanted to. For the first time in his life, he wanted to know everything, understand everything about a woman. He wanted to know Kathleen.

"Jason?"

He cleared his throat. "Sorry. I was thinking. So did you? Get things straight?"

"I'm beginning to. I talked to Tick this morning. He's taking his boat out on the lake later and he asked if we wanted to come along."

"Sounds good." She *knew*. She knew who he was. Uncertainty tempered his relief because from her even tone, he couldn't tell how she felt. He shoved his free hand through his sweaty hair and tried to think.

"Great. So I'll see you at my place in an hour or so?"

"Yeah. Can't wait."

The line went dead, and he returned the phone to its charging cradle.

Going out on Calvert's boat?

Kathleen was going to be his go-between. It made a weird kind of sense, but he wasn't sure how he felt about it. Their dating would be perfect cover and he loved the idea of losing the barrier his lies erected between them.

He wasn't crazy about having her mixed up in the middle of this mess.

He could continue to convince Jim Ed he had her "under control". At the thought, a grin curved his mouth. Like Kathleen Palmer would ever submit to any man's control.

She'd yielded to him, though. The memory of her beneath him, accepting him, widened his grin. He tugged off his shirt and headed toward the bathroom to clean up.

He'd just have to keep her close to ensure her safety.

Really, really close.

ƆℰƆ

The setting sun sparkled off the lake surface, a dazzling array of golds and crimsons. Jason stood on the dock. Kathleen and Altee's soft conversation drifted from the yard above, the words indistinguishable. An odd blend of anticipation and contentment hovered in his gut.

With Calvert gone and Altee preparing to leave, he looked forward to being alone with Kathleen after an afternoon spent on the water, talking strategy and soaking up too much sun. He could think of few things better than the simple pleasure of being in her presence, having the freedom of casual touches—brushing his fingers against her ankle while she lounged next to him, taking her hand to help her from the boat. Little caresses that satisfied the need to touch her yet left him wanting more.

An engine started, the smooth sound of a well-maintained machine, and tires crunched on the gravel drive. Jason turned and watched Kathleen approach. She moved with an elegant grace he associated with ballet dancers, and he smiled. She'd be as comfortable in a designer gown as in the sparkly blue bikini and white board shorts.

She stopped a few feet away, not smiling. "I thought I'd make dinner, since we didn't get a chance last night."

"Sounds good." His hands itched to stroke against the creamy skin exposed by the tiny bathing suit. "Need some help?"

"I can handle it, thanks. I'm not making anything fancy." Her gaze dropped from his. "You got a little sun. Your shoulders are red."

He touched a finger to his skin and shrugged off the slight discomfort. "I've had worse."

"Kuwait?"

"The beach at Panama City."

She laughed, weakening the invisible barrier he sensed. Her head tilted at a curious angle, she eyed him.

He shook his head. "What is it?"

Her gaze shifted away. "I just...you're a stranger. I don't *know* you."

"Yeah, you do." He stepped closer and the coconut scent of her tanning lotion tickled his nose. Lush images of their bodies entwined on a sandy, secluded beach invaded his brain and sent blood to his groin in a tingling rush. "You know what's important."

"And what is that?" Her nervous laugh died when he reached for her hand.

"That I'm the same guy I was last night." He flattened her palm against his chest. Her fingers flexed, a soft caress. Her skin glistened, and if he pressed his mouth to the curve of her breast, she would taste of sun, salt and coconut. "That everything last night was real."

She parted her lips, her tongue darting out to touch her bottom lip. He swallowed a groan, wanting again. She stepped closer, sliding her hand up his chest, over his shoulder to his nape, a burning trail of pleasure-pain in its path. Her mouth whispered over his.

"I'm not really hungry right now," she said.

"I am," he whispered, ready to devour her. He took her mouth, his hands sliding around her waist and tugging her against him.

She circled his neck with her arms, their bare stomachs brushing. She pulled her lips from his and kissed her way along his jaw. A sharp nip at his earlobe wrung another groan from him. "Kathleen."

She rubbed the arch of her foot along his calf. "Still want to make love on my white sheets?"

"God, yes." He pulled his head back and stared down into knowing brown eyes. "How did you—"

"Are you coming?" She spun and walked up the rise toward the house. She tossed him a come-hither look over her shoulder, her hips moving in a soft sway.

He stood for a moment, desire freezing his muscles. If Guinevere had been half as enticing, Lancelot never stood a chance. Forget Camelot. Forget loyalty and honor and everything but the woman who called to him with such a sweet siren's song.

He followed.

Kathleen left the door open and walked down the hall, the wood floor cool under her feet. Desire swirled in her stomach, flowing to a heated ache between her legs. Her body felt open and ready for him, and he'd barely touched her. Not the normal reaction of the good girl her parents had raised.

She wanted to be deliciously, wickedly bad with him.

The door to her bedroom swung inward under her light touch. Remnants of sunlight lay in golden slats across the floor and her bed.

The French door in the living room clicked closed and footsteps whispered in the hall. The pressure in her abdomen built and radiated out, tingling along her thighs and arms, making her breasts swollen and heavy, aching for his touch.

When the footsteps stopped at the doorway, she turned. He stood, a familiar stranger, staring at her with blazing eyes. His gaze flicked to the bed and back to her, if possible, burning even hotter. Her own gaze dropped to the rigid line of his arousal beneath his navy swim trunks.

Without a word, he crossed the room and wrapped his arms around her waist, lifting her against him. He kissed her, a long, sexy kiss, his tongue doing things to her mouth that made her moan and wind her legs around his waist, holding on to keep from melting at his feet.

His erection pressed between her legs and she rubbed against him, wanting to assuage the ache. Stinging pleasure arced through her, intensifying the emptiness only he could fill.

She traced the line of his shoulders and back, the muscles bunching under her touch. His mouth fused to hers, he turned to the bed and they fell into it, her lush featherbed billowing up to cradle them. He broke the kiss, his chest heaving. She eased her hands along his jaw, once again learning the lines and hollows of his features.

He reached for the ties of her bikini top and tossed the brief garment over his shoulder. With strong hands, he molded her curves, thumbs feathering over taut nipples, and her hips shifted in a restless, wanting rhythm.

She shouldn't be this eager. His touch shouldn't make her writhe and scream and beg for more. She should care that she didn't care.

His mouth closed on her breast, and all shoulds and shouldn'ts fled her mind, leaving only the wild, blinding desire.

Hot fingers drifted over her stomach and delved beneath her shorts and bikini bottom. He stroked her wetness, long, deep caresses, and she bit back a scream, the sound emerging as a guttural moan that earned her his satisfied laugh against her breast.

He worshipped the line of her stomach, easing the shorts and bikini from her body. Still clad in his trunks, he paused, poised over her on his hands and knees, and stared down. The mixture of awe and fiery passion in his eyes sent trembles through her limbs.

"You're beautiful," he whispered, one finger trailing from the pulse at her neck, between her breasts, down her stomach to her thigh.

She blinked back sudden tears, frightened by his ability to make her feel complete with a look, a touch, the right words. “Jason.”

He caught the sigh with his mouth, his touch on her pushing the fire higher and higher. She reached for him, seeking the warmth and texture of his skin.

Finally, with a rough groan, he tugged away and shucked his trunks. She watched the muscles and tendons ripple under his sun-warmed skin while he pulled his wallet from the shorts. Visible tremors shook his hands as he sheathed his erection and his shakiness solidified her conviction.

He was right. This was real. She knew enough.

He nudged her thighs apart and his fingers twined with hers, their hands next to her head on the soft pillow.

A breath and a sigh later, he sank into her, filling the aching, pulsing emptiness. Her hold on him tightened. He moved within her, slow, deep thrusts, and she met the rhythm, wanting all of him.

The intensity built, swirling, enveloping, drawing her in to the reality he created until she didn’t know where he ended and she began. When the explosion came, her only awareness was of pleasure and the man calling her name.

They drowsed and woke to make love again, Kathleen taking charge, her knees hugging his hips as she rode him, making him buck against the pure white sheets. After, she lay against his chest, his soft voice soothing her to sleep again.

An insistent ringing jerked her from a dreamless slumber. With Jason’s murmured protest in her ear, she reached for the phone without checking the caller ID screen. “Hello?”

“Put Jason on.” Jim Ed’s malevolence drove the lazy pleasure from her body.

She sat up, hugging the sheet to her breasts as if he lurked in the room with them. Anger and hatred burned in her chest, and she pushed the emotions into her voice. "He's sleeping."

"Wake him up."

The mattress shifted and Jason's hand covered hers on the phone. "Give it to me."

He moved to sit on the edge of the bed, hunched over the phone. "Yeah?" He fell silent, Jim Ed's deep voice a tinny rumble she could still hear. "What's going on? Now?"

Kathleen pulled her knees to her chest. She eyed the distance between them and shivered against the icy sensation slithering through her body. She'd known reality would intrude, that the insulated world they created by making love wouldn't last, but Jim Ed's call dissipated the warmth and security of Jason's touch like heat mirages sliding away on hot asphalt.

"I'll be there." Another tense silence hovered in the room. "I *said* I was on my way. Yeah."

He clicked off the phone and dropped it on the bed. His head dropped, tension plain in the line of his neck and shoulders. Kathleen reached for him, but drew her hand back.

"I've got to go." He stood and tugged on his trunks, sliding his wallet back into the pocket.

He didn't look at her and fear tingled through her chest. "Jason?"

"I'll call you." He jerked a hand through his hair and moved toward the door.

She scrambled from the bed, keeping the sheet wrapped around her body, not understanding the impulse to cover what she'd so freely offered him. But this tense man wasn't the wild, tender lover she knew. "Wait. What's—"

"I don't know what's going on." He turned at the door, a glimpse of that lover showing for just a moment. His hand cupped the back of her head and he pulled her in for a quick kiss. "I'll call you. As soon as I can."

"Do you want me to call Tick?"

A tight smile played around his lips and vanished. "No. Just lock the door and be careful."

He disappeared down the hall, and a few seconds later, the quiet click of the door closing behind him filtered through the house.

Kathleen pressed a hand to the burning fear in her chest, closed her eyes and offered up a swift prayer for his safety. Jim Ed's tight voice played through her head again and she frowned. She knew that tone. Where had she—

The burning turned to cold, slick ice.

The smug malevolence had colored Jim Ed's voice the day the boys had died.

What the hell was Jason walking into?

Chapter Thirteen

Jason tucked in his black T-shirt with awkward movements. His side ached, the result of his bedroom calisthenics. If Kathleen gave him that look again, he would just have to say no.

Yeah. Sure. And if Tick Calvert had the opportunity to spend the day fishing, he wouldn't take that either.

He eased into the passenger seat of Jim Ed's truck. His cousin stared into the darkness behind Jason's trailer. Jason snapped his seatbelt into place. "So what's going on?"

Jim Ed shifted the truck into reverse. "Drug raid."

"Yeah? Is the drug squad coming along?"

"No."

The headlights cut across the blacktop road into the woods on the other side. A pair of eerie green eyes glowed then flickered away. Gravel spit under the tires when Jim Ed turned onto the highway.

Jason shot a glance at his cousin. The red light from the dash highlighted Jim Ed's profile, casting shadows beneath his eyebrows and throwing his cheekbones into prominence. The weird mingling of crimson light and darkness created the illusion of a devilish Halloween mask. A chill trickled down Jason's spine.

"So what's Palmer like in the sack?"

Anger flushed the chill from his body, but he pushed casual arrogance into his voice. "Enthusiastic." He chuckled and made a show of gripping his injured side. "The woman's trying to kill me."

"Yeah?" Jim Ed slowed to make a left. "Always thought she'd be a dead lay. Rumor has it she wasn't giving McMillian any at all their last year."

"McMillian?"

"Her ex. The district attorney."

Curiosity overruled his reluctance to discuss Kathleen with his cousin. "They've been divorced how long?"

"Six, seven years. Stacy knows more about it than I do. That woman loves to gossip. The story is that McMillian didn't want the divorce, but why he wouldn't after going without for a year, I don't know." He reached out and nudged Jason's shoulder, hard. Pain shot through Jason's stitches and he bit back a curse. "Maybe he just didn't find the same buttons you did, huh?"

"Maybe." He didn't want to think about another guy trying to find Kathleen's buttons.

"Now you've got Palmer out of your system, Stacy wants to set you up with her friend Mandy. Talk about a hot little number—"

"Who said Palmer was out of my system? Besides, I thought you wanted me to keep her out of your hair."

"I think she's handled. You *like* her or something?"

He forced another male chuckle. "I like what she does to me, that's for sure. The woman's crazy for me. You think she's gonna stay out of the way if I dump her?"

"She will if she knows what's good for her."

Jim Ed swung into a wide right turn and a street sign flashed in the headlight beams. *Smokehouse Road.* On both sides of the road, Haynes County units sat waiting, including the sheriff's unmarked car.

Foreboding took hold of his stomach and Jason shot a glance at Jim Ed. "Who are we raiding?"

"Johnny Mitchell."

Behemoth. Oh, hell.

He didn't have a good feeling about this at all.

"Jim Ed, man, if this is about what happened—"

"Don't flatter yourself, cousin." Jim Ed's dark laugh filled the truck's interior while he steered to a stop behind the sheriff's car. "Johnny didn't make his payment this month, so he pays the consequences instead. But trust me, he'll pay for cutting you, too."

Before Jason could reply, Jim Ed pushed his door open and climbed down from the tall truck, leaving Jason no option but to follow. Deputies milled around or huddled in small groups, some pulling off uniform shirts to don the bulletproof vests usually left lying on backseats of patrol cars. Others checked firearms.

His own vest was out of commission, the result of his previous dealings with Johnny Mitchell.

Ahead of him, Jim Ed conferred with Bill Thatcher. The sheriff laughed and slapped Jim Ed on the back. Jim Ed gestured, drawing the men around him.

"We're going in on foot. I don't want him to know we're there until we're coming in the door."

The men moved through the woods lining the road. The wet ground and chirping of indignant frogs muffled their footsteps. Jason, reminded of army night maneuvers, walked behind Jim

Ed, using his large frame for cover. Across the road, a dog barked.

Blue-white mercury light spilled over the yard. The broken railing still hung at a drunken angle from the deck. At a signal from Jim Ed, the deputies fanned out to surround the house. Another gesture beckoned Jason. "Stay with me."

Jason bristled at the whispered command, clenching his teeth until his jaw ached. He was thirty-one years old, damn it. A Gulf War vet. Not a wet-behind-the-ears, twenty-year-old rookie. He didn't need his hand held.

The front steps squeaked under Jim Ed's weight and Jason's muscles tightened. Floorboards rumbled inside the trailer. A bead of sweat crawled down his spine. He gripped and regripped his gun, waiting for the door to burst open and emit a cursing, shooting Behemoth. He eyed the line of his cousin's back and wondered if Jim Ed's body would keep a bullet from going through his.

The deputy in front of Jim Ed positioned himself on the other side of the door, Jim Ed took the lead entry point and Jason the backup spot, his side against the trailer wall. Any shots would most likely come high, so he hunched down, his head level with Jim Ed's waist.

In disbelief, he watched Jim Ed back up and prepare to kick the door in. Surely he wouldn't. That was a for-television-only kind of thing that guys without proper training tried. Macho crap that got people killed.

With a loud crack, the door splintered inward.

Surrounded by yells and screams, still anticipating gunfire, Jason followed Jim Ed into the trailer. The aroma of onions and stale grease hung in the air. Jason's heart thudded against his ribs and he gave the small living room a quick appraisal. A thin woman with frizzy bleached hair huddled on the couch, two squalling children clutched in her arms.

No one moved to search her or secure the room. Didn't these guys know how to do anything?

She pulled the children closer and eyed them with a wild expression. "What do you want?"

Jason slanted a look at Jim Ed, who watched the woman with a dispassionate expression as she started to cry. Jim Ed holstered his gun. Jason bit back a groan.

"Shut up, Rhonda Lynn," Jim Ed said, his voice cold. "Where's Johnny?"

She shook her head, but her gaze skittered toward the kitchen. Pulling his gun again, Jim Ed glanced at Jason and tilted his head in that direction. At the kitchen doorway, Jason stepped over a GI Joe doll lying face down and tried to tune out the children's terrified snuffling.

The kitchen held barely enough room for two people to turn around. Jim Ed and Behemoth wouldn't be able to stand together without touching. The room provided no hiding space, but a bifold door lay to the left, the entrance to the standard mobile home utility room. Jim Ed nudged him and moved that way.

Jason eyed the door, a trickle of unease moving under his skin. This was too easy. He glanced around the room again. A metal slab covered a space designed to hold a gas furnace.

No way.

Behemoth couldn't fit in there. Hell, the guy's *shoulders* wouldn't fit in there. But he'd seen Iraqi soldiers in impossibly small spaces. Gaze locked on the slab, he reached out to tap Jim Ed's arm.

His cousin swung the bifold door open.

The metal slab crashed to the floor and Jason stared down the barrel of a handgun.

Behemoth's finger tightened on the trigger.

Jason fired, several shots in rapid succession.

Blood exploded on the yellowed wallpaper. Johnny Mitchell's body dropped to the floor, the revolver clattering against the linoleum. A crimson flood spread out from Mitchell's torso, but his fingers continued twitching. Ice flashed through Jason's body.

He'd seen fingers twitch like that once before, when he'd been an eighteen-year-old kid in desert fatigues and hadn't had a choice but to kill or be killed. Afterward, one of his buddies had held his head while he puked his guts out in the sand.

Hell. Jason glanced at Jim Ed's pale, expressionless face. Bile pushed up in Jason's throat, his teeth chattering.

Jim Ed pushed his hat back and scratched his forehead. He reached for Jason's gun. "Told you the son of a bitch would pay for cutting you."

Fighting the urge to retch, Jason crouched sideways against the wall, head in his hand, elbows on his knees. In the living room, a child wailed, Rhonda Lynn shushing it with a shaking voice.

He'd killed a man.

God, what would Kathleen think of him now?

ଓ෴ഽ

He'd stopped shaking and the nausea passed by the time the GBI arrived. The sensation of being outside himself, hovering above the proceedings as an outside spectator, remained. He'd expected Kathleen and Altee; instead, Will

Botine, the agent in charge of the Moultrie office, put in an appearance.

With a weird detachment, Jason wondered where Kathleen was. In the living room, he recounted his story for Botine. Through the kitchen doorway, he watched the coroner zip the body bag closed. The rasp etched into his nerves.

"Son, did you get hurt?" Botine reached out and lifted the hem of Jason's shirt, clinging wetly to his side. Jason glanced down; blood seeped through the light gauze bandage again. Bet he'd torn a couple of stitches. When he didn't have a clue.

Lifting Kathleen in the bedroom. Coming through the woods. Bursting through the door.

He shut the memory of her out of his mind. He didn't want her connected to this. Later he'd take out the image of her under him on the blinding purity of those sheets.

Blinking, he stared at the pool of crimson on the dingy white tile. The crime scene techs took photos of blood spatter, their conversation drifting over the chatter in the living room.

"Nine damn shots."

"Yeah. Perfect center mass grouping, too."

"Wouldn't want the guy pissed off at me."

Nausea churned in his stomach again.

A young agent wearing a GBI polo stepped to the doorway and held aloft a plastic evidence bag. "Mitchell had a switchblade in his pocket. Looks like dried blood on the handle."

Botine glanced from the knife to Jason's side. "Why don't we finish this conversation over in Moultrie. We can have a cup of coffee and a little sit down."

ઌ

Jason slumped in the hard wooden chair and stared at the scuffed green wall. Did all law enforcement agencies order from some huge wholesaler of puke green paint?

Will Botine entered the room again, bearing two cups of coffee and a wide, jovial smile. The hair on Jason's nape rose. He'd seen that same smile too often on his high school principal's face—right before she suspended him.

Botine set a cup of coffee in front of him and gestured at the man who'd paused in the doorway. "Deputy, this is Tom McMillian, our district attorney. He happened to be over in the state patrol offices across the street. I thought I'd have him listen in on our conversation, if you don't mind."

"Why should I mind?" Jason crossed his arms and eyed the tall man clad in khakis and a starched oxford shirt. So this was Kathleen's ex. McMillian watched him with sharp blue eyes, his dark brown hair showing signs of a receding hairline. Jason couldn't—didn't want to—see him and Kathleen together.

McMillian stepped into the room and closed the door. "Do you want a lawyer present, Mr. Harding?"

Jason lifted an eyebrow. "Do I need one?"

"Your Miranda rights guarantee you one. Even if you can't afford one." McMillian glanced at the open file he held.

"Well, I haven't been Mirandized." Jason narrowed his eyes, anger trembling in his gut. "I wasn't aware I was a suspect, either."

"You killed a man tonight," Botine said.

"A man who was going to shoot me or Chief Deputy Reese."

McMillian looked up, fixing laser-like eyes on him. "Jim Ed's your cousin, isn't he?"

"Yeah. What of it?"

A sharp rap interrupted McMillian's reply. He stepped forward and opened the door. Jim Ed and Thatcher stood in the hall. Jim Ed shot a sharp glance at Jason as Thatcher entered the room with an "aw-shucks" grin.

"Will," Thatcher said, "we'd like to sit in on this."

A knowing look passed between Botine and McMillian, but Botine waved a hand at the two vacant chairs in the room. "By all means, Sheriff. Deputy Harding, I'd like for you to repeat your statement for Mr. McMillian."

Jason recounted the events again, his gaze not wavering from McMillian's.

Thatcher harrumphed. "He didn't have a choice, Will. Johnny meant to kill 'em. He probably saved Jim Ed's life here."

His face a polite mask, Botine looked far from impressed. "Tell me about that cut on your side, Deputy."

"Ran into a barbed wire fence."

Botine leaned forward. "Our lab tech tells me that's human blood on the knife found in Mitchell's pocket."

"That's interesting."

"Type AB negative human blood. Pretty darn rare."

Jason pasted a bored smile on his face. "Really."

McMillian flipped through the documents in the file. "*Your* blood type, Deputy Harding."

"Yeah, it is." Jason nodded, still smiling. "Weird coincidence, huh?"

"Very, since only one percent of the population has that blood type. Pretty coincidental for two people with that rare type to have contact with Mitchell recently, wouldn't you say?"

Jason shrugged. "I couldn't tell you. I failed statistics in college. Not very good with numbers, in case you don't have my bank account information in there."

Jim Ed snickered and McMillian glared at him.

Botine leaned back in his chair, arms crossed over his chest. "About as coincidental as you two being involved in two fatal shootings in a goddamn week."

"One shooting," Jim Ed corrected. "The other was a suicide, remember?"

"Not according to the evidence." McMillian dropped the folder on the table, notes and photos spilling across the scarred tabletop. "Kathleen sure does put together a pretty case, doesn't she, Will? Airtight."

At the possessive pride in McMillian's voice, Jason gritted his teeth. To his right, Jim Ed sat straighter in his chair, gaze riveted to the papers covering the table.

Thatcher rose, hat in hand. "That's enough for tonight. The boy's answered your questions. It was a clean shooting and you know it. Cut him loose."

Botine gestured at the door with one finger. "He's free to go."

Jim Ed clasped his shoulder hard. "C'mon. I'll give you a ride home."

From the hallway, Price's voice echoed. "Hey, Botine. Did you pick up the Haynes County file from our office? Kath can't find it and she's having a fit."

Her voice trailed away when she appeared in the doorway. Her gaze darted around the room and she looked away from Jim Ed as if he were a pile of dog feces she'd stepped in. "What's going on?"

Botine gathered the notes and photos and returned them to the folder. "Little incident during a drug raid. Take this back to Palmer. What are you two doing here?"

"Catching up on paperwork. We went to see her parents, but her mama's not feeling well."

McMillian eased by her into the hallway, eagerness plain in his face. "She in the office, Altee?"

Altee rolled her eyes. "Didn't I just say that?"

"Will, I'll be right back." He strode down the hall without acknowledging the others.

"This should be fun," Altee muttered and followed him.

Frowning, Jason stared after the other man. Territorial urges that had nothing to do with being a Fed struggled in his chest. He didn't want the guy near Kathleen.

As they walked out into the balmy night air, his cousin's gaze lay on him like a soaked blanket.

In the parking lot, Thatcher adjusted his belt and slapped Jim Ed on the shoulder. "I think you've got everything under control here, son. I'm gonna head home and see what Marilyn fixed for supper. Jason, take care of that side, y'hear?"

"Yes, sir."

Thatcher's car eased out of the parking lot, leaving Jason to face his cousin's cool stare. The security lights buzzed overhead, insects fluttering under the seductive glow.

Jim Ed leaned against his truck, arms crossed over his chest. "You were with Calvert today, weren't you? Out on the lake."

Unease tightened Jason's throat, but he adopted a relaxed, unconcerned stance. "I was with Kathleen. But, yeah, Calvert was there."

"This mess has gone on long enough." Jim Ed straightened and stepped closer, the move a clear attempt at intimidation. Jason refused to back up. "This whole thing with Palmer is over. Understand?"

"Yeah." Jason bit the word off, wanting to tell his cousin where he could get off.

"Stay away from her, cousin. If she won't back off, I'll make sure she does. But you're out of it."

Hurt her and I'll break your freakin' neck.

He couldn't say it, but he glared the threat at Jim Ed. The most he could do was warn Kathleen, tell her to watch her back. And maybe find a little comfort in the knowledge that she was probably more capable than he was of breaking Jim Ed's thick neck.

"Get in the truck." Jim Ed jerked his head toward the vehicle.

He bristled then. "I'm not one of your damn young'uns, Jim Ed."

His cousin shot him a withering look. "You might as well be."

The complex's glass front door shot open with enough force to rattle the frame. Kathleen's furious voice carried across the humid night air. "Damn it, Tom, how many times do I have to tell you I don't care about that money. Do what you want with it. Start a scholarship fund. Donate it to the women's center. Buy uniforms for one of the local ball teams. *I don't care!*"

Frustrated tears hovered in her tone and Jason took a half-step toward the sidewalk, forestalled by Jim Ed's steel forearm.

Kathleen shoved files into a soft-sided leather bag, her hands fumbling, and McMillian reached for it. She jerked it out of his grasp. "Kath, I simply thought you'd want some input into—"

"No. You want to remind me of a connection that's long gone. And the fact that you bring this up *every* year at his *birthday* just reinforces how dead that connection is."

McMillian threw his hands out in a tense, frustrated gesture. “What do you want me to do? It’s like you expect me to read your damn mind. God knows I’ve never been able to read you at all.”

Her harsh laugh vibrated with mockery. “Read me? You didn’t want to read me. You wanted me to fall in line with your plans, which is why this whole ‘Kath, I want your input’ crap is just that. Total crap.”

“That is not true. I always consulted you—”

“After you made the decisions.” She walked away, keys jingling. “That’s why we’re divorced, Tom. Because you never wanted to see anyone’s way but your own.”

“We’re divorced because you buried yourself with Everett. I spent eight years trying to dig you out of that grave. Hell, there’s not a man alive who could.” McMillian stalked into the building.

Head tilted back, Kathleen closed her eyes, and the pained fury on her pale face galvanized Jason. He pushed Jim Ed’s arm out of the way and strode across the parking lot.

“Kathleen.” He touched her arms with gentle hands and her eyes snapped open. She glanced toward the building and back at him. A sigh shook her body, her slender frame trembling under his easy hold.

“I guess you heard the whole mess, right?”

“Yeah.” He tucked a stray wisp of coppery hair behind her ear.

She darted a look over his shoulder, her face tightening with dislike. Her voice lowered to an intense whisper. “He’s watching us.”

“I know.”

"Are you all right? Botine wouldn't let me and Altee take the call or allow me in the interrogation room. He wanted to see if he could rattle Jim Ed."

"Was your ex in on it, too?"

"Tom? No. All he had to hear was we possibly had an arrest against a Haynes County deputy and he was over here like a shot." Disdain darkened her eyes. "It's an election year, if you haven't noticed."

"I hadn't." He wanted to pull her into his arms and hold on for dear life, let her soothe away the self-disgust eating at his insides.

Her gaze sharpened, a concerned frown wrinkling her brow. "Jason. You're not okay, are you?"

He shook his head. "I'm fine. I've got to go."

Concern softened her face. "I could take you home."

"No." He let his hands drop from her body. He sighed, a rough, weary sound. "I need you to act pissed off at me."

"What? Why—"

"Because I just dumped you. Under orders." She started to look over his shoulder again and he reached for her arm. "Don't look at him. I want you to shove me away and go back inside. Wait until we're gone. And don't go home tonight. Go to Price's or Calvert's if you have to. I don't want you alone."

She shook her head. "Jason, what—"

"Just do it, Kathleen. Please."

Real frustration slid over her face, but the trust in her eyes gave him hope. She jerked her arm away and pushed both hands against his chest. "You go to hell, too, Harding."

The words rang through the still air, kicking him in the gut even though he knew they weren't real, and she spun, stalking across the parking lot. Jason watched her go, trying to shake the sense of isolation squeezing his heart into a cold, empty knot.

He turned and strode back to the truck. Jim Ed waited, arms crossed over his chest, his face thunderous. Jason met his burning gaze. "Happy now?"

"Yeah." Jim Ed swaggered to the driver's side and slid behind the wheel.

Glad somebody was. Jason climbed into the passenger seat and leaned against the headrest. He stared out the window. A dull ache gripped his temples, but if he closed his eyes, the image of his bullets ripping into Johnny Mitchell's body would play against his eyelids.

He'd killed someone's daddy. He hadn't had a choice, not really. Mitchell would have killed him or Jim Ed, maybe both. His mind accepted that. His conscience kept hanging up on the terrified cries of Mitchell's children. They would grow up without their father and he knew firsthand what that did to a kid.

"You're over there feeling guilty, aren't you?" Jim Ed's voice, full of terse disdain, cut through the darkness.

Jason tapped his fingers against his knee. "What if I am?"

"Then you're a fucking fool. He deserved it and guilt won't get you nowhere."

"Whatever, Jim Ed."

"I suppose you're pining for Palmer, too?"

"I got rid of her because you wanted me to. Ain't that enough?"

"No woman's worth that. The only thing they're good for you can get anywhere."

"I'm sure Stacy would be mighty glad to hear you say that."

"She gets what she wants out of me. The question is what did Palmer want out of you?"

"Maybe she just wanted me."

Jim Ed snorted. "More likely she thought she'd use you to get to me."

"Don't flatter yourself, cousin." Jason enjoyed the small pleasure of throwing Jim Ed's words back in his face. "I don't think her life revolves around bringing you down."

"Shows what you know."

Jason ground his teeth at the sarcasm. The tone reminded him all too much of his uncle's derision—against him, his mother, his cousins, his absent father. "I knew enough to save your sorry self, didn't I?"

The truck swerved. "What?"

"You had your back turned. Mitchell could have emptied that gun into you before you ever turned around. Face it, *cousin*, I saved your life."

"Took you nine bullets to do it, too."

"I suppose you'd have shot him once."

"Damn straight. Right between the eyes."

"You fire until the threat is eliminated."

Silence descended, broken only by the hum of tires on pavement.

Oh, hell. Where had that come from? Straight from his Quantico instructor's mouth, that's where. Sixteen weeks of hearing the statement over and over, delivered with stinging authority. He'd even heard it in his sleep.

His stomach cramped. He might as well don his FBI T-shirt. Or one that read, "Hello, I'm an undercover Fed."

The silence unnerved him, made him wonder what was going through his cousin's head. Would Jim Ed recognize the dictate for the Bureau training mantra it was? No. He couldn't. If he had, Jason would just as likely be staring down the barrel of a gun right now.

Instead, he stared at his own mailbox. The truck slowed, turned into the drive, bounced over a couple of ruts. Jim Ed braked and let the engine idle. "Get some rest. You look like hell."

Relief skittered over him, but the fear returned instantly. He saw himself getting out of the truck and Jim Ed taking a shot at the back of his head. His muscles taut with singing tension, he reached for the handle. "Night."

With every step across the yard, he waited for the bullet to slam into him. He didn't relax until he was on the other side of his front door and Jim Ed's truck rumbled out of the yard. Tremors attacking his limbs, he slumped against the wall and slid to the floor. His forehead rested against his knees, and his body thrummed with a familiar dread.

Waiting for morning, to storm an Iraqi Republican Guard stronghold.

Not sure if one of them would come for him first.

Wondering if he'd live to see home again.

He rolled his head, shoring up his flagging reserves. Forever lay between now and morning.

And he didn't have a clue what morning would hold.

Chapter Fourteen

The dark woods closed in on Kathleen and she welcomed the coverage. This had to be the craziest risk she'd ever taken. The cop in her screamed in protest, telling her to turn around, get back in Tick's truck and drive straight to his place or Altee's. The woman in her, the one who loved Jason Harding, remembered the tortured look in his eyes and pushed her onward through the dense underbrush behind Dale Jenkins's dairy farm.

Dale and Tick went way back and no one would question the dusty white 4x4 sitting next to Dale's battered Jeep in front of the dairy office. And Dale, bless his heart, had merely nodded when she'd told him she'd be on his property for a while. No questions.

Navigating the half mile from the dairy to Jason's trailer took longer than it would have during the day. With every animal that skittered away in the underbrush, her heart thudded harder. *Scared of the dark, Palmer?*

No. Scared witless by what might be lurking in the dark.

Her steps slowed when she neared the trailer. The interior lights were off, the mercury security light bathing the white aluminum siding in a weird blue glow. Jason's beat-up Chevy sat empty in the backyard.

She made a stealthy half-circle of the trailer, making sure no other vehicles waited in front of the tiny building. Listening hard, she crept to the back door. No sounds from inside the trailer. Was he even here?

She eased up the steps and rapped at the rear door. Within seconds, the door swung inward. Hands shot out, fastened on her arms and dragged her inside. Her stomach lurched. The door slammed. Her back hit the hallway wall, hard enough to take her breath for a moment. Jason pressed her closer to the paneling, his chest against hers, his mouth near her ear.

"What the hell are you *doing* here?" Fury vibrated in his harsh whisper. His hands roamed her body, from shoulders to waist to hips, as if he wanted to be sure she was real, safe.

"Making sure you're all right." She breathed the words into his ear, her body reveling in his proximity. His heat permeated her, desire tingling to life deep in her abdomen while her mind whispered reminders of how close she'd come to losing him.

"Are you crazy?" The words hovered on a hoarse groan, his hands under her shirt, molding, caressing the flesh beneath.

She traced his face, pulling his mouth to hers. She was hungry for him, to feel the reality of him, to know he was warm and alive and *hers*.

He seemed as starved for her, invading her mouth with a desperate gentleness, fumbling with her button fly before delving inside to find her wet and aching for him. He moaned into her mouth and shoved jeans and panties down. She stepped out of them, his warm hands wandering over her thighs.

Desire burned, licking at her stomach, her skin, her core. She cupped his erection through his jeans, and he bucked against her, another moan rumbling through him. She popped loose the button and slid the zipper down, desperate to have him inside her. He lifted her higher against the wall, and she wrapped her legs around his waist, wanting no further preliminaries. Wanting him, only him, forever.

When he entered her, he pulled his mouth from hers, his breath coming in hoarse rasps. “Kathleen. God, baby.”

His lips fastened on her neck, sucking, the scrape of his teeth an exquisite torture. Thrilled by the ease with which he supported her, she closed her eyes and held on harder. His strength and masculinity made her more aware of her femininity, and she swallowed against a rush of tears. She tangled her fingers in his hair, pushing harder against him, never wanting to let him go.

“I love you, Jason.” She whispered the words, her lips moving against his temple. The admission brought her a peace and completion she’d missed for years.

The wild tumult was over all too soon, leaving him gasping, his face against her neck. She clung to his shoulders, trying to catch her own breath.

His arms tightened and he brushed his mouth against her skin. She felt the smile curving his lips. “Ah, sugar, how do you *do* that to me?”

Her head jerked up. She told him she loved him and he commented on their lovemaking? She loosened her arms, creating a mental distance as well, and he sighed, still holding on to her.

He nuzzled her neck, but she felt the gulf slipping in between them. He was here, hers, but not. A part of him remained somewhere else.

“Who’s Everett?” He murmured the question against her skin.

She fought the urge to stiffen in his arms, forced herself to remain soft and molded against him. “My son.”

He lifted his head and in the dim light from outside, she could read the surprise on his face. “You have a son?”

“Had.” Glad her face was in the shadows, she swallowed against the lump blocking her throat. “He died.”

He pressed a soft kiss, a whispery caress, to her temple. “I’m sorry.”

“So am I.” Her eyes drifted closed and she lost herself in the feel of him against her. Only him against her. Her eyes snapped open. The firestorm had been on them so quickly they’d not stopped for precautions. “Jason, we forgot to—”

“You’ve got to get out of here.” He pulled back, letting her slide along his body. She felt the shudder that traveled through him with the action.

He bent down to pick up her jeans and she leaned against the wall, her thighs trembling, and tried to pull her mind back into focus. Sharing Everett with him hadn’t been nearly as painful as she’d expected, the twinge of loss, but not the crushing agony she normally experienced. She touched her stomach, imagining carrying another baby. Jason’s baby. One she could be conceiving even now. The hope flushed through her, bringing a simultaneous fear with it.

“Here.” He handed her the jeans. His tight grin, visible even in the dimness, drove the fear away, replacing it with a dull, achy worry.

She stepped into underwear and pants all at once, still watching him, wishing for better light so she could read his eyes. “What’s wrong?”

He jerked both hands through his hair. “Damn it, Kathleen. You need to go.”

“In a minute. Something’s happened, hasn’t it? Something other than the shooting.” She planted her hands on her hips. “What is it?”

"Nothing. It's dangerous for you to be here. You shouldn't have come at all."

She ignored the pang his words created and reached for him, fisting handfuls of his T-shirt to pull him close, his weight and heat a reassurance against her. "This is me, Harding. *Talk* to me."

He sagged against her, the awful tension she felt in him easing with a long sigh. He lifted his hands, framing her face, stroking her hair. "I think I screwed up."

Fear shot through her veins. "What? Why?"

"Jim Ed and I were fussing," he said, his voice a harsh whisper. He wiped a hand over his face before resting his arm against the wall. "He made a crack about the number of shots I took with Mitchell and I said...I said..."

"*What?*"

"That I fired until the threat was eliminated."

"Oh, God." The reality of his words slammed into her chest. How many times had she been on the range and heard Tick beating the phrase into the Chandler County deputies? Words that marked him as a Quantico-trained Fed. Would Jim Ed have recognized them, too? She curled her hands around Jason's rib cage. "What did Jim Ed say?"

"Nothing. Not a damn word. Dropped me off and left."

Hope trembled at the edge of the overriding fear. "Maybe it didn't mean anything to him."

"Maybe." Doubt hovered in his voice.

"I mean, how many Feds does he hang out with?"

"Yeah. You're probably right." He fingered her hair. "But I'd feel better if you weren't here. And don't go home, either."

She forced a smile to trembling lips. “We already covered that. I’ll take Tick back his truck and either camp out on his couch or go to Altee’s.”

He blew out a long breath. “I can’t believe I’m sending you off to spend the night with Calvert. I must be crazy.”

The urge to repeat her words of love lingered, but his failure to respond to her earlier declaration kept them unsaid. She feathered her fingers over his jaw. “No worries there, Harding.”

He stepped back and reached for the doorknob. “C’mon. Let’s get you out of here. I’m going to try for a couple hours’ sleep.”

Cicadas and crickets hummed in the night. At the bottom of the steps, her feet sank into grass already dampened with dew. The reluctance to leave him alone sat in her chest, a physical ache. She turned back, the shadows hiding his face. “Jason.”

“Go on, sugar. It’ll be fine.”

Fine? Leaving him, not knowing what was going to happen? That was fine? Surely the two of them together stood a better chance if Jim Ed tried anything than if she left him alone. “Let me stay.”

“No. I need you to go to Calvert, tell him what I said. He’ll know what to do from there.”

He was right, and as badly as the woman in her wanted to remain by his side, this time, the cop won out. Blinking back hot tears, she jogged up the steps and took his face in her hands, kissing him once more. He crushed her to him, desperation in his touch.

She pulled back, still touching him. “Tomorrow.”

"Yeah. Tomorrow." He turned his mouth into her hand. "Now get going."

Heading into the woods, she felt his gaze on her until the trees and the dark swallowed her again.

ꕥ

"Yeah, Falconetti, I know what time it is. And I know it's Sunday morning. I'm sorry I woke you." Tick leaned forward in the armchair, phone pressed to his ear, the fingers of his free hand pinching the bridge of his nose. "This is important. I think Harding's in trouble."

Knees drawn up to her chin, Kathleen sat on his red couch with Altee and watched him. His eyes closed briefly, listening. A cold lump of fear sat in her belly. With every step through those dark woods and every mile she'd driven away from Jason, that fear had increased.

"Falconetti, I've got Agents Price and Palmer with the GBI here. I'm going to put you on speakerphone." He pushed a button and returned the receiver to its place.

"All right, Calvert, what's going on?" The agent's husky voice filled the room. Tick steepled his fingers together under his chin and stared at the phone, his expression intent.

"Harding killed a suspect last night during a drug raid."

"A clean shooting?"

"Yeah. He didn't have a choice. He'll be exonerated."

"So what's the problem?"

"We think Reese is getting suspicious."

"Why?" The sound of rustling paper filtered across the line.

"He ordered Harding away from Palmer."

"Did he threaten Palmer?"

Tick's chocolate gaze darted to Kathleen. "I don't know. Harding staged a public breakup."

"That's good." A note of relief crept into Falconetti's voice. "Reese expects obedience and loyalty from those around him."

"Cait." Tick paused, and a distant part of Kathleen's mind noted the way his voice tightened around her name. "Harding got into a fuss with Jim Ed Reese afterward. Reese said something about the number of shots Jason made. Harding replied he fired until the threat was eliminated."

"Oh, hell." Stress returned to the husky tone. "Has Reese heard you say it?"

"I don't think so. Harding's a smart guy. He could explain it away if Reese asks. He told Palmer Reese didn't say anything at the time."

"If he asks." A pause hummed over the long distance connection. "So let's assume Reese's suspicions have been aroused. He's a thinker, though. The whole action of forcing Harding to give up Palmer...he's reeling Harding in, keeping him close so he can watch him. He's controlling him."

"Think we need to pull Harding out?"

"I don't know. Reese wants to believe in Harding. He's family. It would be hard for him to believe Harding could betray him. But if he realizes Harding is doing just that..."

The unfinished sentence tightened the icy dread holding Kathleen in its tentacles.

Tick rubbed a hand over his forehead. "You think he'd kill him. Family or not."

"Calvert, the man reads like a textbook example of an antisocial personality. He killed those boys because he could, because they dared to challenge his authority by not stopping once they entered his county. I wouldn't be surprised if there aren't other bodies floating around out there that go beyond the political killings you think he committed. And he's going to spare Harding because he's a relative? No. If anything, the retribution would be more severe."

"So what do we do? Pull him out and blow the operation? Or leave him in and take the risk?"

"Has anyone asked Harding what he wants?" Despite her obvious frustration, Falconetti's tone remained cool and steady.

Tick's gaze darted to Kathleen's. She didn't have to ask, had felt the resolution overriding the fear in him the night before. She clenched her hands, fingernails biting into her palms. "He won't want us to pull him out."

Falconetti's voice crackled over the speakerphone again. "It's a moot point until we can get in touch with the agent in charge anyway. We can't pull him without going through channels. Tick, want me to make that contact for you?"

"That would be great. We'll wait for you to call."

"I'll make it as fast as I can." The line went dead. Tick reached over, lifted the receiver and let it fall again.

Kathleen jumped to her feet and paced the length of the living area, rubbing at her arms. Chills raced over her skin, leaving gooseflesh in their wake. "We can't just leave him alone, Tick."

"We're not."

"We're sitting here waiting for a damn phone call! He's out there alone!"

"He's not helpless, Kathleen," Tick said, an edge creeping into his voice. "Give the boy some credit."

"Your father wasn't helpless, either, was he?" she asked, hating herself when his face paled, his dark eyes burning bright. "And they got to him, too."

"That's not fair." He growled the words. "Damn it, Kath. We don't even know for sure that Reese is on to him."

"But you're willing to take that chance, aren't you?" Bitterness crawled in her throat. "You're willing to risk him to get at Thatcher and Reese."

"What do you want me to do?" He exploded to his feet, his frustrated shout bouncing off the freshly painted walls. "Thatcher had my father killed and Jim Ed's daddy was in on it. I know it, but I can't prove it. Jim Ed... Lord, Kathleen, that body we found in the woods. We don't even know who he was. No dental records because his teeth had been bashed out. Broken bones because they'd beaten him before they killed him. You saw those boys in that truck. We can't let him keep on getting away with this."

"But, Jason... God, Tick." Didn't he see that the same thing could happen to Jason?

"Have some faith in him, Kathleen."

"What if it were Falconetti?" Altee's quiet question jerked Tick's head around. Kathleen stared at her partner.

Tick glared at Altee. "What does she have to do with this?"

Altee shrugged, a graceful movement of her shoulders. "Just answer the question. If your girl Falconetti was in Harding's place, what would you do?"

His mouth thinned. "The same thing I'm doing now. I'd wait for the damned call and hope like hell Reese didn't have a clue."

Altee's perfect eyebrows lifted. "You wouldn't go after her."

"No." A sigh shook his body with a visible tremor. "She wouldn't expect me to. She wouldn't want me playing knight in shining armor, trying to rescue her, putting everything at risk."

"And you could live with that?"

"I wouldn't have a choice. I know she can take care of herself."

Altee turned to Kathleen. "Kath? We can blow off the Feds and all our training, kill our careers and go get him. I'm with you if that's what you want."

Kathleen closed her eyes, trying to make her head overrule her heart. What would Jason want? She blew out a long sigh and looked at her partner's serene face. "No. We'll wait."

ઉ෴ઈ

An hour before dawn, Jason donned his army sweats and running shoes. He couldn't handle the waiting anymore. Ignoring the protest in his side, he set off down the road, loose gravel grinding and crunching under his feet. He should be thinking ahead, planning a way out if Jim Ed tried anything, but all he could focus on was the sound of Kathleen's whispered "I love you".

Just remembering the words slammed warmth into his chest. She loved him. *Kathleen Palmer* saying she loved him. How many times had he fantasized about that?

Was it real? She'd whispered the words with passion exploding between them, with fear hanging around them. Maybe it wasn't real, but he wanted it to be with a desperation that scared him. He couldn't see how it could be, though. He'd lied, shown her only what he could. Was that enough for her to love?

I love you, Jason.

With her breathy whisper, answering words had leapt to his lips and he forced them back. He'd fallen, hard, for the real Kathleen—not the shining icon of his youth. He wanted the flesh-and-blood woman, the one who sparkled with energy and grace and used a tough exterior to hide any softness from the world. He loved her.

He just couldn't say it. Right now, what could he offer her? The uncertainty of his future? More of the fear that had gripped them last night? No way. That wasn't the foundation he wanted for a relationship. Better to wait until his life wasn't a shifting pile of sand under his feet. See if she could love the real Jason Harding.

His feet pounded against the road, jarring his side, a perfect backdrop for the uncertainties whirling in his head. So much remained that he didn't know about her, either. Her marriage, the loss of her son, what she wanted out of life. Too easily, his vision of their future stretched before him like the endless country road—marriage, wrapped in the security of their love, children, a home. A real home, something he hadn't really had, although he knew his mother had tried her damnedest to give him one.

A son. Kathleen had had a son. Would she want a child with him? The thought of making her pregnant, giving her his baby, shot a thrill through him, frightening in its intensity. But hell, what did he know about being a father? He didn't have any models to follow—his own father who'd disappeared from his life overnight, leaving only fuzzy memories, his mother's tears and overwhelming poverty. Jim Ed's father. Yeah. He wanted to be like Uncle Jimmy, browbeating and diminishing his children to nothing.

Guess he knew where Jim Ed got his parenting skills.

Best not to think about Kathleen and babies.

Should have thought about that last night, genius, and remembered the damn condom.

Wiping sweat from his face, he groaned and turned toward home. What if he'd already made her pregnant? Not the smartest thing he'd ever done, letting his need to touch her overwhelm his common sense. All he'd been able to focus on was her presence, her hands on him, and how damned much he *needed* her, how much he wanted to lose the horror and fear in her.

God, what if he'd made her pregnant and he didn't come out of this? The idea of Kathleen in his mother's position, raising a child alone, made him ill. He didn't want that for her. Didn't want her to face the debilitating worry, the derision heaped on his mother by her family, his Uncle Jimmy most of all. Didn't want his child to be an outcast.

It wouldn't happen. Not from one time. Never mind he'd been conceived during one of those "just one time" deals. It wouldn't happen.

But he had to come out of this alive.

Just in case.

The early sun cast fingers of light through the woods in front of the trailer, spilling reds and golds on the damp grass. The light dispelled the fears from the night like mist burning off under the heat of morning. If Jim Ed suspected him, he wouldn't have waited to get rid of him.

He walked toward the trailer, his chest and side burning with exertion, but the tension leaving his body. Relief trembled in his fluttering muscles. Hell, he'd scared Kathleen, too. Doubt she'd slept any more than he had.

Maybe Calvert had been able to reassure her.

He frowned at the thought. Damn it, he'd never been a jealous guy—it smacked too much of insecurity—but he'd developed a sense of possessiveness where Kathleen was concerned. As long as she didn't see it, he was probably okay. He grinned. She wouldn't appreciate it, he didn't think.

He jogged up the front steps. Coffee. He needed caffeine and some food. Anything but Rice Krispies. The day stretched before him, an empty expanse without Kathleen.

What were her normal Sundays like? Probably church with her parents, huge Sunday dinner, lazy afternoon by the lake. Wanting curled through him, the need to just *be* with her.

The unlocked door swung inward and the smell of well-oiled leather hit his nostrils. Adrenaline flooded his suddenly tense muscles and he froze, one foot in the door, his heart pounding a desperate rhythm against the walls of his chest. Nerves jumped in his stomach, huge vulture-sized butterflies fluttering and bumping around.

He stared down the barrel of a forty-caliber handgun.

"Oh, shit."

"My thoughts exactly." Malicious satisfaction filled Jim Ed's taunting voice. His gun belt, duty pistol in the holster, gleamed in the dim light. Jason swallowed a curse. Stupid, careless...damn it, he should have *known*. "And I hope you have hip boots, boy, because you've stumbled into it deep this time."

A deep, cold evil glittered in Jim Ed's eyes and fear wrapped clammy fingers around Jason's insides. He knew that look, had seen the remnants in his cousin's eyes the day those boys had died.

He'd just never expected to face it himself. Not really.

Now he faced more than his irate cousin. He faced the man whose only intent was to see Jason dead.

ന്ദ

Curled in Tick's leather armchair, Kathleen sipped her third cup of coffee and glared at the phone. Altee slumped on one end of the couch, eyes closed and, from the bedroom, the sounds of Tick dressing filtered into the living room—drawers closing, soft whistling, the thud of shoes being dropped on the wood floor. She wanted to scream at his casual cheerfulness.

She wanted to throttle Agent Falconetti for not calling.

She wanted Jason.

Tick's bedroom door opened and he stepped into the living area, his hair damp. "Did you leave me any coffee?"

"Plenty." She waved a hand toward the kitchen and directed a glower at the back of his head. Sooner or later she'd make him pay for this. Maybe help Lynne convince everyone in the county he was gay. Hide his damn cigarettes when he was having a nicotine fit. Tell his mother and hers he *really* wanted help to find a nice girl so he could settle down and have babies.

He returned with a mug bearing the BASS logo. He reached for the Sunday paper lying on the coffee table.

The phone rang.

Kathleen jumped, her heart jerking upward into her throat.

Coffee sloshed over his mug and he cursed, setting the mug down and grabbing the phone. "Hello?"

He closed his eyes, his body relaxing. "Hey, Barbara. What's up?"

His sister-in-law. The urge to scream built in Kathleen's throat again. *Damn it, Barbara, get over it. Get over Del and the separation and over this weird fascination you have with Tick. He's not interested. Get off the damn phone!*

"He did *what*?" Anger tightened Tick's jaw. Even Kathleen could hear Barbara's panicked squawking. Tick sighed and rubbed a hand over his eyes. "Okay. We'll find him. I can't leave right now...I *can't*, Barb, I've got something going on here. I know. I know. I'll call dispatch, put out a bulletin. Let me *go*, so I can do it. I'll call you."

He hit the disconnect bar. "Son of a bitch."

"What?"

"Blake decided to sneak out of the house and take Barbara's car for a joyride. She doesn't know how long he's been gone." He punched numbers with a savage finger. "That boy needs a father. I ought to kick Del's ass for taking off to Atlanta like that."

She frowned. "Does Blake have his license?"

"No. I'm going to—" He bit the words off. "Roger, it's Tick. I need you to put a bulletin out. Late model Toyota 4-Runner. White. If it wasn't stolen, would I be asking you to...oh, hell, Roger, just do it! Yeah. My nephew Blake should be driving it. He's fifteen, about five ten, slight build. Whoever finds him, hold him until I get there. Got it?"

He slung the receiver back into the cradle and jumped to his feet. "I swear, if it's not raining, it's pouring. Last week, he got into a fight at school. What is it with that kid?"

"We did the same thing," Kathleen said, drawing her knees up, glad to have the distraction. "You'd had your license two days and we took your daddy's truck down that old dirt road by the lime mine."

He shot her a lopsided grin over his shoulder. "You convinced me to let you drive. Put the damned thing in the ditch. Cried when your daddy got there, too. He was convinced it was all my fault. You got off with a good talking to and I spent a month working in a tobacco field as punishment."

Footsteps rattled across the back porch. Kathleen rose and moved toward the door with Tick. One hand on the butt of his holstered gun, Tick swung the door open. The two teenagers standing on the porch blinked at him.

One had the dark coloring, straight nose and stubborn jaw that marked him as a Calvert. The other had sandy hair and fearful blue eyes, but his chin drew Kathleen. She frowned. She knew that chin and something familiar about the shape of his eyes nudged at her mind.

Tick clenched the door's edge until his knuckles whitened. "Blake, son," he said, anger trembling in his voice, "you are in a load of trouble. What were you thinking?"

"Uncle Tick, chill a minute, would you? It's important—"

"Chill? You stole your mother's car! And you want me to chill out?"

"You said you'd always listen to me if—"

"Sir, it's my fault." The other boy stood straighter. "I called Blake and asked him to come get me."

Tick turned a glare on him. "Really? Blake, what have I told you about letting people lead you into things?"

"Uncle Tick! Shut up and listen!"

Kathleen stifled an inappropriate smile at Tick's outraged expression. The skin around his mouth pale, he stepped back, arms over his chest. "Delbert Blake, this better be darned good." He turned a narrow-eyed look on the other boy. "Just who are you, son?"

He swallowed, Adam's apple bobbing in his thin throat. "Jamie Reese. And you've got to stop my dad because he's going after Uncle Jason."

Chapter Fifteen

The meaty fist slammed into Jason's stomach. The force pushed vomit into his throat. He fought off the nausea. Gasping for air that suddenly just wasn't there, blinking back unwilling tears, he doubled over as far as possible with his hands cuffed to the arms of the sturdy wooden chair.

Jim Ed grabbed a handful of Jason's hair and jerked his head back, forcing him to look up at Thatcher. Both men smiled with sick satisfaction. Jason stared at his cousin through narrow eyes, hatred and disgust boiling in his aching chest.

"Stupid." Jim Ed flung Jason's head back and let go of his hair. "Just like your old man. Always wanting to do the right thing, the *lawful* thing. I shoulda known."

"You look just like Alex." Thatcher made the observation as though commenting on the weather. He rubbed a thumb over his jaw and eyed Jason. "Talk big like him, too. At the end, though, he begged for his life like all the others."

The breath strangled in Jason's lungs.

His father. He hadn't abandoned them.

He'd been killed. For wanting to do the right thing.

And the same man wanted Jason dead, too.

"Crooked sumbitch." He pushed the words past swollen lips.

Thatcher's thick brows lowered in an ominous frown and he nodded at Jim Ed. Jason watched with queasy, disconnected fascination as his cousin pulled the three-cell Maglite from his belt and swung the heavy flashlight down to connect with Jason's forearm. A nauseating wave of numbness moved up his arm, followed immediately by an excruciating sledgehammer of agony.

Thatcher leaned over him, chuckling. "Now, boy, do you want to tell me what you told Palmer and Calvert?" he asked in his best good-old-boy voice. "Or do you want to play some more games?"

"Go to hell." Jason gasped for air, his jaw clenched in an effort to avoid screaming from the pain radiating up his arm.

With a long-suffering sigh, Thatcher shook his head and nodded at Jim Ed. "Hit him again."

ଔଊ

Impatience thundered with Kathleen's pulse. Tick dragged the two boys into the kitchen, attempting to get the story out of them, with both boys talking over each other at once.

He pointed a finger at Blake. "You, hush." The finger turned on Jamie. "You, talk."

The boy swallowed, his thin shoulders hunched under the Haynes-Chandler High School T-shirt he wore. "I got up early to run before chores. I wanted to go out for cross country, but Daddy doesn't like me being at school late for practice."

Kathleen pressed her lips together, biting her tongue to keep from telling him to hurry up. He had the twitchy look of a scared rabbit, ready to bolt at any second.

"All right." Tick nodded, his voice holding infinite patience. "Go on."

"I let myself back in the house after I fed the dog. I thought I'd have time to take a shower and my dad wouldn't ever know I'd been out." He rubbed his palms down his gray sweatpants. "He was in the kitchen on the phone. I ducked into the laundry room so he wouldn't see me. He was talking to Mr. Bill. You know, the sheriff."

"What did he say, Jamie?"

"He was really mad. I could tell from his voice. You know, the way he talks when one of us doesn't do what we're supposed to the first time. He gets all low and growly and then he starts cussing." Jamie drew in a deep breath. "Anyway, I couldn't move. He was going on and on about Uncle Jason, that he was a traitor and an undercover cop and a whole lotta other stuff, about him and..."

His voice trailed away, and he darted a quick look in Kathleen's direction. "He talked about you the way he talks about my mom. He calls her...he talks to her real ugly and makes her cry. She-she don't deserve that." His hands clenched at his sides, knuckles white. "And I can't do anything about it."

Kathleen met Tick's shuttered gaze and fought back a wave of fear. Damn the regulations. They should have put Jason's safety first.

Tick passed a hand through his hair. "Jamie, how do you know he's gone after Jason?"

"Because he said he was. He told Mr. Bill they'd have to take care of him now. He said he'd go get him."

"Son, this is really important. What time was this?"

"About six-thirty."

Oh, God, please. It was almost eight. An hour and a half. Her mind crowded with images of everything that could happen in that time. Altee's gripped her hand with cool fingers and Kathleen glanced at her partner. With her other hand, Altee rubbed Kathleen's back, a silent source of support.

"There's a code on the phone at home so we can't call out without it. He won't let any of us have it; we have to ask him to put it in for us." A note of panicked apology invaded Jamie's voice. "I had to wait and make sure he was gone, then I ran to the gas station out on the highway. I ran as fast as I could, but I didn't know who to call. It's not like I could dial 9-1-1."

"He called me," Blake said, his voice quiet. "We've been buddying around at school since we took Mrs. Hatcher's drama class together last fall. Kept it quiet because we knew his daddy would have a duck, and I figured you would, too. I guess he thought you could help, since I brag on you so much—"

"All the time," Jamie finished for him. "Uncle Tick this, Uncle Tick that. Like you're danged Superman or something."

Tick looked as dazed as Kathleen felt. He wrapped a hand around Blake's nape. "You did good, kid, but I wish you'd called me immediately."

Blake shrugged away from his hold. "Yeah, but then I wouldn't have gotten to drive Mama's car."

"We'll talk about that later. I see a lot of yard work at Grandma's in your future. Jamie, I need you to tell us where your dad might have taken Jason."

Jamie took a step back, shaking his head. "Not until my mom and my sisters are safe."

Tick looked at Kathleen, then at the boy. He reached out a hand, and Jamie flinched away, suspicion darkening his eyes. The mulish set of his chin punched Kathleen in the chest. He had Jason's chin.

"Jamie," Kathleen said, keeping her voice soft and even, "we have to find him. You know that. And you're the one who can tell us where to look."

"I know." His voice shook and he blinked, a suspicious glitter in his eyes. "I like Uncle Jason. He's a good guy and I don't want anything to happen to him. But I *can't* tell you until I know Mama and the girls are safe. Mama...Daddy hits her. Not where it'll show or anything, and he doesn't hit the girls yet, but...I can't. Not until they're out of the house. Don't you see? I have to take care of them."

Tick nodded. "Okay. We can do that right now." He pulled his cell phone from his belt and handed it to Kathleen. "Call Botine. Have him send someone to get Stacy and the girls. And tell him we need the helicopter on standby."

She did, keeping the conversation as brief as possible and listening to Tick talk with Jamie at the same time. He did so with a patience she found admirable, because hers was long gone.

She handed Tick the phone. "Where?"

"Probably Thatcher's home."

"Oh, Lord." Thatcher's house nestled into a hundred acres of heavily wooded land, the entire compound surrounded by a state-of-the-art security fence. Besides the primary residence, there were various outbuildings and a huge pond. Her throat ached with tears. "Tick, how are we going to find him?"

"We'll find him." He glanced at Altee. "Price, I hate to ask, but I can't leave these two alone."

"Reduced to babysitting." Altee's smile was strained and Kathleen knew it was more for the boys' benefit than hers. Altee's mission here could be as deadly as Kathleen and Tick's, if Jamie's absence had been discovered and the Haynes County boys were looking for him. "Get moving."

“Thank you.” Kathleen moved to embrace her partner.

“He’ll be fine.” Altee tightened her arms for a moment and pushed her toward the door. “Go find him.”

In Tick’s truck, Kathleen fumbled with her seatbelt. Disjointed prayers flooded her mind, jumbling with the fears already rolling around. *Lord, please don’t let it be too late. Let us find him. Watch over him. Please.*

Frightened tears spilled over her lashes and she brushed them away with shaking fingers. They would find him. They had to. She couldn’t face losing him, too, not after he’d reawakened her.

She drew in a deep, steadying breath and tried to pull her reserve around her. Right now, the cop had to win out over the woman. She had to keep it together. The situation would be god-awful ugly, no matter what, and Tick would need steady backup, not a distraught liability.

Tick drove with one hand, taking the curves with skillful speed and familiarity. His other hand held the cell phone to his ear and Kathleen listened as he called in every favor he’d ever earned. In her lap, she curled her hands into tight balls, fingernails biting into her palms. They would need those favors.

He dropped the phone on the seat between them. “Botine and Stanton are up in the chopper, looking for Harding’s truck. It’s not at his trailer, so it’s a good bet if we find that piece of junk, we’ll find Harding.”

Watching the trees blur past, Kathleen hoped he was right and that it wasn’t already too late.

ଓଃ

Jason wasn't sure where one wave of pain ended and the next began. His arm screamed, his chest and abdomen burned from Jim Ed's blows, his mouth ached, and now agony shot through his right foot, because his cousin had just used the flashlight to break his big toe and probably most of the bones across the top of his foot. He leaned his head back, his neck unsteady, and forced a weak grin, the best "screw you" expression he could come up with under the circumstances.

"Hey, cousin," he said, pushing the words out between dry, swollen lips. "Anyone ever tell you that you make UGA's mascot look pretty?"

"Yeah? You make him look smart." Jim Ed slapped the flashlight against his fleshy palm, sadistic pleasure lighting his face.

They were going to kill him. Jason closed his eyes against the thought, fighting the reality. They were going to kill him, but first they planned to make him suffer, see what they could get out of him. He didn't want to die, was nowhere near ready to meet his Maker. He hadn't told Kathleen he loved her yet, hadn't made her any promises. He shied from the thought. He couldn't think of her. If he did, he would break down and Jim Ed would have him and it would have all been for nothing...

"Wake up." Jim Ed tapped his cheek, hard, the contact reverberating through his jaw. Jason's eyes snapped open. Somewhere along the way, Thatcher had slipped from the room, but Jason didn't remember when, the minutes running together in a hazy fog.

"I'm still..." He had to pause and gasp in a breath, his lungs burning. He flexed his uninjured foot. "...still smarter than you. Better trained."

Jim Ed stepped closer, his face threatening. "Yeah?"

"Yeah." Summoning his flagging strength, Jason lashed out with his left foot, making solid contact with the other man's knee. The crack bounced around the room, followed by Jim Ed's furious cursing. "Any idiot knows you...shackle legs."

"You...son of a bitch." Jim Ed doubled over, panting with pain, and Jason grinned, lips aching. He might have to die, but he was going to die fighting.

Like his father.

Enraged, spewing profanities, Jim Ed shoved the chair backward. Jason's head collided with the floor and pain exploded behind his eyes. Jim Ed swung the flashlight down once more. Darkness rushed in on him, his last thoughts of Kathleen.

ଔ

Leaning against the hood of Tick's truck, Kathleen helped him spread the blueprints over the aerial map. They were a mile up the highway from Thatcher's home, the closest place the helicopter could land without being in sight of the house. Unmarked units and a couple of state patrol cars lined the road, agents waiting, talking quietly with state troopers.

Tick scratched his temple and glanced at Botine. "Y'all didn't see anything?"

"Jim Ed's truck is in the drive. There's three garages. Harding's truck could be in any one of those." Discouragement hovered in Botine's voice.

Stanton Reed, newly appointed sheriff of Chandler County and Tick's longtime partner from the FBI, circled an area on the map with his finger. "What's the deal with the fencing in the pond?"

Botine shook his head. “The fool raises alligators. Goes out and feeds them like they’re pets or something. Dangles chickens over them. He’s just begging to get eaten.”

Cold certainty dropped Kathleen’s stomach to her feet. Horrified, trying to block the images Botine’s careless words invoked, she lifted her gaze to Tick’s and saw her own shocked realization reflected in his dark eyes.

She shook her head, a strangled moan slipping past her lips. “No.”

Tick wasn’t the kind of guy to mouth empty reassurances, but right now, she really wished he was. She wanted someone to take the terror away.

Instead, Tick crumpled the map and plans together and flung them into his truck. “We’ve got to get in there.”

Botine and Stanton exchanged a look. “What?” Botine demanded. “What did I miss?”

“If you wanted to get rid of a body without any evidence, what would you do with it?” Tick pulled a rifle from the rack behind the seat of his truck.

“You think he’s going to try to feed him to the gators?” Disbelief colored Stanton’s voice, but he pulled his own gun from the holster, checking the magazine.

“Yeah. That’s exactly what I think.”

“We can’t take the chopper,” Kathleen said, remembering the brick and wrought iron fence bordering the property. A thin wire along the top of the sedate fence hinted at an electrified surface. “If they hear us coming, they’ll shoot him. How are we going to get in there?”

“The iron fence stops at the edge of the pond on the back acres. There’s just chain link there.” Botine rubbed his chin, brows meeting in a thoughtful frown. "It shouldn't be electrified."

Hope jumped in Kathleen's chest and she glanced up to meet Tick's resigned gaze. She forced a smile, all of her focus on Jason, getting him out alive. That's all that mattered, not that he'd never said he loved her, not that there was still so much they didn't know about each other.

The only important thing was saving his life.

Tick sighed and tugged his cell phone from his belt, handing it to Stanton. "What's a few alligators? Come on, Kath. He's *your* boyfriend."

"Fifteen minutes," Stanton said, pocketing the phone. "And then we're coming in after you, even if we have to use the chopper."

Kathleen jogged into the woods, taking the lead and using the underbrush as cover. She struggled to keep her breathing even. Panic tapped at her resolve, looking for weaknesses, and she refused to give in. Panic was deadly. Control was everything.

Brambles pulled at her jeans and scratched her arms. She ran harder. With every step, memories flickered in her mind. Jason in uniform that first day, a small smile curving his mouth. On her deck, hungry for more than food, wanting her to see beyond the lies. Kissing her with more desire than she'd ever experienced with any other man. Making love to her, their bodies wrapped in white Egyptian cotton. Clinging to her last night, wanting her close but wanting her safe more. Making her walk away.

Tears blurred her vision, and she blinked them away. *Focus, Palmer. Tears later.*

The woods opened up at the wild border of Thatcher's pond. The chain link fence stood a few feet out in the murky water. Stopping at the edge of the woods, Kathleen took deep, even breaths, her throat aching. The water lay still, sparkling in the early morning sun.

"They sleep during the day." Tick gasped the words near her ear. "Or sun themselves."

She glanced at him over her shoulder. His chest heaved and she shook her head. "You've got to quit smoking."

He waved off the comment and gestured toward the far corner of the pond. "The water's shallower over there. We can go over the fence and use the woods for cover again. I want to be in that water the shortest time possible. They only look fat and sluggish."

Kathleen nodded, eyeing the motionless water and the empty banks beyond. The house rose over the water. Nothing moved. She'd thought getting in would be the hard part. Now she knew it was only the beginning. Once inside, they still had to find Jason. And she had no idea where to start looking.

Tick tagged her arm and moved toward the water. "Come on."

ଔଷ

Jason hit the packed ground face first, the impact driving the air from his chest. He lay for a moment, his lungs clawing for oxygen, fingers curled into the coolness of damp red clay. Beyond the burning in his chest was the pain in his arm, his foot, his face, his head. He didn't want to move. He wanted it over, for Jim Ed to finish this however he chose. He just wanted the waves of pain to end.

Kathleen.

She wouldn't want him to give in, give up. And he wanted to give her whatever she wanted.

Finally able to breathe again, he pulled together what strength he still had and pushed up on his good arm. Eyes closed against a wave of dizziness, he made it to his knees.

Jim Ed's booted foot slammed into his stitched side. The stitches gave with a sick tearing and the momentum flipped him to his back.

"God!" He thought he screamed, but knew the plea came out a muffled moan instead. Tears slipped from his swollen eyes, joining the blood dripping down his face.

"You just won't quit, will you?" Jim Ed leaned over him, unwilling admiration glittering in his eyes. "Give it up, cousin. It's over."

"No." Spitting blood with a weak cough, Jason rolled to his side and struggled to his knees again.

Jim Ed grasped the collar of his T-shirt and dragged him to his feet. He half-pulled and half-pushed Jason forward, Jason's mind so fogged now that he didn't care where he was headed or what would happen. The training, the focus, the mission—everything was gone except the images fluttering in the last cognizant part of his brain.

Rich brown eyes with flecks of gold. Creamy skin under his fingertips. Full mouth kissing him. A rare sparkling laugh dancing along his veins like champagne.

"Sorry," he mumbled, his head flopping forward. *I'm sorry, Kathleen.*

"Why?" Betrayal choked Jim Ed's voice. "Why'd you do it?"

"Right thing to do." He wasn't even sure if he spoke the words aloud.

"Well, the right thing got you killed, boy. I was good to you, Jason. And you pay me back like this." Jim Ed flung him forward and this time his body collided with a wood surface. The soft lapping of water soothed his ears and he opened slitted eyes, closing them immediately against the harsh brightness of sun sparkling off water. "Now you're really gonna pay."

He took a breath, his lungs weak and jittery. "Only care about yourself. Not me. Not...anyone. Yourself."

"Yeah? Look where it's gotten me. Look where you are."

"Reese!" Calvert's voice rang through the still air. "Move away from him."

Safe. The word hovered in Jason's mind, the concept still unreal. Maybe he dreamed that deep drawl, full of steely command.

"Go to hell, Calvert." Hatred vibrated in Jim Ed's growl.

"Drop it! Get away from him."

Gunfire cracked, over Jason's head and in the distance. The booted foot connected with his body again and he rolled with the force, falling, until water closed over his head. Cuts stung, needled by the icy water, and he gulped, his lungs filling before he struggled upward. He surfaced, gasping, his movements stiff and uncoordinated. Shouts filled the air, broken up by the whup-whup of a chopper landing. God, he was so far gone, he was hallucinating, imagining things.

Black dots danced at the edges of his blurred vision, the pond sucking him under again. Water rushed up his nose, choking him. Something brushed his leg and he tried to recoil, his limbs refusing to obey his fuzzy mind.

He kicked upward again, barely getting his head above the surface before he sank once more. The blackness tunneled in, his only awareness of cold, rank water around him, filling him.

Any sense of panic disappeared, swallowed by blessed resignation.

A strong arm looped around his chest, pulling him up. His head broke the surface. Oxygen invaded his body, weak coughs wracking his lungs. The arm holding him moved with the rhythmic strokes of a strong swimmer.

"Stan, help me get him out." Calvert's urgent voice, next to his head.

He floated, an arm supporting his neck and back. A sensation of movement, then hands under his armpits, dragging him up while other hands kept his body stable. Pain shot through him, water burbling from his throat and out his mouth.

Lying on his back, light on his face, but he couldn't open his eyes. His pulse thundering in his ears. Hands on him, assessing, sending more pain along his nerves. Blood and water in his throat, chest aching as he vomited. Hands turning him.

Darkness flooding his mind, voices around him.

Jim Ed yelling in the distance, pain ravaging his shouts. Vestiges of the Miranda rights floated to him.

"Pulse is over a hundred." Male voice, one he didn't know.

"Going into shock." Calvert's voice again, grim and raw. Something covered his chest and stomach. "C'mon, Harding, stay with us. Hell, there's a *dent* in his head."

"Did you see that gator?"

"See it? I *felt* it. Damn thing brushed our legs."

On his back again, his head tilted back. A cloth wiping his face.

"Lifeflight's in the air." Botine? "ETA five minutes."

Memory flickered. He wanted...he needed to...

"If he makes it that long. We're losing his pulse."

"Jason?" Kathleen. Tears in her voice. "Jason!"

"Get her back, Botine. Damn it, where's the EMTs?"

Kathleen. Love you.

A black void closed in.

Nothing.

Kathleen fought Botine's restraining arm. "Damn it, Will."

His hold tightened. "Stop it, Palmer. Let them take care of him."

Sobs ravaged her chest. Tears streamed down her face, and she didn't bother to brush them away. This wasn't happening. *This wasn't happening.* He wasn't dying in front of her on the dock, with Botine keeping her from him. She wasn't losing him, too.

"No pulse." The look Stanton Reed exchanged with Tick stabbed at her.

Tick leaned over Jason, shaking his shoulder. "Harding? Harding?" He caught Stanton's gaze. "Unresponsive. Starting CPR."

"Oh, God." The sobbing moan slipped past her lips, her body sagging against Botine. She couldn't close her eyes, couldn't turn away.

"Clear his airway, Stan."

"I'm *trying,* damn it. There's too much blood."

Oh, please.

Finally, Stanton puffed two breaths into Jason's mouth. Tick knelt beside him, hands ready to begin compression. The steady chop of a helicopter grew in the distance.

Don't be too late. Please don't be too late.

Stanton and Tick moved with the precision of a well-oiled piston, a puff of air for every five compressions. She held her breath, her focus on the artificial rise and fall of his chest. Around her controlled chaos reigned, agents swarming the grounds, tending to an injured Jim Ed, keeping Thatcher in custody on the deck.

Her existence narrowed to the scene on the dock. Nothing else mattered. Stanton lifted his head. Tick's hands stopped moving. Stanton turned his head over Jason's mouth. Listening for breath sounds. His fingers slid to Jason's pulse.

"Continue CPR."

Her face crumpled, fresh tears spilled over her lashes. The chop-chop grew louder, the water rippling with the helicopter's approach. An engine whined. Tick pushed down on Jason's chest, Stanton breathed for him.

Footsteps pounded on the wood, a stretcher rattling in time with the beats. An EMT knelt by Jason's body, obstructing her view. "What have we got?"

Tick's terse voice filled in the details, the EMT already busy placing a blood pressure cuff on Jason's arm and inserting an IV line. After moving his body to the stretcher, they bagged him, taking over the CPR, and Tick moved out of the way. He looked up, his gaze locking with Kathleen's.

The hopelessness in his dark eyes took her breath. He thought Jason was gone. She could see the knowledge in his face, guilt and sorrow etched into the tense lines bracketing his mouth.

She shook her head. "No. He's not. He can't be."

Tick moved forward and Botine's arm dropped away.

Kathleen sniffled, her nose running, and brushed tears from her face. "He's not dying."

The helicopter lifted off, dust and bits of grass blowing across the pond.

Enfolded in Tick's shaking arms, his damp clothing smelling of pond water, she cried and pounded a fist against the wall of his chest. "He's not dying, Tick. He's not."

He cupped her nape, stroking her hair. He didn't offer reassurances. She shook her head, trying to catch her breath between the harsh, racking sobs. Her voice cracked with each word. "We weren't too late. We weren't."

Tick stepped back and looked away. He swallowed, his throat moving. Kathleen dropped her gaze to his hands, specked with blood. Jason's blood.

He reached for her. "Come on. We'll meet them at the hospital."

She let him lead her away, paralyzed by a fear beyond prayer.

Chapter Sixteen

"He'll be just fine. Some nerve damage to the arm, possibly some long-term numbness, but he should retain full use of it." The doctor's reassuring voice filtered into Kathleen's numb consciousness. "No reason why he shouldn't make a full recovery."

Weary shoulders aching, Kathleen lifted her head and studied the doctor. He stood a few feet away at the entrance to the surgical unit. Stacy Reese, her tear-stained face lit with relief, smiled up at him. Kathleen looked away, unable to stand it. Of course he would be okay. Jim Ed always was. Even locked away in prison, he'd be okay.

Jason wasn't okay. He lay behind those heavy steel doors, too, and doctors were doing more than taking a bullet out of his shoulder. Somewhere behind those doors, doctors struggled to save his life. Radiating skull fracture. Hemorrhage. Possible brain damage. Death. The surgeon's words swirled in her head, echoing.

But Jim Ed would recover fully.

Bitterness choking her, she looked up and for a moment met Stacy's blank blue eyes. What kind of woman was she? Her children were at the women's shelter, waiting for an emergency foster home, and she was here, supporting her husband. A murderer.

Maybe Jason's killer.

A victim. The words whispered across the surface of her mind. That's what kind of woman Stacy was. Another of Jim Ed's victims.

Her mother patted her hand. "Honey, let me get you something to eat."

She shook her head. "I don't want anything, Mama." Just Jason. Warm and alive, holding her close, calling her sugar.

She felt her mother move to peer at Altee over her head. "Altee? Can I get you something?"

Altee's hand slid down Kathleen's back in a soft, comforting sweep. "You know, some coffee would be great, Mrs. Palmer."

"I'll be right back."

Altee leaned her head against Kathleen's, tucking strands of hair behind her ear, a slow, soothing motion. "She needs something to do."

"I know." Kathleen swallowed against fresh tears scratching her already swollen throat. "I just...I can't stomach anything right now."

"It's okay." Altee's lips brushed her head. "It's okay."

"No." The tears burst free, strangling her, falling from her burning eyes. "It's not okay. Not with him...oh, God, Altee."

"Sshh." Arms wrapped around her, Altee rocked her. "Don't do this, Kath."

Kathleen clung to her, sobbing. "I can't lose him. I can't."

"You won't. You *won't*. He's strong. You know that."

A hand cradled her head, and she pulled back, glancing at Tick standing beside her. He'd changed clothes, his wet shirt and jeans exchanged for department polo and khakis. His dark hair fell on his forehead, looking as if he'd ruffled it in frustration more than once.

She brushed tears from her face, the skin raw. "Hey."

He squeezed her knee. "Hey. Any news?"

"Yeah." The bitterness poisoned her voice. "Jim Ed's going to be just fine."

"Well, he can be just fine behind bars. For the rest of his life. Thatcher rolled on him. Wants a deal in exchange for testimony."

Anger burned in her chest. "Tell me Tom isn't dealing with him."

"Tom laughed in his face. Good thing, too, because Botine and I had already decided to kick his ass from here to Atlanta if he offered up a deal."

"Good." She clasped his fingers, grateful for the warm steadiness of his presence. "You were awesome today."

He glanced away. "I almost got the boy killed following regulations."

She remembered him taking a shot at Jim Ed and diving immediately into alligator-infested water to drag Jason to safety. He'd worked over Jason's body, performing CPR until his arms shook with fatigue. "You saved his life, Tick. I won't ever forget what you did."

A flush colored his cheekbones. "Does this make up for running your cheerleading bloomers up the flagpole?"

"Yeah. I think that's covered now." A smile trembled at her lips and died.

He rubbed his nape. "Talked to Falconetti. She has Jason's file. He had a couple of emergency contacts listed. Looked like army buddies of his. She's going to give them a call."

"Good." Kathleen nodded and stared at her lap. Jason had been in there for hours now. Why didn't they come tell her something?

More hours crept by. The waiting area slowly emptied—Chandler County deputies and GBI agents spoke to Kathleen in quiet voices and wandered out. Worried by her mother's pallor, she convinced her father to take her home, overriding his reluctance by pointing out she didn't need to be anxious about her mother, too. Tick settled into a vinyl chair and leaned his head back, seeming to doze. Altee held Kathleen's hand and didn't try to talk.

Kathleen prayed, bargained and wept silent tears.

The surgical unit doors remained closed.

At last the door opened and a doctor emerged. Kathleen leapt to her feet, Altee beside her. Tick unfolded himself from the chair. The doctor looked around the room and focused on Kathleen. "I'm Dr. Grady. Are you Jason Harding's next of kin?" she asked.

"I...yes. He has no family." Her knees trembled. She searched the other woman's face and found only solemn compassion. Altee's fingers tightened around hers. *Oh, God. He was dead.*

The doctor's mouth thinned. "Your relationship to him?"

This was not good. Next of kin and talk of relationships and no mention of his condition. Dots danced at the edges of her vision, and she struggled to breathe. "I'm...we're involved."

Involved. What a weak, ineffective word for what he'd become to her. He was everything.

Tears burned her eyes and she gripped Altee's hand, a cool, steady lifeline. "He's dead, isn't he?"

"Oh, no." Dr. Grady's face softened, her mouth curving into a compassionate smile. "No, he's not dead. We've just sent him to recovery."

"Oh, my God." Her knees liquefied, Altee's supportive arm keeping her upright. She covered her mouth with shaking fingers. "Oh, thank You, God."

"He's in recovery, but he's not out of the woods yet." Despite the sympathy, Dr. Grady's voice remained sternly realistic. "With any type of brain injury, well, you face a wide range of complications. And he's at an increased risk of pulmonary problems because of the water inhaled. These first few hours will be critical."

"I understand." Kathleen didn't bother to wipe away the tears. "May I see him?"

"From recovery, he'll go to the surgical intensive care unit. Usually, the only visitors allowed are immediate family members." She tempered the words with a smile. "I think we can let you have five minutes with him. I need to prepare you, though. His face is very bruised and there's extreme swelling. He's on a ventilator with the respirator breathing for him. His appearance might be frightening to you—"

"I don't care," Kathleen murmured. "I don't care what he looks like." She only cared that he still lived.

"It's going to be a while still," Dr. Grady said. "He'll be in recovery an hour or so, maybe longer. You might want to grab something to eat."

"Thank you." Her voice threatened to break and she took a deep breath. "For everything."

The doctor smiled and walked down the hall. Elated, Kathleen turned to Altee and flung her arms around her partner's neck. "He's all right, Altee. He's going to be okay."

"Yeah." Altee rubbed her back in a soothing circle. "I heard."

ଔଛ

Her first glimpse of him drove away the elation. Tubes and monitors invaded his body, the bandages and bruising making him unrecognizable. He lay still as an open grave, the artificial movement of his chest in time with the hissing respirator making him seem like a grisly mannequin.

Kathleen touched his unresponsive fingers and remembered how they'd felt against her skin. She leaned close to his ear. "Jason, it's Kathleen. It's over. You're safe."

No movement, no change in the monitors, nothing to let her know he heard.

She feathered her fingertips along his jaw. "You did it, honey. Jim Ed and Thatcher are both behind bars." He remained immobile under her touch, as though the very essence of him was far away, already out of reach. Touching Everett's body had been like this. Her heart contracted, and she swallowed back a fresh wave of tears. "Jason, you have to get well. You have to wake up. I need you. You have no idea how much."

The shushed click and hiss of the respirator answered her.

"What if I'm pregnant, Harding? I don't want to raise our baby alone. You *have* to wake up. Do you hear me? You have to. You can't let him win."

"Ms. Palmer?" A nurse touched her shoulder. "It's time to go."

Kathleen nodded, loath to leave him, and leaned over, her mouth next to his ear. "Jason? I love you."

ଔଛ

A deep voice jerked Kathleen from an uneasy sleep. She blinked and struggled to an upright position. Her neck ached from its unnatural angle against Altee's shoulder. Altee stirred as well.

Beyond the waiting room, a nurse guarded the ICU entrance. A man stood over her, arms folded across his chest, muscles in those arms tight under skin the color of rich Colombian coffee. The man was huge, at least six inches taller than the blond man behind him and almost a foot taller than the brunette next to him, who tapped her foot against the floor and glared at the nurse.

The guy with the broad shoulders leaned forward. "Look, lady, I'm telling you. We *are* his family."

"We're his brothers," the blond man said. "And she's his sister."

The nurse didn't look impressed, her narrow-eyed gaze moving from the tall black man to the thinner blond to the curvy brunette. "Brothers, huh?"

The blond spoke up again. "Half-brothers. And she's adopted."

"Shut up, Fish," the other man ordered. "You're not helping."

"But—"

"We just want to see him," the first man said, his tone gentling. "Please."

The brunette stepped forward, dark curls tumbling over her shoulders. "We've come a really long way. We won't stay long or bother him."

The two of them glanced at the blond. He threw out his hands. "What? You know I'm not any good at sucking up."

A harsh sigh shook those impossibly broad shoulders. "Please?"

The nurse relented, sympathy softening the line of her mouth. "I'll check with the doctor. She's with another patient, so it may take a few minutes. You can wait with his other visitors."

She walked away, her rubber-soled shoes muffled on the shining linoleum floor. The tall man turned his head, fixing Kathleen with a penetrating look.

Kathleen passed a hand over her burning eyes. They were obviously here to see Jason, but who were they?

The trio entered the room. The black man was the obvious leader and he moved with an ingrained sense of authority. Kathleen stood, brushing back her disheveled hair, aware of Altee at her side.

Kathleen forced a weak semblance of a smile. "You're here to see Jason."

One corner of his full mouth tilted in a grin. "Yes, ma'am, we are." He held out his right hand. "Bull Jones."

"Kathleen Palmer." His huge hand enveloped hers in a firm handshake. He didn't let go, but continued to eye her with a knowing expression.

"I see." He chuckled, the rich sound filling the quiet room. "Hot damn."

His reaction puzzled her, but she was too weary and heartsick to work it out right now. She pulled her hand from his and he gestured toward the others. "Fish Williams. Angie Francesco."

She nodded, aware they stared at her with the same measuring expression. She half-turned, drawing Altee forward. "My friend, Altee Price."

More handshakes and Angie stepped closer, low-slung jeans attempting to hang on to her hips. “Have you seen him?”

Kathleen nodded and bit her lip, determined not to cry again. “For a few minutes. He…it’s bad.”

Despite her resolve, her voice broke. Angie reached for her hand. “Hey. Don’t.” The remnants of a New Jersey accent lingered in her voice. “If anyone can come out of this, it’s Harding. The man can do anything.”

“Yeah.” A grin played around Fish’s mouth, but didn’t reach his blue eyes. “Leap tall buildings. Drag Bull’s huge butt out of a firefight. Eat Angie’s cooking.”

Angie elbowed him, hard enough to make him wince. “Put up with your sense of humor.”

The young nurse walked in. “Dr. Grady says you can see him for a few minutes.” The three moved forward as one, and she shook her head, smiling. “*After* she examines him again. She’s on morning rounds, so it’ll be about an hour. Go get some coffee or something to eat.”

Altee smoothed Kathleen’s hair behind her ear. “That sounds like a great idea. You’ve got to be starved.”

Not with worry gnawing at her stomach. There wasn’t room for hunger. Kathleen shook her head. “I’m not—”

“I don’t remember asking you. I’m telling you—you’re going to eat something. Now.”

Respect lit Bull’s shiny ebony gaze. “Damn, woman. I like you.”

Fish chuckled. “He has a thing for authoritative women.”

“At least he knows what authority is,” Angie muttered. “You’d think after more than a decade in the military, you’d have figured it out, too.”

"All right, children." Bull chuckled again. "Let's find the cafeteria and feed Harding's lady."

Kathleen darted at glance at him, finding that speculative glow in his eyes again. The force of them overwhelmed her. She could see Jason enfolded by this group of people, his makeshift family. People he cared about deeply, people who cared about him. He'd left them behind to go into a dangerous situation that kept him isolated, alone. A wave of admiration for the honorable man she loved cascaded through her.

The cafeteria was quiet and almost deserted at the early hour. A sleepy intern downed coffee while a couple of nurses chatted over eggs and toast. Kathleen let Altee bully her into choosing a muffin, a bowl of strawberries and coffee, echoing Angie and Altee's choices. Fish's plate held three times as much food as Bull's—eggs, grits, toast, sausage and bacon.

They chose a corner table graced by a patch of early morning sunshine. Fish lifted a spoonful of grits and let them drip back onto the plate. "Dude, what *is* this?"

Bull forked up a mouthful of eggs. "Just eat it."

Kathleen picked at her muffin and listened to the good-natured ribbing flying around the table. Under Altee's pointed look, she took a small bite, the rich bread like Styrofoam in her mouth. She swallowed with difficulty and slid the plate away. Images of Jason's bruised face, his shaved head swathed in bandages invaded her mind.

Bull covered her hand. "He did, you know."

She looked up, blinking. "Did what?"

"Dragged my huge butt out of a firefight." He pointed to his chest. "I took three rounds. Thought for sure I was dead. And here's this scrawny eighteen-year-old private I'd known for two weeks running through heavy fire to get me to cover. Didn't realize until later he'd gotten shot doing it."

The scars on his shoulder and hip.

Fish gulped his coffee. "That's Harding for you. Always in the middle of everything. Do the right thing, worry about the personal risk later."

Angie nodded, her lips trembling under a soft smile. "They sent us out to help the National Guard with a flood one time. Bull and me, we're filling sand bags. Jason and Fish? Shimmying down ropes from a helicopter to pull out stranded people."

Fish laughed. "Then we found these radical whitecaps and went rafting. Dude, if we'd had boards...you should see him surf."

"Dude," Angie said, a mocking lilt in her voice. "You're from Ohio, remember? Not the California coast."

"It's that time we spent in San Diego. I'm a transplant. Me and Harding? Born surfers."

Lord, so much she didn't know about him, so much she wanted to learn. She just needed a chance. She needed him to come back to her.

"Hey." Tick set a cup of coffee and a half a pack of cigarettes on the table and pulled out the chair next to her. "How's Harding?"

"The same."

His dark glaze flickered around the table while Kathleen made quick introductions. He reeked of cigarette smoke. Kathleen wrinkled her nose. "God, Tick. Do you just spray the nicotine on now?"

He shot her an apologetic smile. "Stress. Chain smoking." He lifted the pack. "Second one since last night."

Fish pointed at him. "Dude, those things will kill you."

Angie rolled her eyes. "This from a guy who jumps out of planes for kicks." She looked at Tick, appreciation glowing in her luminous brown eyes. "You just need a new addiction. You know, to take your mind off the craving."

Altee laughed, the sound weary. "Give it up, hon. He's pining for a lost love, drowning his pain in a never-ending string of young, dumb blondes and empty flirtation."

A deep flush reddened his face. "Damn it, Price."

The levity grated on Kathleen's raw nerves. "Tick. Where'd you go?"

He'd disappeared shortly after midnight. He aligned his lighter on top of the cellophane pack. "First, I went down to help subdue Jim Ed. He went off the deep end when he woke up. We strapped him to the bed." A grim satisfaction lit his face, but died under a darker expression. "Then I went back out to Thatcher's with Botine. They started draining the pond, but we're dragging the bottom in the interim."

"Oh, God." A sick expression pinched Altee's face. "What?"

He shuddered. "I have never...hell, none of us have. Loose bones. I can handle that. It's the drums. Sealed fifty-gallon drums with remains inside. We've recovered nine of them so far. You don't want to be around when they're opened either. Ten times worse than an autopsy lab. I tossed my cookies after the fourth one."

Kathleen closed her eyes, fingers pressed to her forehead. *Jason.*

"We'll start excavating the grounds later today. No telling what we'll find." He paused, rubbing his thumb along the rim of his coffee cup. "One of the barrels...well, anything fabric or leather is long gone, but the plastic and metal is generally intact. We pulled a driver's license and one of those seventies-style ID bracelets out. It's...it's Harding's daddy."

"So he didn't just leave him." Angie's voice was soft.

Tick shook his head. "No. He didn't leave him. Thatcher and his boys probably got rid of him for some transgression or to keep him quiet. Looks like they took care of anyone who got in their way."

"It's over then," Altee whispered.

"No." Kathleen struggled to keep her voice steady. "It won't be over until Jason wakes up."

"Don't worry," Bull said. He exchanged a glance with his comrades. "We'll wake his butt up."

ᘓᘏ

Jason was on a troop transport. He had to be. He didn't hear the rhythmic drone of a C-130, but over him, Fish and Angie argued, something about her cooking and his ancestry. Why wouldn't they shut up and let him sleep? Hell, they should sleep, too. There would be little time for rest when they got wherever they were headed.

Where were they headed? He tried to concentrate, running into walls in his head. Thoughts jumped around like wild phantasms, nothing he could reach out and grab. He couldn't even hold on to the pain hovering at the edge of his consciousness. He hurt. He knew it, but even the pain seemed unreal. Drugs. Somewhere beyond the painkillers, that pain was gonna be huge.

What had happened? Had he been shot? Again, he nudged at his memory. The walls refused to give.

He sensed motion over him.

"Dude, wake up." Fish's voice, the ditzy surfer tone that didn't match the sharp mind underneath. "Come on, Harding.

Wakey, wakey. Two days is long enough for a nap. You're breathing on your own. You can do this, too. C'mon. Open your eyes. Hey, if you don't wake up, Bull is gonna give me the keys to your car."

Like hell. Bull knew better. He wanted to chuckle, but oblivion sucked at him again.

Pain. Real this time, the drugs not dulling it. Pain everywhere—his foot, his arm, his chest. His face. Sweet Jesus, his head. What had happened to his head? Little sledgehammers slammed against the surface of his skull. He recoiled, seeking the dark where he didn't hurt.

"Jason? Buddy, you there?" Bull, his deep voice heavy with concern.

He could hang on to Bull. A guy had buddies, and then there were *buddies*, the ones who could be trusted with a guy's life. Bull was one of those.

Blood brothers, Bull said, because Jason had shed his saving Bull's sorry self.

With Bull here, he could brave anything. Even the overwhelming, all-encompassing agony. Whatever had happened, Bull could help him fight back from it.

"Hey, man. Wake up." Bull's voice dropped, close to his ear. "You were right about that Palmer chick, man. She is hot. You gotta wake up and give me the details."

Kathleen.

Jim Ed. The walls of his memory gave way, anger and hatred and agony flooding back.

His head hitting a concrete floor.

A booted foot slamming into his side.

Water closing over him.

The son of a bitch had tried to kill him and damned near succeeded.

Jason. I love you.

He wouldn't let his cousin win. He had to fight his way back, for Kathleen. She'd said she loved him and he had to find out if it was true. He had to tell her, too.

"That's it, man. Open your eyes." Urgency flooded Bull's voice. "C'mon, Harding. You can do it."

Light blinded him. He blinked, everything fuzzy, his lids fighting to close again. Bull leaned over him, a wide grin splitting his face. "All right! How you feel, buddy?"

His tongue lay thick in his mouth, his throat dry and on fire. He opened his mouth, trying to force out a sound. Trying to tell Bull what he really needed. A croak emerged.

"Kathleen."

ଔଓ

In the ladies room, Kathleen leaned over the sink and splashed cool water on her gritty eyes. Three days. Small improvements—the respirator removed, Jason breathing on his own now, his brain waves registering normal activity. But he hadn't regained consciousness, although his condition remained stable enough for Dr. Grady to have him moved to a private room and out of the ICU.

The door burst open and Bull rushed in. The elderly woman reapplying too-red lipstick shrieked and smeared it across her cheek. Kathleen stared at him, his wild-eyed look striking another type of fear in her heart.

She backed away, shaking her head. "No."

He nodded, a huge smile showing off sparkling white teeth. “Yes. He’s awake. And he wants you.”

“Oh, my God!” Kathleen launched herself into his arms and, with a booming laugh, he swung her around and out into the hallway.

He pushed her toward Jason’s room. “Go. I’ll get the doctor.”

She didn’t need to be told twice. Heart pounding, she dashed to the end of the hall, to the corner she’d haunted for two days now. Her hand trembled on the door latch, a shakiness that attacked her entire body as she slipped into the dim room.

His eyes were closed again. Some of the swelling had receded over the last day and he looked more like himself, though deep blue and purple bruises still covered his face.

Kathleen eased closer, struggling against crushing disappointment that he seemed unconscious once more. Bull had seen him awake. He would wake again.

Next to the bed, she reached for his uninjured hand, careful of the IV line. She leaned over him. “Jason?”

His lashes fluttered, lifted, dropped again.

Her heart jumped, a huge thud against her ribs.

She feathered a touch across his dry lips. “Jason, it’s Kathleen.”

His mouth twitched under her thumb. His eyes flickered open, the sea green depths murky with pain and drugs. Tears spilled over her lashes. *Thank You, God.*

She smiled, stroking his hand. “I love you.”

His throat moved. His lips parted and, under her hand, his fingers flexed. Recognition shone through the confusion in his eyes. “Kath.”

She shook her head, his shallow breath a whispery warmth against her skin. "Don't talk. It's okay. Everything's okay. You're safe."

His eyes closed, lashes dark against his pale skin. His mouth moved again. "Love you."

A tear dripped onto his chin. "Good. Because I'm never letting go of you, Harding."

Epilogue

A bass broke the surface of Lake Blackshear, sending a spray of silver droplets into the air. An egret lifted from the water and flapped away into a stand of cedar trees.

"Rain's coming." Jason rotated his wrist, trying to relieve the deep ache in the bone. Ever since the fracture had healed, the increased pressure of a coming rain sent a throbbing through his entire forearm.

Tick reeled his line in and cast a skeptical glance at the sky. "There's not a cloud up there."

Jason chuckled, the sound blending with the gentle lap of water against the boat. "Trust me. My wrist hurts. It's going to rain."

"Sure it's not overuse?"

"One semen sample does not constitute overuse." Jason tugged his cap lower over his eyes. Being handed a little plastic cup and ushered into a bathroom did constitute one of the most awkward events of his life. But worth it. Kathleen wanted his baby, the old fashioned way wasn't getting it, and he wanted her to have whatever she wanted.

Enough that he'd be playing sperm donor again tomorrow, this time for the artificial insemination. He wanted the procedure to succeed, not just so Kathleen would have the baby she desired, but because he missed his wife. For the last six months, their love life had been regimented, ruled by temperatures and fertile dates. Not that he wouldn't make love with Kathleen whenever, wherever she wanted, but he missed the playful, spontaneous woman he'd discovered under the layers of Kathleen's reserve.

Thunderclouds gathered on the distant horizon. Jason nudged Tick's foot with his own. "Told ya."

By the time they loaded the boat on the trailer, fat drops of rain pelted them. They made a dash for the cab and Jason laughed. "I'm telling you. The wrist never lies."

Tick glanced at him. "You finished with the physical therapy?"

"Yeah." He flexed his fingers. "It's not ever going to be as strong as it was, but it's a lot better than at first."

A silence descended on the truck while Tick navigated rain-slick roads. The wipers slapped in rhythm across the windshield, rebellious rivulets making their way down the side of the glass.

"I saw Stacy yesterday," Tick said, his voice quiet.

Jason straightened. "How is she?"

"She's different. Tori can't say enough good things about her. She's completely reorganized the front office at the women's center. The divorce is final. Did you know that?"

"Jamie told me." He was coaching a county rec baseball team this year, which let him spend time with his cousin's son. He'd been afraid he'd see too much of Jim Ed in the boy, but instead kept seeing flashes of himself at the same age. "He's proud of his mom."

"He should be. Starting over completely couldn't have been easy."

"The family counseling's been good for all of them."

Tick pulled into the driveway of Jason and Kathleen's home. "Good luck tomorrow."

"Thanks." Jason grabbed his rod and tackle box from the truck bed and made a dash for the house. Only his unmarked car, bearing the H-1 tag signifying his rank as Haynes County's appointed interim sheriff, sat under the carport. Kathleen wasn't home yet, probably still at her late appointment to have her hormone levels checked before the next day's procedure.

Jason left his boots and equipment on the deck by the door. The house enveloped him with Kathleen's essence when he stepped inside. He loved walking into their home, the first real one he'd ever had. But home wasn't the house, the furniture, the wedding photos and honeymoon snapshots.

Home was Kathleen. Home was the incredible love and affection that flooded every aspect of their lives with light and healing.

In the bathroom, he stripped off and dropped his bait-scented clothing in the hamper. He stepped into the shower and groaned with satisfaction, hot water pelting any residual tension from his muscles. The week had been rougher than usual, from trying to hire a new investigator to attending Jim Ed's sentencing hearing.

He wasn't sure what he'd expected to get out of going, and he and Kathleen had argued over it. Whatever he'd looked for—a confession, an apology, an admission from Jim Ed that what he'd done had been wrong—Jason hadn't gotten it. But that part of his life was over.

He couldn't think of any better way to begin the next chapter than having a baby with his wife.

Once out of the shower, he rubbed water from his hair and wrapped a towel around his waist. He pushed his damp hair away from his face, brushing the ridge of his surgical scar.

"Jason."

He startled, heart pounding against his ribs for one uncomfortable moment. Clutching his ribs, he chuckled and glanced at the bedroom door. "Geez, Kathleen."

"I'm sorry." An apologetic smile on her face, she reached for him, her arms going around his waist. "I didn't mean to."

"I know." He rubbed his face against her neck, inhaling her clean scent. The increased tendency to startle easily was normal, at least according to his doctor, and should fade, just as his getting the words for colors mixed up had in the three months after his head injury.

"Mmm. You smell good." Kathleen pressed closer, nuzzling his jaw. She kissed down his neck and he shivered, a tingling arousal rushing to his groin.

"Sugar, this isn't a good idea." He leaned against the vanity and slid his hands to her waist. "I've got that..." She mouthed his nipple, taking his breath, and his hands tightened. "...thing tomorrow."

"What thing?" Her teasing tone matched the mouth traveling over his stomach. The towel fell to the floor.

"The appointment thing." She nipped his thigh, and his fingers tightened on her shoulders. "Ah, God, Kathleen. We can't."

Her tongue smoothed the spot where she'd bitten him. "Why not?"

He tried to remember why not, but she was driving him out of his mind, and all he could think of was tumbling her down on their bed or right here on the thick rug.

"Because it'll lower my count." He gasped the words and felt her smile.

"I don't think that's a problem. I canceled the appointment."

That got his attention. He gripped her arms and pulled her up. "What? Why?"

She touched his mouth, smiling. "I didn't ovulate."

He groaned and closed his eyes. "Hell, sugar, I'm sorry."

"Jason." She cupped his jaw and he opened his eyes, meeting her shining brown gaze. "I didn't ovulate because I'm already pregnant."

He laughed. "Really?"

Her arms wound around his neck. "Yes. Really."

Wrapping her in a tight embrace, he swung her around, their joyful laughter bubbling in the small room. His mouth found hers and the laughter ceased for a long time.

ƆƐ

Later, they lay sprawled among rumpled white sheets. Sated, he rested his head on her chest, his hand on her stomach. Kathleen sifted through his hair, the easy caress making him drowsy.

He flexed his fingers against her flat abdomen. "Hard to believe there's a baby in there." He lifted his gaze to hers. "Is it okay for us to be doing this?"

Her sparkling laugh warmed him. "Now you ask, *after* we've done it. Yes, it's fine. I asked."

He moved up on the pillows and pulled her into his arms, her cheek against his chest. She sighed, stroking his side. "I have never been so happy in my life."

"I'm glad." He caressed her back, sleep pulling at him.

"Are you happy, Jason?"

She had to ask? He smiled, her tousled locks tickling his lips. "Yeah, sugar, I'm happy." He tightened his arms. "I've got everything I've ever wanted, right here."

About the Author

How does a high school English teacher end up plotting murders? She uses her experiences as a cop's wife to become a writer of romantic suspense! Linda Winfree lives in a quintessential small Georgia town with her husband and two children. By day, she teaches American Literature, advises the student government and coaches the drama team; by night she pens sultry books full of murder and mayhem.

To learn more about Linda and her books, visit her blog at http://lindawinfree.blogspot.com or join her Yahoo newsletter group at http://groups.yahoo.com/group/linda_winfree. For more fun information on her *Hearts of the South* series (including free reads!), visit the *Hearts of the South* blog at http://heartsofthesouth.blogspot.com. Linda loves hearing from readers. Feel free to email her at linda_winfree@yahoo.com.

Look for these titles by

Linda Winfree

Now Available:

What Mattered Most
Truth and Consequences

Coming Soon:

His Ordinary Life
Hold On To Me
Anything But Mine
Memories of Us
A Formal Feeling

The sheriff has the hots for her prime suspect.
What's a girl to do?

Too Good to be True

© 2007 Marie-Nicole Ryan

Sheriff Rilla Devane has sworn to serve and protect, just as her father did before he was murdered. An influx of party drugs has killed two teenagers, but she has a suspect: handsome, rich newcomer Mackenzie Callahan, a published author seeking small-town atmosphere. To build her case, she moves closer to Mackenzie and his dangerous brand of seductive charm. She'll risk everything for her investigation, even when it means letting her guard down and falling for her suspect.

Mac Callahan lives and breathes for undercover work. But his last mission ended in near disaster, and he has one last chance to prove his value to the DEA. Taking sexy Sheriff Rilla to bed might ruin his career—or lead him to the love of his life.

Enjoy the following excerpt...

"Let's impress this crowd with our terpsichorean prowess."

She scowled and muttered, "Just because you pretend you're a writer, you don't have to talk like one around me."

"Come on." He stood and held out his hand, palm up.

"You're almost as smooth as Rob Wyler." She smirked and placed her hand in his.

Mmm. Warm and strong.

"I'll show you smooth." He pulled her to his chest and took off in an easy one-two, one-two-three swaying glide around the small dance floor.

Her body was warm against his chest. "You're pretty good at this," he whispered in her ear.

"You're not so bad yourself." She gazed into his eyes. "I must say I'm surprised."

"Why? Haven't you found me skilful in other physical endeavors?"

"Have I complained?"

He laughed. "No, you haven't at that."

The music continued and he drew Rilla closer. Her body molded to his...and felt damned good. "Dare I say it? Your beeper hasn't gone off once tonight."

Her eyes widened. Placing an elegant finger to her lips, she shushed him. "You've done it now, but maybe not. This isn't a real date."

"It isn't?" Mac nuzzled her neck. "Hmm, sure feels like one."

She gave a small shake of her head. "No, it's a pretend date so we could backup Kit."

He turned to leave the dance floor "Well, that's it. Ready to leave?"

She laughed, a low sensual growl and tugged on his hand. "Oh, no, you don't. The music's still playing."

She slipped her arms around his waist and slid her hands into the back pockets of his jeans, cupped his ass and pressed against his dick.

"This is feeling less like pretend," he said. Pretend, hell—she was teasing him and having a great time. His dick was hard as a rock, and if she kept it up...

But damn, he loved this playful side of her. He couldn't help but wonder if they'd met under different circumstances...

Her head went back, revealing the long column of her neck. She laughed then emitted a delicious giggle which sent a searing jolt straight to his groin. Did she have any clue how she affected him? "You're having too much fun."

"Is that even possible?" Her eyes glittered with amusement.

Possible? He swung her around and headed for the door. "Let's find out."

The Porsche was parked along the side of the roadhouse in the shadows. They made it to the car.

Barely.

He backed her against the passenger door. His lips fastened on hers and she welcomed his kiss. He eased his hands under her halter top while he kissed her neck and blew a soft puff of air into her ear.

Skin—God—so soft. Her nipples hardened under his touch. She arched against him and moaned. She gazed up at him, her dark eyes glazed with heat. Could she possibly want him as much as he wanted her?

“Mac, we can’t. Not here.” Her breath was warm on his neck. God. He needed her so much. More than any woman he’d ever known. He pulled down her halter top and lightly raked her brown nipples with his teeth, pulled at them and sucked.

Again she moaned, a sound of desperation…for more?

“Lift your skirt.” He fumbled with his zipper. His dick sprang free, ready for battle. And make no mistake about it, making love to Rilla was like a battle between two warriors.

Her skirt shielded their bodies, but if anyone saw them, there’d be no doubt what was happening. Underneath the full skirt, her slim thighs parted.

Thank God. No panty hose. She wore another one of those scraps of lace she loved. He ripped it off.

He dipped a finger between her thighs and slid into her warm, honeyed slit, rubbing her sensitive clit with his thumb.

Her body shook and trembled against his. She gasped ragged breaths against his chest, and whose pounding heart was whose? Why couldn’t he have four hands? So many sweet places he wanted to touch and so little time.

His lips fastened on her mouth again. She opened to him, her hot tongue battling his for possession. He slid another finger inside her slit and she started moving against them.

“No, wait.” He removed his hand and adjusted his stance for a better position and access.

“No.” Her voice rasped in his ear.

“This is better,” he promised and nudged the head of his cock up and down her outer lips then thrust into her wet warmth.

A low moan ripped from her.

“All right?”

“Yes,” she hissed and trembled as he tried to bury himself deep within her. He cupped her ass cheeks and impaled her securely her onto his straining cock. Keeping her light weight cradled, he moved her up and down. Her inner muscles clenched around his dick so fiercely he nearly lost control.

“Easy, girl. Easy.” He panted and tried to slow her bucking pace.

“No. Not easy.” She clung to his jacket and wrapped her legs around his waist, forcing his cock even deeper inside. “I don’t want it easy.”

Exquisite pressure grew in his balls until he exploded in waves of hot release. He pumped into her over and over, unwilling to leave the blistering heat of her sweet body.

Her head whipped back as she gave a long, low moan. Her body vibrated under his hands. God. What made this woman so hot, so in tune with his needs?

Her climax took her. She stiffened and her teeth fastened on his neck, her nails digging into his shoulders as she rocked against him.

He slid a free hand under her halter and pinched her nipples, then nipped the silken skin of her neck. Another low moan, more of a groan.

Her muscles rhythmically gripped his dick even tighter as she milked him of every last drop of cum.

Printed in the United States
109531LV00002B/121-168/P

9 781599 987712